TOO WYRD

BOOK I: THE RUNESPELL SERIES

SARAH BUHRMAN

BLACK✿ROSE
writing

ISBN: 978-1-61296-752-3
PUBLISHED BY BLACK ROSE WRITING
www.blackrosewriting.com

Printed in the United States of America
Suggested retail price $16.95

Too Wyrd is printed in Adobe Caslon Pro

To my children, Logan and Dharma

– you are the reason I would save the world. I want to thank my husband, Stormcrow, for making suppers and putting kids to bed so I can write, and for telling me it's good. I would also like to thank my dear friend, Phil Kessler, for being my Joseph.

TOO WYRD

TOO WYRD

CHAPT 1

I knew better than to answer the phone when the Animaniacs ring tone was playing. Yakko, Wakko and Dot tried to warn me that what followed would be "totally insane-y", but I didn't listen. That particular song indicated a call from my dearest friend.

"Nicola, it's about Keith," the smooth, bedroom voice said.

"Seriously, Joseph?" I did not want to hear about the ex, certainly not at 10 o'clock at night on a weeknight. I wanted him left in the past, six years past, where he'd put himself by denying his child. "What about him? Is this about Ella?"

"Just answer the door."

I stalked to the door, still talking into the phone. "It would be exactly what you deserve if I was naked right now." I flung open the door to find Joseph grinning at me. We both put our cell phones away and stepped into each other's arms for a hug.

Joseph held me at arm's length and raked my body with his eyes. "Not naked."

I craned my neck to look up into his face, more than six inches above mine, and saw the fatigue in the tension around his blue eyes; that worried me. I forced a grin and rolled my eyes. "Like you'd even appreciate my naked awesomeness, gay man."

I stepped back and led him into the house. "Come on. You want something to drink? Water? Red wine? Hard black cherry lemonade?"

Joseph gazed around, taking in the practical arrangement of furniture and the portraits of my daughter covering most of the wall behind the sofa and in the hallway. I couldn't blame him for being a little nosey; he had never visited me at home before. Living so far away from each other made that nearly impossible.

"Red is fine." He nodded to the most recent picture on the wall, Ella's dark brown hair framing her tan, heart-shaped face with honey-colored eyes sparkling. "She looks good. Happy."

My eyes narrowed as I poured a glass of red wine for him. "She is. Happy." It was a gut reaction to be upset. I was always sensitive to comments like that. Being a single mom was filled with little digs and insults, even though most of them weren't intentional.

I grabbed a hard lemonade for myself and gestured for him to go through the sliding door onto the patio. We sat in the overstuffed patio chairs and I dropped the drinks on the low table between us. "You gonna tell me what this visit is really all about? It must be good for you to leave the city."

Joseph sighed and rubbed his face with his hand before reaching for the wine and taking a long drink. He'd never been a heavy drinker, so I took that as a bad sign. "I'm not really sure. I wish I knew what was going on, but this... It just doesn't make any sense."

I took a sip and a deep breath. "Well, tell me what you've got."

Joseph sipped his wine again. "A couple weeks ago, I heard a rumor about Keith."

I nodded. Joseph was a kind of neutral entity in the Indianapolis Pagan Community. He kept his nose out of drama and his ears open, so most of the stuff that went on came to his attention quickly.

"I blew it off at first, 'cause it was so... out there. But people kept talking. I figured there might really be something to it, but I never thought it could be what I'd heard." He looked at me. "They were saying he was invincible. And that he could show people, prove it. They said he could stand in a fire and come out with no burns. He could be sliced with a knife and not bleed. They said he couldn't be killed."

I cocked my head to the side, considering this. If Joseph was telling me these rumors, there was some truth to them. Neither one of us was the type to believe in stuff like that without proof, Pagan or no. We didn't just buy into the whole fireball-and-lightning kind of thing. "So, you checked it out?"

Joseph gulped down the rest of his wine. "Yeah, I did."

"And?"

Joseph stared at his glass for a long moment, then he reached into his pocket. "I got vanillas." He waved a pack of cigarettes in my face. "You want one?"

I raised an eyebrow. I'd quit smoking nearly a decade ago, though vanillas were the one exception to that. "I don't know how you get that kind of contraband snuck into this country, and I don't want to know." I reached for the smoke and grabbed his Zippo lighter, too. "Why are you avoiding telling me what happened?"

Joseph sighed and lit his own cigarette when I returned his lighter. "Because it's one of those things that makes you wish you were a normal, mainstream, Sunday-Christian, non-magic using, non-magic knowing human."

Both my eyebrows went up this time. "That bad, huh?"

Joseph nodded. "I crashed one of his events. I slipped in with a group of initiates from the Golden Cauldron and hung out in the back. I don't think Keith saw me, but I caught most of what he did."

I shifted in my chair, waiting for Joseph to drop the bombshell. With as much as he was avoiding saying what happened, it had to be pretty serious.

"I swear on Hecate, I saw them cut him. They took a big machete or something and cut through a watermelon – to show how sharp it was – then they hacked at his arm. And nothing happened." Joseph rubbed at his face again. "There was no bruising, no blood, no scrapes, nothing."

I chewed on my lower lip as I considered this.

"And before you start picking it apart, Nicola, that's not all," Joseph interrupted my thoughts. "They set up a big fire, about 5 feet across. The flames were going at least 3 feet high. He stepped right into it."

Joseph leaned forward, his gaze boring into me. I could feel his need for me to believe him. "I saw the coals in the center break under his feet. You could walk around the whole thing and see him surrounded by flames. In a sleeveless shirt and shorts." Joseph swung his face away from me, like he couldn't stand to watch my reaction, and stared into the stars overhead.

I finished the cigarette in my hand and tossed the butt into my cold, freestanding fire pit. We sat silently for several minutes, sipping our drinks. I went through every possibility, but I couldn't think of one that either Joseph would not also consider or that he hadn't discounted with the details of his story.

Finally, Joseph took a deep breath and sat up. He looked at the dead cigarette in his hand and tossed the butt at the fire pit. He pulled out another smoke and lit it, dragging deeply a few times.

I shifted in my seat. "Okay, so Keith gets to be superman, or whatever. Even if that's the case, so what? Why do I need to know this? People get to show off their special skills all the time. That's why there's so many Tarot readers, healers and such at the fests."

Joseph rolled his shoulders as if to relieve tension. I remembered it as a sign that he was about to drop a surprise in my lap. "He says he's starting an army of magic-users. He's recruiting for a battle."

"A battle? Against who? Al Qaeda?"

Joseph glanced over. "He says it's for Ragnarok."

•   •   •

Okay, I shouldn't laugh so much. But really? Ragnarok? The end of the world and the death of most of the gods according to the Norse pantheon and its texts?

Joseph stared at me until the hyena cackling had subsided. "You done?"

I wiped the tears from my eyes and nodded. "Yeah, for now. But come on... Ragnarok? That's a battle between the gods. Humans, when they are involved, would be nothing more than cannon fodder, with or without witchcraft."

Joseph shrugged. "I'm not arguing that he is being rational or anything. I'm just telling you what he said."

"Yeah, but there's something else to it, something that makes you take it seriously, or you wouldn't be sitting here telling me about a mythological battle of the future, and the man who would be Sergeant Major." I stood up and grabbed his glass and my empty bottle. I gestured with the glass and he nodded. I stepped inside to get the refills, calling through the patio door. "So what takes this from psycho circus with optional admission to a crazy train running us down at the crossing?"

I heard Joseph move to stand in the doorway. "I don't know. It's mostly just a gut feeling. I think he's up to something more than just the impossible parlor tricks he's been pulling. I just don't know how to figure it out." He sighed. "And I don't think me confronting him will give us any answers. Keith has always had that slick as goose-shit feel to him."

I came out of the kitchen with fresh drinks and stopped. Joseph had that look on his face. He was going to ask me to do something, and I wasn't going to like it. "So you want me to talk to him."

"You could be just the thing to throw him off balance. Besides," Joseph scrambled to make his case before I shut him down, "you are the only person I know who can read anyone at anytime. You have a gift and it could give us the information we need."

I walked slowly back to Joseph, handed him his drink and sat down. He sat back down in his seat and let out a sigh. He was sure he'd convinced me. But I still had a case to make. "Why?"

Joseph choked on his swallow of wine. He coughed a few times and choked out his words. "Why what?"

I smiled innocently, knowing Joseph wouldn't buy the innocent part. "Why do we need the information? Why do we need to know? Why should we get involved?" I cut him off as he started to break in. "What is the worst possible scenario? And how is it our fucking problem?"

Joseph stared at me, and I got a sinking feeling. He hadn't told me everything. He hadn't told me the thing that *I* would see as the most important.

"Muriel disappeared from her usual hang-outs about four weeks ago, and rumor has it she'd joined Keith's army before she did."

I stared at Joseph, wanting to disbelieve. But, no, that was exactly the kind of thing that my step-sister would do. "Crap."

"I know."

"You are sure she's gone?" I sighed when Joseph nodded. "How can anyone be so oblivious?" I lifted my drink to my lips, fighting the urge to gulp it.

Joseph snorted. "How should I know? Your little step-sister can find the only broken chair in a room."

"Truth." Without taking my eyes off the bottle I was drinking from, I reached out to give Joseph a fist-bump. We missed. "So,

Muriel is missing and probably involved in some deep shit. If she wasn't such a damned innocent, I'd let her sink. Well, if we were a hundred percent certain her deep shit was this thing with Keith, at least. Maybe then she would learn a few things."

I saw Joseph nod his agreement from the corner of my eye.

I considered the situation from as many angles as I could come up with. Best case scenario was that we were wasting time and we'd leave Muriel to putz around with a fraud until reality set in. Worst case was that Keith could really pull out the big guns and drag her into something that was way over her head.

I looked at Joseph. He glanced at me expectantly. "Is this just about building an army, or do you think Keith is turning to the dark side?"

Joseph shook his head. "I don't know. I hope not, but..." He shrugged. "I just don't know."

"Fine." I heaved a sigh. "Tracking down Muriel might take a few days. I'll need to get some stuff in order before I just take off. I can finish my current orders and get those mailed off. Ella can visit grandma for a week. I'll just tell her I'm checking out a workshop possibility. I can be back in Indianapolis on Monday."

Joseph nodded.

I was able to pull in a few workshops and seminars through nearby festivals and conventions, which boosted my income from the online sales of magically charged herb and oil blends, and video-conferenced Tarot readings. I would have to set up my sites to let customers know I was away for a while.

I stood up. "You want the guest bed?"

Joseph gave me a questioning look. I grinned and led him into the living room. I tugged an ottoman towards the wall.

"I got an inflata-bed that plays dead as a foot stool." I popped the top off of the ottoman and unfolded the bed platform. I tugged out the plug and jammed it into the wall socket. A soft buzz filled the room.

Joseph chuckled. "Beats staying at a hotel, I guess. Let me go out and grab my overnight bag."

As he walked out the front door, the smile fell from my lips. I closed my eyes, hoping that this was just a dream. Muriel was my responsibility by default. Her father, my step-father, had died a few years ago. Her mom had fallen off the face of the earth a few months before that. I was the closest thing she had to family, and family duty was a sacred duty.

I opened my eyes, resigned, when Joseph walked back into the house.

● ● ●

Somewhere in my mind, I knew I was dreaming.

I ran through narrow hallways, feeling the presence of something chasing me. In that dream way, I couldn't tell you what it was chasing me, but I knew what it was. It was a monster. Or several.

I ran, keeping just ahead of the monsters in a way that can only happen in a dream. I could feel the way the monsters reached for me, barely missing my back. But when I threw a glance over my shoulder, there was nothing there.

I ducked around a corner and stopped dead in front of an old wizard. He looked a lot like a certain gray wizard from a certain story about a certain ring, but it wasn't the same guy. This one had an eye patch over one eye, for one.

The wizard held out a piece of parchment to me, and a raven-feather quill. I took it and looked it over. It listed a bunch of random things, none of which stayed in my mind once my eyes left the words.

I put a check mark next to several of the items and handed back the parchment. The wizard bowed his thanks, turned and walked away.

As soon as the wizard left, I started running again. The monsters were behind me and had taken up the chase again. But they were no longer the only things chasing me.

There were men working with the monsters. I heard the yelling, growling and snuffling of their chase, felt their claws graze my shirt.

I ran around a corner and entered a huge warehouse storage room. I stared at the room for a moment, surprised. It was filled with huge piles of grain, over 8 feet tall. The different shapes and colors told me that they were different kinds of grains, but I didn't recognize any of them.

The monsters approached the door and I ran into the room. I

dodged behind one large pile of grain and hid. I could hear the men and monsters looking for me as I edged around the pile, digging my hand into the grain, searching for something. I wasn't sure what I was looking for, just that I needed to find it.

Once I was far enough away, and they were too close, I ran to the next pile of grain and did the same thing. This time, I pulled a piece of paper out of the pile of grain. I glanced at it and saw lines scratched on it, like symbols.

Over and over again, I ran from one pile of grain to the next, digging for pieces of paper, hiding from the monsters and the men. Soon, I had four pieces of paper clutched in my fist. I bolted from the room and ran across the hall into another room.

As I ran, I saw warriors running towards me. They looked like barbarians or Vikings. They attacked the men and monsters on my heels. I slammed the door shut behind me, somehow sure that they were here to protect, not me, but the pieces of paper.

The sounds of battle frightened me, but they soon stopped. The door opened and the wizard stood in the doorway, this time dressed in jeans and a t-shirt. He held out his hand and I gave him the papers. They turned into silver pendants in his hand. He checked each one against the check-marked list that I had filled out before.

"You are the one," he said. "I'm sorry."

I sat up in my bed, cursing loudly.

CHAPT 2

The concrete street reflected the early summer sun with a matte glow that gave me a headache. Even the colorful paint on the bricks along the top of the bridge and artistic graffiti on its short sides and on the buildings nearby couldn't relieve the blinding brightness.

I took a deep breath, coughing a little on the dry air filled with exhaust and the smell of warm tar. A thick silence surrounded me, the sound of a neighborhood stiffled. The street wasn't a busy one, the businesses didn't draw many customers, and the Bridge Kids gathered in small groups, conserving their energy for their money-making efforts throughout the night.

I already missed the hills and trees surrounding my home, filled with noisy birds and rustling leaves.

Joseph shuffled his feet next to me as we peered into the reflected light at the people around the Rainbow Bridge. This was one of the major places that the young and homeless ended up in Indianapolis. It was Muriel's favorite stomping ground.

"Hey, rich girl!"

I looked toward the gruff, tenor voice and smiled.

"Sup, Hound Dog," I called out. We walked a few feet down the sharp incline and reached out to take the hand of the scruffy young man with a faded black tribal tattoo covering the back of his neck and his ears gauged to make room for two-inch wide plugs in the stretched lobes.

"Not much. Keepin' things going."

I nodded. Hound Dog had been on the streets since he was fourteen, having left his parents' home more than a decade earlier when his dad decided to beat the gay out of him. He was well-known for taking the new young homeless under his wing and teaching them how to survive. He was a man of his word and got a lot of respect for what he did.

Joseph shook Hound Dog's hand and nodded. "We need to find Muriel," Joseph said.

Hound Dog looked us over and ran a hand through his dirty blond hair, making it stick up in uneven spikes. "No messing around then." He sighed. "I heard from Mercy that Muriel had gotten herself involved in some deep shit."

"Mercy?" I hadn't heard the name before, so she must be a newer Bridge Kid.

"Yeah, she showed up about two months back. She really helps take care of the younger kids. Wicked right hook, too," Hound Dog grinned. "Muriel's been gone for a couple weeks, so I doubt you'll find her here, but Mercy might know where she's gone off to. She took a special liking to Muriel."

"How so?"

"She just seems to latch on to the most vulnerable kids and keeps 'em from jumpin' into the fire." Hound Dog scratched at his unshaven chin as he scanned the people around the bridge. "Lemme see. I saw her hangin' around just a bit ago. There she is." He gestured to us to follow him and jogged up the steep shoulder and across the bridge.

Joseph and I scrambled our way up the shoulder and ran to catch up to Hound Dog just as he slowed to a walk and approached a group of five kids sitting on the bank and sharing a bag of bruised-looking apples, probably gotten from a recent dumpster dive.

Four of the kids looked underage, but a blonde woman in a red flannel shirt seemed closer to mid-twenties. She looked up as we came near, locking her ice blue gaze onto me and Joseph.

"Hey, Mercy," Hound Dog said. "This is Nicola and Joseph. They're friends. Lookin' for Muriel."

Her eyes flicked over to Hound Dog before raking over us again. "And what're they gonna do with her?"

I gave Mercy the eyebrow. "We're tryin' to find out how much trouble she is actually in. And if it's something we have to get involve in."

"How you gonna do that?" she asked, her smooth alto voice dripping with disdain. "You got super powers or somethin'? Maybe you think throwing money at a problem solves it."

I frowned. The dig was blunt – how could we possibly help a street kid, since we obviously weren't a part of that culture?

Hound Dog cleared his throat. "Mercy, back off. These two have the juju to find this stuff out."

"Prove it." Mercy stood up. She was a bit taller than I was, and I could see her muscles move under her skin. She had the kind of muscle build you get from actual work, not from lifting weights or other controlled workouts. "You gonna give me the winning lotto numbers or tell me about my troubled childhood?"

I sighed and let my eyes go unfocused for a moment. I drew on the energy within me that was part of the source of all magic. Some people called it willpower, and that made some kind of sense. Both science and religion stressed how humans could make changes through acts of will and faith.

But I hated the word "willpower". It reminded me of my few desperate stints in weight loss programs, where they told me that those last 10 pounds would drop off if I would just have the willpower to ignore the food and deny the cravings.

Denial is the problem. In my personal experience, the way to magic is through full-contact participation. You have to love and lose, hate and hope, have wonder and let yourself weep. Those experiences feed the emotional well inside your mind and soul. And those emotions are what you tap into to make magic.

Without those emotions, you make wishes without a star. Without that energy, the most profound spell is nothing more than a rhyming pentameter chanted in the darkness.

I tapped into that energy now, bringing up the memories of the first time I was overjoyed and shocked at being able to see auras. I let that feeling wash over me, fueling my second-sight. I looked for what her energy was telling me by way of random thoughts, images and impressions, ideas flickering through my mind.

"You are a warrior," I said, verbalizing what I saw. "But not one for an earthly kingdom. Not too fond of the Christian stuff either. You are more of a kickin' ass and takin' names type, answering only to one who embodies honor, sacrifice and wisdom."

Mercy stared hard at me, and Joseph took advantage of her

distraction to take her hand. He stared at her palm for a moment. "Odd. You have no past lives, but this isn't your first incarnation. What is you right now is all of your experiences, and you are totally aware of them."

Mercy jerked her hand away and stared at each of us for several minutes. I felt like she was trying to see my soul. I glanced at Joseph and, by the slight frown on his face, he'd experienced the same feeling.

"Fine, you've got some mojo." Mercy turned and tossed the rest of the bag of apples to the kids. She nodded to Hound Dog and, turning back to us, jerked her head up towards the road going over the bridge. "Let's talk."

I glanced at Joseph and shrugged. I followed Mercy up the embankment with Joseph trailing behind.

Mercy climbed the short, steep path with goat-like skill and turned to wait for us to catch up. She stomped her worn hiking boots several times to get the bits of grass and mud off of them.

"So, you wanna know how deep Muriel is?" Mercy said. She paused while Joseph lit a cigarette. I shook my head when he offered. "Well, it's real deep. And skills or not, I'm not convinced you can handle it."

I sighed and tried not to roll my eyes. "I think that's for us to determine. We just want to find her right now."

Mercy shrugged. "No one has seen her in a couple weeks. She and her family just up and disappeared."

Joseph frowned. "You mean her street family?"

Mercy nodded.

I rubbed an itch on my nose and thought back several years to when I had been more involved in the street culture. I'd never been homeless, but my drive to help Muriel had led me to the edges of the complex web of support and sharing of resources that kept street kids alive despite their harsh situation.

Most street kids fell in with others around their same age, forming small, tight groups of three to six people. These "families" were extremely loyal to each other, sharing food, money and shelter with each other.

Often, one or two in the group took the lead, guiding the others using experience, wisdom and even charisma. These "parents" were usually the ones who collected and distributed resources, giving the group more buying power, organizing the time and skills of the family, and ensuring that none of the group was left out.

Rarely, a family's parents would use their influence to abuse their family, pimping out the family members or demanding participation in risky criminal activities, such as breaking-and-entering or holding up convenience stores.

Muriel's connection to me had given her family an advantage, since I could often spare a little cash or food to help her out. Because of this, Muriel had become the "mom" of her family, which gave her opinion in family decisions additional weight.

If Muriel had gotten into a cult, she very well could have pulled her entire family into it. But, just because a parent made a decision that the family obeyed didn't mean that the whole family agreed with it.

I turned my attention back to Mercy.

"Is anyone from Muriel's family still showing up from time to time?" I asked.

Mercy pursed her lips. "Well, I heard from Hallie that she heard from Big Ralph that he saw Jada over at the city mission's soup kitchen last week."

I scowled, trying to mentally follow the connections. "So, where's Big Ralph now?"

"Probably at the city mission," Mercy said. "He got a job there doing some clean-up before and after supper. He keeps an eye on some of the others and keeps them from giving everything to the thumpers."

I nodded. The city mission offered one free meal each day, complete with conversion attempts by the thumpers, as in bible-thumpers. Most street kids blew it off as the price of admission, but some got sucked in and ended up caving to the evangelicals' pressure to tithe most of their money to a church or charity.

The little bit of cash that those kids had was from low-wage or under the table jobs, or from long days of panhandling. It pissed me off because too many of those kids got into dangerous situations to earn so little. Some punk high-schoolers liked to make a game out of beating on panhandlers and buskers - people who performed on the streets for donations. People professing to be helping, but taking homeless kids' money - that kind of hypocrisy got my blood boiling.

Joseph stubbed out his most recent smoke, crushing it on the gravel. "Well, if we head out now, we can catch this Big Ralph before all the good Christians get there."

• • •

We stepped through the open back door at the city mission's kitchen, Joseph and I hesitating at the doorway. My nose wrinkled at the stale smell of cooked pasta that permeated the kitchen.

"Hello?" Mercy called out, striding through the dark kitchen towards the swinging door that probably led to the dining area. "Anybody home?"

I glanced at Joseph before hurrying after her. Joseph was on my heels as we burst through the door.

It was, in fact, the dining hall - a large open space filled with long tables packed around with folding chairs. The room had that vaguely eerie feeling of a room that should be full of people but isn't.

Mercy was already talking to a huge black man who looked like he was in his early 20s. At around six and a half feet tall - a bit taller than Joseph - and close to 250 lbs, he looked like he could lift cars off of small children. His white teeth flashed against the dark brown of his skin as he chatted with Mercy.

I smiled in recognition. Big Ralph used to go by Little R around a decade ago. Obviously, he'd grown out of the "little", but based on what I was getting from his body language and a glimpse of his aura, Big Ralph was still a big teddy bear of a guy.

I was proven right when I walked up and Big Ralph grinned. "Nicola! How have you been, girl?" He pulled me into a big hug. "How's the baby?"

"Hey, Big Ralph! She's not much of a baby anymore," I laughed. "She's in kindergarten already, and the smartest little girl ever, too!"

Big Ralph puffed up his chest. "'Cause of them books, right?"

Ralph had decided that it was his job while I was pregnant to find my baby some books. I had accepted them gratefully, knowing how hard it was for the street kids to get and keep books. They didn't usually have the luxury to encourage reading when they had babies. Food usually won out against books when you were homeless.

I'd considered it a sacred duty to pass on as much of my daughter's toys, books and clothes to the homeless when she'd grown out of them. I'd also begun teaching my daughter about the importance of passing along such items to those less fortunate.

I nodded. "It was definitely those books," I assured the man.

Joseph stepped up and offered his hand to Big Ralph. "I'm Joseph. Nice to meet you, Big Ralph."

Big Ralph shook his hand firmly. He grinned at us all before grabbing the dust mop propped up against a nearby chair and continuing his work while he talked to us. "So, what can I do for you guys? Don't tell me you missed me so much you had to come look me up at work?"

I shook my head. "Sadly, no," I said. "We heard that Muriel has gone and disappeared. You know me – I can't just leave her hanging. We're trying to find her so we can check up on her, but no one's seen her or her family in weeks. Except we heard you did."

Big Ralph nodded as he turned the corner to go down the next row between tables. "I seen Jada 'bout a week or so ago. She come in for the chili." He grinned. "Ms. Pauline makes the best black bean chili outside'a the Deep South."

Joseph smacked his lips. "Sounds good!"

Big Ralph turned to face us. "We ain't got chili today. Sorry. We only do chili on Wednesdays." He turned back to his sweeping. "Today, we got chicken fried steak with mashed potatoes, peppered white gravy, creamed corn, an' a little lettuce salad on the side. Mm hmm."

He hesitated a moment before he continued. "I dunno where Jada is now. Or Muriel. I didn't get a chance to talk to her much. Just said hi and that's it. But," he threw a sly grin at us, "you could stay an' volunteer at the supper tonight. Maybe she'll come in."

I smiled. "That sounds like a great idea."

• • •

I talked Mercy into helping us convince some of the Bridge Kids to come with us to the city mission for supper. I knew most of them could use the meal, but the walk was too far for most them to make the effort. Plus walking meant taking the risk of running into trouble with a capital fist to the gut.

With Mercy and Joseph helping, I piled as many kids as I could into the car and we headed for the kitchen. Joseph grimaced and shifted in the passenger seat under the two teens on his lap. I drove slowly, hoping we wouldn't get pulled over.

At the mission, a flustered woman thanked us for our help and gave us our assignments. Joseph got put on door duty, greeting people and directing them towards the end of the line. Mercy walked the floor, keeping an eye on the people standing in line and sitting at the tables in case someone needed help, or on the off chance someone started trouble.

I was put at the end of the food line, helping people with walkers, wheelchairs and kids get all their silverware, food and drinks to their seats. I smiled and chatted up the guests, knowing that half the reason they came to the kitchen was for the small degree of human interaction they got.

I turned back from chatting with an older woman who had promptly cut her chicken fried steak in half, wrapped up one of the pieces and put it in her purse for the dog, Betsy, she'd left tied to a tree outside. Big Ralph stood at the end of the row of tables, gesturing me over. I walked quickly to his side.

"There she is," he said in a stage whisper. "Jada. The girl in the red shirt." He poked his finger towards the front of the line, holding it close to his chest to keep the movement from being seen.

I followed the direction his finger showed and saw the girl he was talking about. She was a strikingly pretty and very young-looking Hispanic girl with shiny auburn hair and piercingly brown eyes. I glanced around and found Joseph chatting up a middle-aged couple near the door. Mercy had disappeared for the moment.

I walked back to the drink table and helped a middle-aged woman with three kids get their food to a group of empty seats, keeping an eye on my target the whole time. I set down the last drink and tucked a napkin into the lap of the youngest girl, then turned to check on Jada.

She had just sat down at a table a little closer to the door. She seemed to be here alone, but she was making small-talk with an older lady sitting nearby.

I made sure that the others helping with getting people seated weren't too busy for me to take a few minutes, then I grabbed a glass of tea and plopped down in the chair beside Jada, my body turned toward her. She glanced at me warily and turned back to the lady.

I grinned. So she thought she could ignore the crazy chick sitting next to her and staring, huh?

I cleared my throat, "So, Jada, how's it going?"

Her head whipped around and she stared at me with a slightly confused look. I sat up and turned my body to face her.

"You're Muriel's family," I accused. Her face went pale, and I took a moment to rethink my approach. "It's okay. I'm her other family. We need to talk." I glanced at her half-eaten food. "Soon."

●   ●   ●

It took about 5 minutes for Jada to finish eating. She'd watched me with a guarded look the entire time, like she was afraid I'd take her food or smack her at any moment. I felt bad about it, but I played on her fears to hurry her up. For some reason, time had started to feel... slippery. Like it was getting away.

I'm sure it was just an effect of all the hoops we were jumping through to find Muriel. But my experience told me that the feeling might mean something else, something more sinister.

When she finished, I led her to the door. I caught Joseph's questioning look and shook my head. He didn't need to abandon his post as well.

We walked down the sidewalk several feet before stopping. Jada leaned against the building, while I stood in front of her with my hands in my pockets, angling my body sideways so I wouldn't appear too intimidating. I wanted her to be able to open up to me.

"So, Jada," I began, keeping my voice low and calm. "Do you know who I am?"

She shrugged and shook her head.

"I'm Nicola Crandall. Muriel is my step-sister. And you are part of her street family. We both have an interest in keeping her safe, right?"

I waited for Jada to nod before I pushed on. "I'm not after her for anything. If she's safe, I'll be going home happy." I turned towards her. "But if she's not safe, I'm gonna drag her ass out of whatever fire she's in. You got me?"

Jada sighed and opened her mouth as if to speak, but she hesitated. I relaxed my stance and waited for her.

"She got a job," Jada said. "She's got us a rental house, too."

I performed an actual double-take. Playing white knight didn't usually end with getting such good news. "Well, that's... good," I said. But Jada didn't look like she was giving me good news. "So what's wrong?"

She flinched. "I don't know," she said. "Muriel got the others jobs, too. And me. We share a place in a pretty decent neighborhood. A four-bedroom over in Ravenswood."

"But...?" I pressed her.

Jada shrugged. "But Muriel goes to these meeting things all the time. And she's always trying to get us to go with her. Most of the others do, once in a while. But they also try to schedule their work so they won't have to. I won't go. I just... don't like them."

"You mean the things with Keith Ludlow?" I asked.

"Yeah, that's the guy's name. And that freaky, controlling older guy who's usually with him. I don't know what it is about either of them, or that group. I just get a sick feeling in my stomach about it."

Jada's nervousness got the better of her. She pushed off the building and bounced on her toes. "No one else seems to get that, so I don't hang out with the family as much."

I nodded my sympathy.

Jada shifted uncomfortably. "And 'cause we got jobs and stuff, we've stopped going down to the bridge or anywhere else the other kids hang."

"So you come here once in a while?"

She shrugged. "It's hard to explain. I'm not really a street kid anymore, now that I got a house and a job, but I miss them all. I miss being part of them."

"I get it, I really do," I said. "Look, we are gonna be checking into what Muriel and Keith are doing. If there's something wrong, we'll find it, okay?"

Jada nodded, putting her hands in her pockets.

I caught her eye and sent a little push with my will to give her more motivation to help us. "Now, I need to know where to find Muriel."

• • •

I pulled in to the convenience store late the next day and shook my head. Showing up at Muriel's work was the best guarantee to find her, so Joseph and I had spent the day catching up on each other's lives before heading to the run-down gas station. Muriel had been in some crappy places, but this place was full of red flags.

Two guys in parachute pants (seriously? what decade is this?) and should-have-been-white-not-yellow undershirts eye-balled each other from where they slouched against the brick wall on opposite corners of the store.

The parking lot was empty of cars, but three people were sitting on the curb in front of the store drinking from bottles hidden in paper bags. A woman in leggings that had seen better days and a tube-top (it's the 90s isn't it...) was thrusting out her hips and shaking her booty at cars driving by.

I unfocused my eyes to check out the energy. The two eye-ballers showed up as red imps - aggressive, but not as badass as they try to come across as. The drinkers had various parasites hanging on them - stress and depression were draining them of any fight. The woman in the tube-top showed a hot pink but emaciated energy - she didn't hate her job, but there was a desperation about her, so it probably wasn't going well at the moment.

I glanced at Joseph who looked like he'd just eaten a bad lemon.

"What are you getting?" I asked him.

Joseph took a deep breath and checked out the scene again. "Sorrow, depression, posing. Nothing big, just nothing good."

I nodded and opened the car door. "Let's see if they have an iced coffee machine."

The bell rang out our arrival with false cheerfulness. We went straight to the counter. The entire check-out area was surrounded by

Plexiglas.

A short brunette in her mid-twenties came out of the back office. Her clothes were clean but worn and some lines had begun showing around her eyes. She met my gaze and stopped.

"Nicola. Joseph. What the hell are you doing here?"

I put my hand up to the Plexiglas, reaching out for my family. "Muriel. We heard you were in trouble. So..."

"So you thought you'd come rescue me?" Muriel crossed her arms across her chest, aggression rolling off of her in waves. "You and your holier-than-thou white fucking horse can turn around and go home! I don't need you to save me. I got a job and a place and I don't need you to come charging in and fix shit!"

I dropped my hand and glanced at Joseph. We needed to short circuit her anger or we wouldn't get anywhere with her

Joseph met my eyes briefly. He stuck his hands in his pants pockets and smirked at Muriel. "Muriel. Did you just call me a horse?" He tossed his head and made a pretty realistic-sounding whinny.

Muriel cracked a smile and her energy changed. Joseph always knew how to diffuse a tense situation.

"So-o-o-o," I turned back to Muriel. "We thought we'd come find out what's going on, and find out IF you needed any help."

Muriel's shoulders slumped and her arms dropped to her sides, losing some of her defensiveness. "Oh. Well. What's there to know? I'm getting my life on track. I've got some people on my side and things are going really good."

"People like Mercy?"

Muriel nodded.

"And Keith?"

She scowled. "Jealous?"

I chewed my lip, letting her see me thinking. "I don't know. Is there something to be jealous of?"

"We aren't fucking, if that's what you want to know," she moved around the counter area, straightening things that didn't really need it. "He's helping lots of people. Giving them a purpose."

"Like you?" Joseph asked.

Muriel raised her chin. "Yeah, like me."

"How?"

"He gave me ambition, a reason to work for a better life that isn't selling out, and then he helped me find this job."

Joseph leaned on his arms on the counter. His nose almost touched the Plexiglas cage. "This job gives you a purpose?"

"Yeah," Muriel lifted her chin again. "I contribute to the cause."

I met Joseph's eyes. "Tithing?"

Joseph shrugged.

Muriel continued as if she hadn't noticed our exchange. "We've been fighting through our lives for so long. Now we have something to fight for. We've been losing so much of ourselves. Now we have a reason to win. We've been barely surviving. Now we will live."

I nudged Joseph. "Sounds pretty rote."

He nodded and we turned back to Muriel. "Is that how he says it?"

Muriel crossed her arms over her chest. "Yeah. So?"

I shrugged and filed away the information. "So... what else does he do? Any activities? Classes? Stuff like that?"

"We learn to defend ourselves, if that's what you mean," she said. "He hosts a self-defense class and hand-to-hand combat. A few of us get to learn some energy work and how to do spells. And we learn the history of the gods, about how the human world got screwed over by the Ay-seer."

I blinked. "You mean, the Aesir? Like Norse gods?"

"Yeah, them."

"Oh. But..." I hesitated, trying to figure out how to phrase things so Muriel wouldn't get defensive and shut down. "How did they screw over the human world?"

"Well, see, Odin, the king god, won't let Ragnarok happen 'cause all the gods will die. And when they die, it will bring the cleansing waters over the earth. But Odin wants people to keep going the way we are so there is enough pain for him to feed on."

I tried to follow what she was saying and match it to my own understanding of the Norse myths. "Odin? Feeds on pain?"

Muriel nodded. "Yeah. That's why he captures souls of the dead and brings the one guy's head back to life."

"You mean, uh..." I wracked my brain for the name. "Mimir?"

"Yeah, him. He was beheaded and Odin brings his head back to life so he can torture him – Mimir – for information."

"Well... Okay." That was certainly a new interpretation of the myths. "So are the Aesir the enemy, then?"

Muriel nodded. "Yeah. And the only way to defeat the Aesir for good is to bring about Ragnarok."

I pinched the bridge of my nose, trying to think. The basics of the myths were there, but they had been seriously warped against Odin and the other Aesir.

Joseph jumped in. "And how do you bring about Ragnarok? Is that what the endgame is?"

Muriel turned to him. "Well, yeah. That's how we bring the Peace of Ages to the earth. We have to be ready to fight in Ragnarok, but Keith has the hardest job. He's the one who has to start Ragnarok. I dunno how he's gonna do it though."

The bell rang cheerfully as a few teenagers pushed in and headed for the candy aisle.

"Muriel, me and Joseph are going to have a smoke outside while you get these kids taken care of. What time do you get off work?"

Muriel glanced at the clock. "I'll be out of here in about 10 minutes, depending on when Johnny gets in."

I nodded. "We could go out for a burger and talk some more..."

She nodded and turned away as the first customer approached. Joseph and I headed out and we each lit up a vanilla.

"Did you see anything?" I asked Joseph.

Joseph sucked air through his teeth to make a loud hissing noise as he inhaled. "Her energy is dulled unless she is talking about Keith and his cause. Then she is focused. Manic, even."

I nodded. "That's what I got, too."

I glanced around the lot, trying not to be obvious about keeping an eye on the loiterers. My eyes widened when I saw Mercy striding towards us. She looked a little miffed.

"Mercy," Joseph said in greeting.

I nodded at the woman as she took up a position next to me.

"It took me all morning to catch up to you," she accused.

I shrugged. "Never said you were coming with us today. That was your assumption."

She frowned at my comment, then we fell into an uncomfortable silence.

I noticed she was watching us as we smoked. My hackles raised, always sensitive to other people's judgment. "What?" I snapped.

She cleared her throat. "I thought that... well, doesn't smoking do something to block psychic... powers or whatever? If you have those kinds of... abilities, why do you guys smoke?"

Joseph laughed.

I grinned. "I quit a while back but this is a special occasion."

Joseph took a drag and blew it out. "And smoking does kind of stifle psychic 'powers'. That's why we do it."

Mercy frowned.

"You like music?" he asked.

She nodded.

"Favorite song or group?"

She nodded again.

"So what if you had to listen to that song or group or whatever over and over for days... How would you like that? It'd be great for the first few hours or so, right?"

Mercy shrugged.

"But then you'd start to get numb about it," Joseph continued. "After a full day of hearing the same thing so many times, you'd start to hate it, right? Then it might even start to piss you off, drive you crazy, you know?"

I jumped in. "That's what psychic powers can be like, especially when you are actively using them, like we are now. We usually keep them turned off, but we need them right now. Smoking, drinking, even harder drugs, sex... all that can be used to dull the effects without shutting it off. It keeps us more or less not crazy."

"People who don't learn to turn them off tend to go one of two ways," Joseph said. "They use the suppressors, sometimes to an extreme. Or they stop living this life, and the other worlds, other lives – as in reincarnation, spiritual identities and such – they treat those like the priority."

"Forget working a job just to pay rent, 'cause ancient Sumerian princesses are better than that," I ticked off examples. "You were a warrior in another life? Try to live like a samurai in this one, buying expensive weapons at every urge. Haven't gotten groceries yet this month, but dropping a hundred bucks on a necklace 'cause it reminds you of the one you had when you were an elf lord."

Joseph took another hissing drag. "People forget to successfully live this life because their abilities give them insight into a more romantic or dramatic life. They want that one, not this one, so they focus on that one in a game of Ultimate Escapism."

"And they refer to those other lives, past lives and spirit selves as their 'true' self." I shook my head. "'Cause living this life, rocking the here and now, isn't 'true' enough in comparison."

Mercy chewed her lower lip. "So why didn't you guys do that?"

Joseph laughed. "Who says we didn't, at one point?" He gestured to me. "Nicola struggled for a few years before she figured out that being an herbalist in a past life doesn't mean she automatically knows how to be an herbalist in this life with the differences in plants, modern knowledge and FDA regulations."

"Not to mention that past life memories aren't photographic memories. You forget stuff. Can't remember what you had for supper last Tuesday, but you think you're gonna remember details about your last lifetime?" I shrugged. "But I got over it. Just like he got over the asshole boyfriend who had been his one true love in another incarnation. Three years and twenty-five thousand in debt later."

Joseph sighed at the memory. "Hard lessons. Basic idea: turn it off so you can live your life."

I nodded. "Most of us don't get to make a career out of our abilities. So..."

The bell chimed behind us as the kids took off and Muriel came out on their heels. "My relief came in on time for once, so I'm free to go."

"You remember Mercy, right?" I indicated our third.

Muriel grinned and walked right into Mercy's arms for a hug. Joseph caught my eye over their heads and raised his eyebrow.

I shrugged and headed for the car. "Get in. I'm buying burgers all around."

• • •

We grabbed a couple bags of loose-meat on hoagie sandwiches and a half-pound of mozzarella sticks from a local sandwich shop before heading to a park to eat. We laid claim to a picnic table and spread out our paper-wrapped loot. After we'd all gotten a few bites down, Joseph swallowed some lemonade to wash the sandwich out of his mouth.

"So," he said, looking at Muriel. "You are hoping to start Ragnarok, huh?"

Mercy choked on her mozzarella stick. She grabbed her drink and gulped it down, her eyes darting from Joseph to Muriel and back.

Muriel was unfazed. "Yeah, Ragnarok will wash the world clean. It's like, a fresh start."

Mercy laughed with a trace of bitterness in the sound. "That's one way to put it."

Muriel frowned. "What do you know about it?"

Mercy shrugged and gave her full attention to her sandwich.

I jumped in. "Muriel, did you ever think that maybe Keith isn't telling the whole truth on the Ragnarok thing?"

Muriel shrugged. "No one ever tells the whole truth. But, so what? This life sucks. There's so much wrong that it's pretty much impossible for regular people like me to get ahead. Better to start clean, even if it isn't as rosy as what Keith says."

"Rosy?" Joseph said. "How about most people are supposed to die during Ragnarok? And you are talking about fighting in it? You wouldn't survive. You wouldn't get to see that shiney, clean new world."

Muriel raised her chin. "That's a sacrifice that some of us are willing to make for everyone else."

I blinked. Muriel had never been a mean or selfish girl, but this level of self-sacrifice was a little on the extreme side. I touched her arm. "You would do that? Why? Who are you saving?"

Muriel smiled sadly. "My life isn't going anywhere. I got nothing to work for. I got no goals, nothing. But I got you, and you got Ella. And there's millions of other little kids out there. They can survive.

They can have a better life than what I got."

I drew my hand back and covered my mouth in shock. She was willing to die for my daughter. That was crazy. It was beautiful. It was... wrong. I blinked at the tears that came from nowhere. "No."

"What?"

I reached for my anger, wrapping it around myself like armor. "You don't get to throw my daughter under the bus for your cause." I stood up and grabbed a handful of wrappers to throw away. "Find something else to salve your ego on."

I walked away, bristling. How could she do that? She effectively laid her life at my daughter's feet as if it was her right to put that kind of emotional burden on someone. It wasn't that it was a bad thing to do, but really? I would never be able to tell my daughter why her aunt died because, well... Imagine the guilt that it would leave on my child.

I threw the papers into the trash bin.

People have a hard enough time living up to living when someone dies saving them from fires or car accidents or normal things. Survivor's guilt was a real thing.

Starting a war of gods and volunteering to die in that war so my daughter could have a better life? That was too much for me to deal with. And it was too much to be putting on a little girl. I stalked back to the table.

Muriel stood up as I approached. "Nicola..."

"No!" I pointed at her. "You sit down and listen."

I stared at her until she dropped into her seat. "You cannot use my daughter - or any other kids - as an excuse for your actions. You can't do that to them. How would you feel if you were told that someone you loved started a fucking war and died so you could have a better life? Would you be thrilled? No pressure?"

Muriel swallowed hard and shook her head.

"Damn right," I continued. "That's a really crappy thing to do to someone. And just so you can feel like you finally have a purpose in your life, right?"

She shrugged.

I pressed on. "You need to seriously reconsider your motives on this little jaunt into the jaws of the hounds of war. And stop making it out like you are doing people a favor. You don't know that it's really a good thing."

I paced in front of her, grabbing at the words flooding my head, hoping it would make sense to Muriel. "It doesn't matter if this war thing is real or not, if what you believe is real or not. You are taking risks and placing the result of those risks at the feet of a Kindergartener. I need you to see how unfair that is, how hurtful that is, even if it seems to be for the best intentions."

I plopped down and grabbed a mozzarella stick, chomping down so hard I almost bit the inside of my lip. "If you feel have to die for Ella, at least have the decency to not tell us that."

Everyone sat in silence for a moment. Mercy chewed on her sandwich, eying me as if sizing me up. Joseph kept his head down as he finished off his drink - a smart move, him having experienced my rages before. Muriel sat with her hands in her lap, staring at me and chewing on her lip.

"Now that we've gotten that straight," I said, finally breaking the ice. "Muriel, it's time for you to really explain what is going on and why you are so into doing this... whatever it is."

She nodded and gulped down her diet soda before she started talking.

• • •

"You have got to be kidding me," Mercy said.

Muriel sat with her arms crossed on the table, having finished telling us what she's said to Joseph and me at the convenience store, though with fewer interruptions. "That's the plan. Start up Ragnarok, fight in it, let everyone else live happily ever after without the tyranny of Odin."

Mercy stared at her. "Do you even know the first thing about Odin? I can't even begin to explain how many things are wrong with what you just said."

I interrupted. "Hold up a minute. Let's do a little background first. Mercy and Joseph, if you think what I'm saying is off-base, jump in."

They both nodded.

"Okay," I began. "First off, Odin doesn't feed off of pain and suffering. He may not always be the nicest guy, but he isn't a total asshole, either."

"He has human-like flaws," Joseph said. "It's one of the more fascinating things about the Norse gods. They were very human-like in their characteristics. Neither good nor evil, per se, just massive strengths and normal flaws."

I nodded and ticked off a second finger. "Odin brought back Mimir's head so he could learn more. It wasn't a great thing to do, but it was an ends and means kind of thing. And Odin collects knowledge from all over the world, by way of Mimir and the ravens - whatever their names are..."

"Huginn and Muninn," Mercy offered.

"Thanks," I said. "He uses this information as a way to try to put off Ragnarok, not because he feeds on pain and Ragnarok will end it, but because Ragnarok will destroy the world and most of the people in it long before the happily ever after ending."

Muriel frowned, thinking about this.

I continued. "He tries to put off massive and really painful death, knowing that no matter what he does, it will still come someday and that he will die during the battle."

"Then Baldur takes over, right?" Joseph said.

"Wait a minute. Who's Baldur?" Muriel asked sitting up. "Keith never said anything about any Baldur."

"Baldur is the Norse god of love and peace," Mercy said. "Flowers spring up where he steps. All of nature loves him. His rule will usher in the era of peace, but only when most of the other gods sacrifice themselves in the battle to save the remnant of humanity."

Muriel seemed confused by this information. "There is a Norse god of love and peace?"

"Yeah," I said. "It's not one of the stereotypical Norse things, but Baldur is beloved of all the gods."

Muriel shook her head in denial. "Keith said that only by destroying all the Norse gods in Ragnarok could humans live in peace. Under the rule of the savior."

I frowned. "Well, some people do see Baldur as a kind of savior god, but I always thought of that as a carryover from the Christianization of our worldview."

Mercy nodded. "That is a very liberal interpretation of Baldur, but not really wrong."

Muriel shook her head. "No. I mean, I don't think Keith was talking about a Norse god. He seemed pretty sure that all the Norse gods needed to be killed."

"Maybe we should be asking Keith about this savior," Joseph said.

I nodded. "Perhaps it's time to check out Keith's little events." I looked at Muriel. "Where do we find him?"

Muriel shrugged. "He's doing a show tomorrow at Circle Centre Mall."

"Great. We'll be there."

"No way!" Muriel said. "You guys are gonna get in there and cause a bunch of trouble and I don't want anything to do with that. You leave me out of this."

"Fine," I shrugged. "Stay away from the show, then. But you need to get somewhere safe."

"I'll go to work and then straight back home."

"Safer than being alone, Muriel." I looked at Mercy. "Can you babysit?"

Muriel jumped up. "Jesus! I don't need a babysitter. The rest of my family is at home. We can look out for each other."

I frowned. "Fine. But please don't get into trouble. If we are going to be rocking the boat, I don't want you falling out."

Muriel scowled. "Maybe you shouldn't be rocking the boat, then."

I grinned. "If you can tell me that this little discussion hasn't given you some reasons to question what Keith's been saying, I'll drop it right now and head home to Ella."

Muriel lifted her chin and stared at me for a long moment before dropping her eyes. "Fine. Talk to him. Make him prove what he's saying. But then you have to leave us alone."

"Deal." I tossed half the bags of remaining food to Mercy and half towards Muriel. "Take it and let's get going. We need to get some rest before we face off tomorrow."

Muriel picked up the food I'd tossed on the table in front of her and stood up, her gaze falling on the parking area. "Uh oh."

I followed her eyes to a spot near the car and let out a string of curses under my breath. "Just what I need," I muttered.

A tall man in a black trench coat and top hat stood on the side of the road with his hands in his pockets. His eyes were hidden by small, round sunglasses with dark red glass, giving him the appearance of Dracula a la Gary Oldman. He never moved as I walked over to him with Joseph, Muriel and Mercy on my heels.

"Theo," I said with forced cheer. "How's Rowan?"

Theo's mouth tightened before he spoke, his voice a smooth tenor. "Lady Luna Rowan Lightfeather", he emphasized each word as if correcting me, "sends her greetings, and a warning."

I raised my eyebrow and crossed my arms over my chest. He hesitated as if he wanted me to say something first, but I kept my mouth shut. I refused to give him an inch.

"My lady wants you to know that she is aware of your presence in the city," Theo continued in his buttery voice.

I might be wrong, but I think he was a bit pouty that I wasn't playing along.

"You were banished for your disgraceful behavior some years ago. Your sentence has not been revoked. You will leave."

I cocked my head to the side. "Uh hmmm," I drawled. "And if I don't?"

Theo turned his head to face me with his sunglasses. "You don't want to find out."

I dropped my arms and laughed in his face. Probably not the most diplomatic approach, but really.

"You and your lady can try whatever it is you want to try," I said. "But your so-called banishment had nothing to do with my leaving and has the same effect on my decision to stay or go in this city as does a mosquito bite."

I brought my finger up to hover barely an inch from the bridge of his nose. I barely hid my smirk when he flinched slightly.

"You have no right to tell me to leave," I continued. "I'm here on family business that has nothing to do with you or Rowan, or your little group of whatever the hell you are calling your coven these days. I will finish my business and you will leave me the hell alone while I do so."

I turned on my heel and walked to the car. As I reached for the handle, I called over my shoulder. "And tell Rowan it's a shame she is still so bloody butt-hurt about what I said. No one but her thought it was even a thing." I glanced back at Theo. "Maybe her ego really is that fragile."

I got in the car and turned on the ignition. The other three jumped in as I put the vehicle in reverse.

Theo had removed his glasses and stood glaring at me, lips pressed together. I grinned at him as I drove away. Theo was still really big on having the last word in any conversation, no matter how small, and my exit had cut the opportunity for that off. Oops!

Muriel gave me directions to her neighborhood in a low voice that stood out in the silence that had fallen over the four of us. We dropped her off where she asked, even though I gave her a look when she asked to be let out at a local park. However, our run-in with Theo had really pissed me off, and I'd already started to fume over the situation. So I just left her on the sidewalk and headed back to the Rainbow Bridge to drop off Mercy.

After a few more minutes of driving quietly, Mercy leaned forward from her seat in the back. "So who's Theo and Rowan? And what was that all about?"

I frowned. This was not my favorite topic.

Joseph jumped in. "About five or six years ago, Nicola was offering a class in one of the local shops. What was it? Astrology?"

I nodded.

"Yeah, anyways. She asked Rowan if she would like to help, since Rowan was always trying to get a foothold in that particular shop to do her own classes. It seemed like a really good partnership. Nicola got to have someone help her with the natal charts, because they are so time consuming. Rowan got to give a class in the shop so she could get some history with them."

"I should have known better," I bit off. "Rowan always was a crowd chaser. She wanted to be famous, well-known, whatever. I should have known that that would be her priority."

"You are just too willing to give people a chance," Joseph said, patting my shoulder. "So, during the class, one of the students asked a question about... what was it?"

"Progressions. He wanted to know about progressing through the signs."

"That's right. So, Rowan jumps in with this long speech about how progressions give you a way to predict how people are going to behave. Essentially, she said you could use them to predict your future." Joseph shrugged. "That's one way to look at it."

"Rowan finished answering and then I said that that was one way, but not the only way, that astrologers interpret progressions." I glared at Mercy in the rearview mirror. "I told the class that most astrologers don't mess with trying to predict the future, unless they are writing horoscopes in a daily rag or something like that. I said that progressions are usually interpreted to show how the person is likely to develop their personality over the course of several decades. Frankly, I was being diplomatic."

I paused, thinking back to that moment, years ago. Seeing Rowan's face when I turned back from telling the class the more common view on progressions, the rage and disgust she'd shown. The moment of numbing confusion I'd felt in response to her intense anger.

Rowan had immediately slammed her notes down on the table and walked out of the shop. The shop owner had sworn she'd never invite Rowan to teach another class.

"She didn't like what I'd said. It seems she felt I was contradicting her in front of her students. She announced - announced! - that I had betrayed her, set her up. When she found out I was moving, she declared that I was banished from the city for my actions and that I was no longer welcome in any coven in the city." My grip tightened on the steering wheel. "As if she could even hope to have that kind of authority over me."

Joseph nodded in sympathy. "She's been after Nicola's blood ever since," he said. "She never passes up an opportunity to tell people how horrible a person Nicola is. She's gone after me a few times just because I won't disavow Nicola. It's BS politics and I won't play the game. Unfortunately, there are a lot of people that believe Rowan, go along with her, or just don't bother to argue the point."

Mercy sat back. "So she pretty much gets away with it."

I nodded. "Yeah, though only people new to the local community believe what she says about me."

"Will she follow through with her threats?" Mercy asked.

I stared silently at the road ahead of me. I didn't know the answer.

CHAPT 3

I stared around, feeling a slight panic building in my gut. My eyes darted from the busy streets to the busy sidewalks and past the businesses lining both. I flinched as a car honked its horn while driving past. I did not miss the crowded streets of Indianapolis at all. Particularly downtown.

I looked down the sidewalk, knowing we still had a few blocks to go. We were lucky to have parked so close to the Circle Centre mall. The meeting would be starting in a few minutes and we were hoping to be just a little bit late to avoid running into Keith before the show. I wanted to see what was going on before we had to confront him.

I gasped a little as we jogged through an intersection, coughing on the fumes from the passing trucks.

Joseph eyed me. "Getting too used to that fresh country air, are you?"

I snorted and coughed again. "I knew there was a reason I kept smoking for so long after I left. I had to wean my lungs off the CO2."

Joseph laughed and picked up the pace. I flipped off his back before increasing my own walking speed.

We entered the mall and headed for the escalators to the third floor. It was obvious where we were headed; in the busy mall full of trendy clothing and flashy gaming stores, the white-papered windows and hand-painted signs stood out.

We got to the storefront just as the last person in line closed the door behind him. I eyed the sign, painted on the glass, announcing the meeting times for the Covenant of World's End.

I turned to follow Joseph inside, but a pleading "Miss!" brought me to a halt.

I looked over my shoulder and saw an older gentleman walking towards me. He held out a clipboard and pen, and I decided he was looking for signatures for a petition. Since I'm always up for a good damn-the-man petition, I shrugged at Joseph and turned to smile at the man.

"I am Dr. Corvus with the University of Indianapolis. I'm doing a study on randomization and random choice clusters. Could I take a moment of your time and have you fill out our survey?" He thrust the clipboard into my hands.

I held the man's gaze while he spoke to me, though I noticed that his eyes didn't quite match up. I looked down at the clipboard. A single sheet of paper asked for my demographics and one question.

"Just this page?" I asked.

The man nodded, and I noticed the eye thing again. Not a lazy eye; maybe glass.

Joseph moved to my side and peered over my shoulder as I turned my attention to the form. I quickly checked "female", "unmarried" and "multiple race", then scratched out "32" for the age.

I read the question: randomly select 4 items from the list below, then I skimmed through the options, which seemed to be a granary inventory list. I picked ones that caught my eye or had meaning to me, which is my MO for random picks.

I scrawled my signature on the bottom, dated it, and handed the whole thing back to the man. He smiled and turned to leave, and I headed back to the storefront. Joseph opened the door for me and we took our places at the back of the room.

The number of people was a bit too much for the size of the room, especially since there was a large stand-alone fire pit cordoned off just a little back from the dead center. A wooden table-like thing stood over the fire pit, and I wondered what it was for. Several large pipes with vent openings hovered around the ceiling above the fire pit.

Joseph nudged my arm and I turned my attention to the small group entering from the back of the room. My eyes went straight to Keith.

He looked a little more haggard and older than he should be from the six years since we'd been together. He'd put on some weight, losing the little bit of toning he'd had and hiding any wrinkles on his pale complexion. His hair seemed to have a lot more gray, but then he was a brunet and the gray showed more.

I turned my attention to the three in his entourage. The first guy was about 20 years old, dressed like an army vet, and strutted around like he was in charge. Too much ego for any real power on that kid.

The second was an older man, around Keith's age of nearly 40. He had a predatory look about him that raised my hackles. This guy was what that kid only wished he was.

The last one, a woman in her 20s, hung on Keith's arm in a skimpy shirt and tight jeans. My lip curled in disgust.

Joseph leaned over. "Jealous?"

I turned to look at him in surprise. "Of what? Keith?"

Joseph nodded, sympathy showing on his face.

I smiled. "It's sweet of you to care. I just don't like women who allow themselves to be used just to display some guy's masculinity."

I turned back towards the procession and nodded my head at the woman. "She's only there to make Keith look manly-like. He doesn't touch her, talk to her or make eye contact with her, and she doesn't do any of that outside hanging on his arm. So their being together isn't about his feelings for her, or even her feelings for him."

Joseph looked back toward the couple approaching the fire pit; the two men had dropped out of sight. "You got all of that from them walking together?"

I shrugged. "Isn't that why you dragged me into this?"

We fell silent when Keith dropped the woman's arm and stepped onto the table over the fire pit. I nodded. Clever use of space.

Keith held up his hands, and I focused on making mental notes.

"Quiet please!"

He still wasn't confident in his ability to work the room, so he yelled instead of waiting for people to simply fall silent.

"I would like to welcome you all to our presentation. Tonight, you will see some things that only hint at the power that I can access. Power that I will use for the benefit of those who would follow me."

"Follow you where? "

People's heads craned to pick out the voice in the crowd. I noticed the kid in the area where the voice had come from. He manipulates the crowd with a lot of micromanagement. He may be afraid that he could lose control. Insecurities? Or just over planning?

"I am gathering a legion of warriors, destined to reshape the world into a paradise," he said. "We will take the mess that has been created here on earth and transform it in a way that the politicians haven't been able to do, despite their campaign promises, because of their political fighting and back-stabbing. We will make this world a better place for ourselves and our children."

I winced. The man had abandoned his own child, but was preaching parental responsibility?

The crowd, however, was loving it. I couldn't blame them.

We lived in a world where people in power were just as likely, or more, to believe that the Christian God would provide a miracle to save us, as that there was a looming disaster in the environment and climate. I suppose that would be okay, but this God never seemed to follow through these days, and super storms were becoming frighteningly common.

A loud clink and slow roar of the ventilation kicking on drew my attention back to the fire pit. Keith was holding out his bare arms, and the older guy had reappeared, holding a two-foot-long machete that he was sharpening with a stone. How classic, but it sets a good scene.

I leaned forward, trying not to miss any details, as the man set the whetstone aside and raised the machete above his head over Keith's arms. I suppressed a flinch as the machete came down on the bared flesh. I could see the sharpened blade glint as it struck and glanced off.

The man drew up the machete again, and Keith took a handkerchief that the girl offered up to him. The machete came down on the cloth and sliced through it cleanly. The crowd gasped.

I bit my lip as Keith stepped down from the small platform. The short table was removed and the fire pit was lit. Tensions built as the flames got higher, dancing in the breeze created as the smoke was sucked into the vents.

The older man used a poker to move the burning logs around the edges of the pit, leaving a small space in the center. Keith poured a cup of some kind of liquid into the fire, which then leapt even higher.

"Lighter fluid," Joseph murmured beside me.

I nodded. "Or gasoline."

I couldn't help but hold my breath as Keith lifted his leg to step into the center of the tall flames. He stood there, arms spread for a moment, before I saw his lips move briefly. The flames instantly died down to cinders, and I watched as, one by one, the red embers went out.

"Fuck me," I breathed.

I stared in shock, trying to process what I'd seen, as Keith took up his position on the small table again. The ventilation system ground to a stop as Keith began speaking. It was much the same as what he'd said before, though more drawn out. I wrenched my mind from Keith's so-called miracles and dragged my focus on to what he was saying.

I tried to pay attention to the series of clichés and trite phrases that Keith was using to get the crowd riled up, but it was like listening to an infomercial after an action movie. I caught several of the phrases that Muriel had used the day before.

I knew the sales tricks Keith was using, and I could sense the excitement and drive when he yelled out a call to action. But I couldn't help wanting to shake my head at how transparent it was to anyone who was familiar with the techniques.

I could tell that the crowd wasn't feeling the same way. They were lapping up every word and embracing the emotions Keith was calling for. The faces had gone from passive curiosity at the beginning of the event to barely contained ferocity.

I focused on the energy he was putting out. It was well-done, though not subtle. Keith had always been great at inspiring people, using natural charisma with a magical oomph to inspire passion. This time, Keith had tapped in to people's basic need to have faith in something, and he offered himself up as that thing.

I looked around at the crowd, and I felt a sinking feeling in my gut. As Keith began closing out his speech, I grabbed Joseph's arm and tugged him towards the door. He shot me a look, but he let me drag him back from the crowd.

I glimpsed Keith and his small entourage moving towards the back of the room where they had entered just an hour before. The crowd was pressing forward, pressing inwards on each other.

Joseph and I were just outside the crush and nearly to the door when I heard a high-pitched wail of pain and fear. I whipped my head towards the sound and spotted a small figure drowning in the crowd.

I nudged Joseph and pointed at the scene. He was already straining with his greater height to see over the frenzied group.

"Looks like a young girl," he said. I didn't wait for him to say more.

I pushed my way into the crowd, tapping into the feelings that I wanted. I projected confidence and regality to encourage a sense of awe, as well as giving off feelings of rejection and submission to keep people at bay. I tightened my gut and let the feelings wash down my arms and fingers, and into the space around me.

Now, this stuff doesn't work like it does in the movies. There's no concussive wave that knocks people back with an almost visible force. It wasn't even a parting of the sea of bodies as people got out of the way. The crowd still bumped into me and jostled me around, but they tried much harder to avoid it. They moved away from me, even as they mostly ignored me.

Two twenty-something guys hesitated in their surge forward just as I passed in front of them. A large man held his ground just a moment longer to keep from being pushed into my path. A woman slipped her thin frame between two other bodies just before I stepped into the space she had been the moment before.

I quickly made my way to the young girl, a brunette of about 13 years. I grasped the girl's arm, and felt her fear even before I saw it in the hazel eyes she turned towards me. I sent feelings of calm and safety down my hand, and indicated the back of the room with a jerk of my head.

We quickly moved away from the press of bodies, despite her heavy limp, and I handed her over to Joseph. I sent out a feeling of avoidance while Joseph sat the girl down in one of the few chairs along the back wall.

I kept an eye on the crowd and grounded my energies a bit while listening to them talk.

"What's your name?" Joseph asked.

"Liz. Who are you guys?"

"Joseph. Nicola. Are you okay?"

"Just a sprain, I think. Someone stepped on my ankle."

"Do you have friends here? Family?"

"Yeah, my friends are... " Liz trailed off as she looked into the mass of people in front of us.

"We can just wait here for things to calm down," Joseph assured her. "You can find your friends when people start leaving."

I caught Liz's nod out of the corner of my eye. The crowd was still pushing, but the initial frenzy was dying down. It didn't look like anyone else had gotten any injuries more severe than some bruises from people elbowing.

"Joseph." I caught his eye and waved him over. "Time to accelerate the calming and the going away of the masses."

He nodded and stood next to me. We put our hands at our sides, palms facing forward. We grounded and centered, and let our energies join where our bodies were nearly touching.

I hesitated a moment to see if Joseph would take the control, but he didn't. I quickly reached for the emotion I wanted: laying back with a cool drink in the shade of an umbrella, with a warm breeze, the soft roar of ocean waves, and the warm colors of a tropical sunset. It was calm, content, and sedate. I sent that feeling into our combined energies and projected it out in a broad arc over the crowd.

The result was subtle but quick, taking hold in a matter of minutes. People who were hyped up and bouncing on their toes, stepped back, rolled their shoulders and relaxed their stance. The crowd stopped its steady press forward and, after a momentary hesitation, began shuffling towards the doors. Instead of the aggressive shoving, people began to display more courtesies, letting people go before them, saying "thank you".

I rolled and cracked my neck before turning to Liz. "You see your friends?"

She peered around us to the crowd. "Well... Oh yes! Kate! Becca! Over here!" She stood and waved her arm as two other girls walked towards us. After a moment of catching up, the three girls walked off with the remaining crowd.

I sighed. "Keith still knows how to get 'em riled, but never stays to clean up his messes."

"The more things change..." Joseph grabbed my arm. "Speaking of Keith, we need to leave unless we are doing a confrontation here and now."

I considered facing the man now, but I shook my head. Joseph and

I were both going to be feeling the effects of the energy work, and I didn't want to face Keith while fighting the exhaustion and the mania that often followed magical efforts.

I turned to follow Joseph and we slipped out the door with the remaining crowd. I let Joseph take the lead as we headed back to the car, with my mind drifting over what I'd just experienced. I paid just enough attention to my surroundings to not get run over when we crossed the street against the light, and I tailed Joseph to the parking lot.

When we got to our car, I felt a jolt of anger and frustration. We were blocked in by another car. The rage crashed over me before I could get a hold of my emotions.

"Dammit! This is why I have sudden urges to pull a gun and start taking out idiots!" I moved around the vehicles to take down the license plate number so we could call the police about it. I imagined keying the car for good measure.

"Freeze! Put your hands where I can see them!"

I stopped dead, shock and fear ran cold down my limbs and washed away the rage. I tried not to think about how often a minority of cops in Indy got a little carried away with their jobs. At least, I hoped it was a cop. It sounded like a cop thing to say.

I held my arms out, slowly raising my hands to the side. I saw Joseph doing the same from the corner of my eye.

A slightly sweaty, middle-aged man dressed in a cheap, charcoal gray suit stepped into my field of vision. This guy screamed detective, with his crooked tie and spare-tire belly. The thin, graying hair slicked into an uneven part topped off the look.

He held out his badge in his off hand, but the gun in his right hand is what held my attention and made my throat dry up. In fact, I was working up to new levels of terrified. I don't often get a gun pulled on me.

I cleared my throat, trying not to squeak the words. "What can we do for you, Detective...?"

The man edged up to me and lifted my shirt hem a few inches to check my waistline for weapons. Then he moved to do the same to Joseph before he answered. "You Nicola Crandall?"

I raised my eyebrows. Asking for me by name? Not a great sign.

My pulse galloped while I focused on not showing my fear. "Yes, sir. What is this about?"

The detective angled his head to talk to Joseph, keeping his gun on me. "And who are you?"

Joseph lifted his chin. He was pretty good at bravado, though I could see the sweat on his brow. "Joseph Andress."

The detective paused, the gun wavering as if he wanted to move it to point at Joseph now. "How do I know that name? You in trouble a lot, Joe?"

"No, sir," Joseph said with a barely concealed sneer. He didn't like people calling him Joe. "It's Joseph. I have a show on the local radio station. And I write for the newspaper once in a while."

The detective seemed disappointed by Joseph's answer. "Huh." He turned back to me. "Well, you need to come with me, Ms. Crandall."

"Am I being arrested, detective?" I looked the man in the eye, despite the nerves that seemed to be turning my muscles into jelly. He was definitely the type who used bully tactics people, not for pleasure but out of insecurity about his own capabilities. "I would like to know the charges, if I'm being arrested."

The detective frowned. He seemed to be thinking it over. His eyes fell on the gun in his hand and, as if he'd forgotten he'd pulled it out, he hurried to put it back in his shoulder holster. "No, you're not getting arrested. We need you to come in for questioning."

I lowered my hands, just slow enough to not spook him. "Questioning in regards to... what?" I crossed my arms over my chest and lifted my chin.

The detective scowled. "In regards to a case, Ms. Crandall. Now, come with me." He reached for my arm.

I dropped my arms and stepped back, only slightly, to avoid his grasp. "If I'm not being arrested, then I can go to the station in my own vehicle and at my own convenience, so long as it is within a timely manner."

The detective's hands clenched into fists and he blew out a breath. "Yeah. That's right." He tried to stare me down for a moment, but I didn't blink.

The detective snorted in disgust and reached for his wallet. He dug out a business card that had seen better days and flicked it at me. It took more will power than I thought I had at the moment, but I didn't flinch as the card hit my cheek and fell to the ground.

I watched him fume for several seconds before I bent over to pick it up. I kept my motions slow and calm, hoping he wouldn't notice how much my hands shook.

"Well, Detective..." I read the name on the card, "Brett Ames." I looked back at his face, refusing to hide from eye contact with him. "It just so happens that I am relatively free this afternoon. Shall I ask for you, specifically?" I managed a small smile that I didn't think was too shaky.

Detective Ames sneered at me. "Yeah. I should be at my desk all day."

It wasn't my fault. I'm just so used to using sarcasm as a shield. Plus, he opened that door wide and begged me to walk through it. So, I did. I gave him a head-to-toe look, smirked and replied, "I have no doubt of that."

Probably not the smartest move of the day.

Detective Ames snarled wordlessly and got into his car.

"You are gonna pay for that one," Joseph said, quietly moving up beside me as we watched the unmarked car drive away.

I nodded and let out a shaky breath that was just a hair from becoming a whimper. "Don't I know it."

•   •   •

A few hours later, after taking the time to calm down from the morning's events, we pulled into the police station indicated on Detective Ames' business card. I was still worried about why I was being called in for questioning, but at least at the station it was unlikely I would get shot at by a detective with an itchy trigger finger who was bitter about his dead-end career.

I had told Joseph that he didn't have to come with me, but I think he felt that his local reputation might protect me a little. It was a nice thought.

We walked into the station and asked for Detective Ames. The woman at the front desk shot me a look that I could swear was sympathetic before she pointed us in the right direction.

The bullpen was a decent sized, open room that seemed much smaller than it really was since it was crammed full of desks. We stopped and asked a young deputy where Ames' desk was at. He pointed at a desk across the room unsurprisingly piled high with papers.

Detective Ames was reading a file, sitting in a chair that was probably older than he was. He was leaning back with his feet on a tiny spot on the desk that wasn't filled with manila folders and dot-matrix printouts. When he saw us walking towards him, he quickly dropped his feet down and stood up, straightening his unbuttoned jacket.

"You came," he accused me.

I raised my eyebrows. "I said I would. Now, can we get this over with? I have places to be and things to check out."

Detective Ames looked at Joseph and pointed to the hard, wooden benches outside the bullpen. "You can wait there. Ms. Crandall, come with me."

We went to an interview room, a tiny dark space with a large table, three chairs and a full-wall mirror. I primped my long dark hair with a smirk before sitting down. I wondered what the people on the other side of the mirror were thinking.

Detective Ames brought in a digital recorder and a legal pad, and dropped them on the table in front of me. A younger officer followed him in with a banker box marked with several letters and numbers. The officer dropped the box on the table and left.

Detective Ames opened the lid with a flourish and pulled out the manila folder on top. He sat down, flipped open the folder and scanned through the top page before pinning me with his eyes. "Where were you around 1 am on April 8th, 2010?"

"What?" I gave him the are-you-crazy look.

"Where were you on the morning of April 8th, 2010, at approximately 1 am?" Detective Ames repeated, leaning forward.

I stared at him in shock for several minutes. That was more than five years ago. Why would I remember that?

I realized he was serious and I began searching my memory for any information to give him. "Well, I would have been around 6 months pregnant with my daughter. So, home, alone, in bed, asleep."

Detective Ames sat back and stared down his nose at me. "Are you certain of that?"

I snorted. "More or less. I mean, I don't specifically remember, but I don't recall ever going out that late during my pregnancy. I kinda became a hermit."

"How so?"

I shrugged. "I went to work. I went to doctor's appointments. I went to the grocery store. Sometimes picked up some drive-through." I leaned forward on my elbows. "Most of my socialization was by phone, text or internet, if I bothered to do that much. And I was pretty tired throughout my pregnancy, so I got in the habit of going to bed early. Since I don't recall any specific event that would have changed that pattern for that specific day, it's a pretty good guess that that's where I was."

Detective Ames huffed and flipped to another page in the folder. "So, you were alone. And no one can verify that you were home all night?"

I pressed my lips together. "I was alone, so... no, no one can verify my whereabouts."

"And how did you know Jim Addison?" Detective Ames asked.

I frowned. "I don't recognize that name."

"Jim Addison. A security installer. Engaged to Erica Dansby. Lived in the neighborhood of Glendale." Detective Ames bit off the words, raising his voice.

I sat back and folded my arms over my chest. "I don't know him. I don't recognize those names. I didn't hang out much in Glendale."

The detective watched my face for several moments before he turned his attention back to the folder. He flipped to another page. "Tell me about your involvement in the group known as Thor's Hammer."

I blinked. "I've never been involved in Thor's Hammer. Aren't they a white pride type of gang?"

"You know what kind of gang they are but you've never been involved with them?" Detective Ames smirked at me, with a disbelieving expression.

I cocked my eyebrow and stared at him for a moment. I caught my reflection in the mirror behind him and I nearly laughed aloud at the idea of being in an Aryan gang, with my dark complexion and curly black hair.

It wasn't uncommon for people to think I had some African in my ancestry, and that wasn't wrong, though my roots were more Italian and Romani thanks to my father's lineage. I would stick out in a white-pride group like a wolf among sheep.

"I've heard of Thor's Hammer," I admitted. "Just enough to know to stay away from them. That's it."

"But you are Heathen, aren't you?" Detective Ames asked with a sneer. "You are all over these Heathen chat groups online."

I sighed. "Yes, but..."

"And this Thor's Hammer gang is a Heathen gang. But you are claiming you aren't associated with them at all?"

I leaned forward, glaring. "Are all Baptists the funeral protesting fanatics, Detective? Are all Seventh-Day Adventists part of the Branch Davidians?" I gave him a brief moment to process that, then sat back. "No, I'm not associated in any way with Thor's Hammer. Yes, I am Heathen. The connection between the two is circumstantial at best."

"So you say." The detective muttered before he looked down at the folder again, reading through several pages. I watched the bulge of his double chin change size as his head moved while he read down the pages.

After several minutes, he looked up. "And how often did you visit the Zoot Suit during that time?"

I jerked my eyes from his wobbling neck. "The what?"

"The Zoot Suit."

"I'm not familiar with that name," I said. I barely kept from rolling my eyes at his attempts to "catch me" by phrasing his questions as if he expected me to know these people and places.

Detective Ames poked his finger into the table between us. "It's a jazz bar. In Broad Ripple."

This time I rolled my eyes. "I never really went to any jazz bars. Unless there was karaoke. I'm a bit of an introvert that way." I pulled my phone out of my pocket and checked the time.

Detective Ames reached across the table as if to grab the phone. "Hey! You can't use that in here."

I glared at him, holding the phone out of his reach. "I'm checking the time."

I put it back in my pocket, taking my time just to annoy him. "Speaking of which, I've given you enough of my time. If you don't have any important questions," I put a lot of emphasis on "important", "I am in town for a reason, and I'd like to get back to that now."

The detective stood up and leaned forward on his hands. His face was close enough that I caught a whiff of garlic and pickles from his breath. "I'm not entirely satisfied with the answers you've given me, Ms. Crandall. We received a tip that you are involved in this case, and I intend to find out how."

I stood up calmly, reaching for my power to give me presence and a tiny bit of intimidation. I was sick of this treatment.

"I am NOT involved in this case," I said. "I never have been. Unless you have decided to arrest me - and you'd better have good evidence to do so - I am leaving." I walked around the table and opened the door.

"You have my number if you decide you need to ask me about any other neighborhoods in Indy." I stepped out the door, but I couldn't resist calling over my shoulder, "Or just buy an atlas."

I picked up Joseph on my way out of the station. He seemed to sense that I wasn't up to talking about what had happened yet and kept quiet as we headed to the parking lot. As we approached the car, a tall woman stepped out of the shadows of the tree we'd parked under.

I froze a moment, then relaxed and sighed. "Mercy. What are you doing here?"

"Following you," she folded her arms across her chest. "Find anything interesting?"

I exchanged a look with Joseph and he shrugged. I looked back to Mercy and nodded. "We checked out Keith's little show. It was impressive."

"And Nicola nearly got herself shot and arrested due to excessive snark in the presence of an officer of the law," Joseph said, opening the passenger door. "Let's go grab some food. I think better when I'm chewing."

Mercy headed for the back seat. "Sounds good."

• • •

We settled into the corner booth of a local diner, sliding in along the torn vinyl seat and propping elbows on the worn table. Mercy ended up in the middle.

The server, an older woman, juggled our three iced teas, a Cobb salad, a double bacon cheeseburger, and a breakfast platter. Once all the food was delivered safely and we started digging in, Mercy brought up Keith's show, talking around the sausage link she popped into her mouth whole.

"So, what did you guys get from Keith's display?" She paused. "You ain't gonna be joining his little coalition, are you?"

I laughed. "Not today." I chewed on a french fry. "But he's got a very dramatic display going on. I can see why he's got a following. I wonder how many are actually in his... coalition, as you called it."

Mercy nodded. "From what I've seen and heard, he's got a couple hundred general followers. Maybe two or three dozen hard core." She gulped her tea. "The hard-core ones are the ones who give him the real money."

"Yeah, the tithing." Joseph crunched down on a crouton. "How much does he ask them for?"

Mercy shrugged. "Don't know for sure. He asks for 10%, so about seventy, eighty bucks a month, I'd say. I heard one guy gives over a thousand a month."

I choked on a piece of bun. "Wow! Estimating an average of a hundred bucks a month, times thirty-some people? That's around three or four K a month!"

Joseph rubbed the bridge of his nose. "There's something off about the whole thing, though. He knows how to get people's attention, and bring them into his game, but he doesn't seem to really know where to go with them."

I nodded. "His goals are all very vague and he never gives any firm plans."

"Like he doesn't know the endgame," Joseph said.

I considered this for a moment, chewing my last bite of burger. "Maybe he doesn't. Maybe he doesn't have the plans. Maybe he just plain doesn't know what comes next."

Joseph frowned, thinking about this. "But, then... that means he isn't the head honcho of this little horde."

"Then who is?" Mercy asked.

Joseph sipped on his tea. "That, my dear, is an excellent question."

"How do we find out?" I asked, leaning back in my seat. "We can't just corner Keith and make him talk." I paused and sat up.

Joseph must have read my mind, because he started smiling and it was an evil smile. "Well, maybe we could do just that."

I grinned back at him. "Or something close to it."

Mercy rolled her eyes and stuffed the last half of a pancake into her mouth. Her words were muffled as she talked around the syrupy glob. "You'alls crazy." Joseph and I nodded. "And what was this about getting shot?"

I snorted and flagged down the server for refills of our drinks while Joseph told Mercy what had happened in the parking lot. Then I sighed and told them both about the interrogation.

Joseph shook his head. "Damn! He seriously thought you were involved in that stupid Thor's Hammer gang? What was he thinking?"

I frowned. "He was doing the ignorant, all Pagans are the same thing crap. You know how that goes." I slouched in the booth. "What bugs me, though, is that he said they got a tip that I was involved. There is no way I had anything to do with this."

Joseph sucked down half his tea. "We know this..."

I sat forward. "So where'd he get a tip about me from?"

Mercy frowned. "What about that guy from the park?"

"He wouldn't," Joseph said. "Not without Rowan's say-so... Holy crap!'

I growled. "That bitter, whiney, butthurt little... Grrr! She totally would do that kind of underhanded BS move." I grabbed the bill and scooted out of the booth. "I should hex her with so many boils on her ass that she can't sit down without thinking of me!"

CHAPT 4

Cornering Keith sounded like an easy plan when we were talking over iced tea and french fries. Finding the man, however, proved to be more complicated. We just had no idea where he would be at the moment.

We finally decided to try finding Muriel again, this time, at her house. The small one-story home had peeling white paint and a chain-link fence keeping the weeds on the outside from invading the crabgrass on the inside.

I tried to keep in mind that this was a step up from living on the streets, but I couldn't help wincing when beer bottle glass crunched under my shoes. We walked up the broken sidewalk and knocked on the weathered door.

Nothing.

We glanced at each other and knocked again. Surely with four people living here, someone was home.

This time we heard some muffled bumps and bangs as someone made their way through the house, either drunk or half-asleep. The door cracked open and a dark eye peered out.

I smiled. "Hi, Jada. Remember me?"

The door opened wider to show the young woman in an oversized night shirt and loose-leg pajama pants. "Yeah. Whaddaya want?"

"Is Muriel home?"

Jada yawned and scrunched her face as she peered at me. "Ain't you found her yet?"

I shrugged. "We found her. It's just, we need to talk to her again. Do you know where she's at now?"

Jada rolled her shoulders, working out kinks in her muscles. "Um, well... she ain't at work. It's her day off." She scratched at the side of her nose. "She sometimes hangs out with Keith's group downtown.

Circle Centre Mall. You know where that is?"

I shot a look at Joseph. "Yeah, we know where it is." I turned to leave. "Thanks, Jada. You've been a big hel..." The door closed on my words.

Mercy cocked her head to the side. "We should have considered looking for Keith where he holds his events."

I shrugged. "I'm entitled to a duh moment once a year."

Mercy laughed. "So, off to the mall?"

Joseph snorted. "More like back to the mall. I haven't been to that center of mass consumerism so much since I was a teenager."

I nodded wry agreement as we all piled back into the car.

• • •

We returned to the mall, this time scoring a spot in the underground parking garage. Hopefully, we wouldn't find a SWAT team when we left this time.

We walked with silent determination to the storefront that Joseph and I had visited just this morning. The doors were locked and the windows were still covered. Mercy put her ear to the door and Joseph and I held our breaths while she listened.

"I hear voices," she whispered. "It sounds really muffled though. They are probably in the back."

"So how do we get to them?" Joseph asked.

Mercy and Joseph both turned to me. That's what I get for being the idea person.

I rocked back on my heels and considered the situation. We couldn't just knock and expect to be let in, or even answered. There was no telling who was there or what kind of secret meeting they might be having.

My gaze wondered around, landing briefly on the woman and little boy getting a giant hot pretzel from the soft pretzel place. I mentally licked my lips. I love pretzels.

My eyes flicked to one side as an employee for the shoe store next door began pulling displays inside in preparation of closing time. I pulled out my phone to check the time. The mall would shut down in ten minutes.

I glanced to the other side and saw another mall employee, a big guy in a referee shirt, coming out of a tiny hallway next to Keith's storefront. My eyes flicked over to the next store, a women's lingerie shop. I wondered if the employee worked there. Not likely.

He probably worked at the sporting goods store several storefronts down. But then, why was he coming from that hallway? The hallway must lead to a back area with storage and employee areas and access to several storefronts and...

"Ha!" I barked out a laugh as I turned my attention to the little hallway.

I glanced around and gestured Joseph and Mercy to follow me. I quickly walked into the long, dark hallway and jogged to the door at the end. I sent out a plea and a push of energy and tried the door. It opened. I could tell by the way it pushed open that the latching mechanism hadn't caught completely.

We moved through the door and looked around. It was a hallway going left and right with doors along on both sides. The doors were all labeled with a letter-number designation.

I caught Joseph and Mercy's attention. "Move like we belong and know where we are going. If we do something wrong, just keep going like it ain't no thing."

They nodded and I took a deep breath. I turned down the hallway in the direction of Keith's storefront and stopped in front of the first door. It was most likely the back door into the space. I reached for the handle and tried the latch.

It rattled, loudly, but didn't turn.

I dropped my hand and moved on to the next door. I grabbed the handle and felt a jolt of surprise go through me as the handle turned itself in my hand.

I swallowed a scream and jerked my hand back. I stepped back in time to see the door swing in.

A young man appeared in designer jeans and a t-shirt that I recognized from the window of one of the over-priced stores we had passed on our way in. He did a double-take when he saw us, but then flashed a quick smile and stepped out into the hallway. He headed further down the hallway and turned where an exit sign hung from the ceiling.

At least a dozen other people followed the first young man. Men and women, late teens to mid-twenties, even a few I would guess at being in their 30s. Some wore business casual, some had on torn, dirty jeans. Several looked like they were modeling for college brochures, young and a little preppy.

One young man looked like a walking stereotype for Computer Science. He actually had a white plastic pocket protector. I didn't think they still made those.

Mercy, Joseph and I just watched, wide-eyed, as all these people filed out. No one said a word. They just stepped out of the door, glanced our way, and walked to the exit. It was really creepy.

Finally, the last person stepped out, glanced at us and walked away, letting the door close behind her. Mercy jumped forward and caught the door with her hand before it could latch. Joseph and I both let out huge sighs of relief, then chuckled at each other.

Mercy grabbed the door and slowly pushed it open, holding it for us. I peered into the darkness. Joseph was so close behind me, I could feel the warmth of his body on my back. I glanced back to see Mercy on Joseph's tail just as close.

We slowly walked into the dark room, letting the door close quietly behind us. We paused a moment to let our eyes adjust. I grabbed Joseph's hand to help us stay together in the dark.

We walked carefully through the room, and I hoped it was as clear a path as our brief glimpse in the light from the hallway and the dim light in the room now showed. We moved towards the source of the light - a door into what seemed to be a hallway and another door opposite the hall into what looked like a small meeting room. We could hear muffled voices drifting out of the room.

Joseph kicked something that skittered along the floor. The noise sounded obscenely loud and we all froze, waiting for the voices to come for us.

Nothing happened.

In the back of my head, a little voice popped up. Why were we sneaking around? We were here to talk to Keith, and he was very likely one of the people in the room across the hall. Why didn't we just walk in and announce ourselves?

That was a valid point, I thought, continuing my careful walk across the room. But we might stumble on some information this way.

Oh, the little voice said, starting to annoy me. It wasn't that we didn't want to get caught, it was that we wanted a chance to eavesdrop first.

I sighed silently. I hated admitting that my intentions were less than straightforward, but this opportunity was just too good to pass up.

We continued sneaking up to the room, reaching the door to the hallway without incident. I crouched down, listening carefully to the voices in the other room, two distinct voices now. One voice was high-pitched and feminine, the other lower-pitched.

Joseph crouched down beside me, and Mercy stood, guard-like, over us. I stretched tendrils of energy into the other room, tasting the mood.

I quickly recognized Keith's voice as the deeper one. I swallowed my fear when I realized that the female voice was Muriel. I could sense there was a third person in the room as well.

"If you don't believe in the cause, you don't have to stay with us," Keith said, his voice the same smooth showman's voice that he'd used during the earlier event. There was an oily feel to his energy. "There's nothing keeping you here but your own choice."

"It's not that I don't believe, Keith," Muriel said, a pleading note to her voice. "I'm just saying that... Well, I've learned that some of the myths don't back up what you've been telling us. I just want to know why."

There was a pause. A slight squeak of shoes on linoleum indicated that someone was walking. Maybe pacing?

"There's always going to be misinformation when you are dealing with tyrants," Keith said. "And, don't be fooled. We are dealing with centuries-old tyrants."

Keith paused before continuing in a softer tone. "Do you think Odin would allow information – information that actually proves him wrong – to be passed on for centuries? No. He wouldn't. We have been given the truth that has been destroyed, truth that has been hidden, truth that most people will never know. We have been entrusted with the destiny of all mankind."

"But how do we know that this new information, that what we've been told is the truth, really is the truth?" Muriel asked. I silently praised her clever question. "How do we know which is the real destiny? And who is the real tyrant?"

Keith laughed. "Who else would be the tyrant than Odin? Who else would be trying to control how things end?"

Muriel was silent for a long moment before she responded. "I - I don't know."

I waited for Muriel to continue questioning, but Keith spoke instead. "Sit down, have a cup of coffee."

The sound of a chair being dragged across linoleum echoed in the empty space. "I realize you've been struggling with these doubts," Keith continued. "And that's a good thing. It means you are growing past the level of blind acceptance. You are nearly ready to fully embrace this destiny, and accept your part in it."

I could feel Muriel's energy drop. Her confidence was broken down and she didn't have the energy or passion to fight Keith's spin on the situation. I realized that we should move now, or we would lose Muriel to Keith's propaganda, possibly for good this time.

I stood up and strode into the other room, Joseph and Mercy at my back. I caught the surprised look on Keith's face and bit back a smile as he struggled to hide it. I glanced around the room and noticed the older, military looking man sitting at the table and staring at us with narrowed eyes.

My eyebrows went up. I wouldn't have guessed that the third was this guy, but I quickly understood why Jada didn't like him. He was putting off an odd vibe, sitting calmly with his right ankle propped up on his left knee and a can of soda in his hand.

"What about telling us who's giving you this 'truth' that you're calling destiny?" I said, pushing our advantage of having surprised him.

Keith frowned and took a step back. "I cannot reveal the name."

"Because you don't know?" Joseph asked, pressing forward at my side. "Or because no one would believe you?"

"Or because it's just you making shit up?" I added. "Must be nice to have your life funded by the people you've conned with your line."

I realized I'd made a mistake in my assumptions when Keith's shoulders relaxed and he smiled. He shook his head and tsked.

"Nicola," he drawled out my name. "You've grown so bitter and cynical. It's sad that you don't have something like what we have here, our purpose, something to live for."

I smirked. "I have Ella," I reminded him quietly.

He blanched and seemed to stumble for a split second. I frowned and filed that away. I hadn't expected his reaction to be so... obvious.

From the corner of my eye, I saw the older man drop his foot and shift forward in his chair.

"I'm not bitter," I continued. "Just because I don't buy what you're selling? That's not bitter, that's having half a brain."

Joseph jumped in. "And you didn't answer the question. Why can't you tell us the name of your source?"

Keith swallowed, his eyes flickering over to the older man for a second. "My source has worked long and hard to provide humankind with the opportunity to break free of Odin's control. His name is... unimportant."

"Him?" I said. "That narrows it down a bit."

I watched Keith squirm as I took my time to consider the information. "Loki is probably bound by now, so it wouldn't be him. Besides, he starts Ragnarok after being triggered in some way, and we are talking triggers here, aren't we?"

I smiled when Keith's eyes narrowed. "I'm not telling you who it is," he growled. "I won't ruin more than two thousand years' worth of planning."

"Two thousand years, huh?" I narrowed my eyes while Keith swallowed nervously. "So not a mortal, then."

The older man stood up, his movements slow and steady, and took a step forward. "You have no idea what you are getting yourself into."

I shrugged. "It doesn't matter," I said. "Whoever he is, he's a coward. He won't take responsibility for what he is doing."

Keith fumed. "He is taking responsibility for the entire world! He is gathering his flock and will save those who have followed him. Those who have helped him complete his task!"

I laughed. "And do what? Be dead somewhere?"

Keith stepped forward in a rage. The older man put a hand on Keith's shoulder to stop him.

"He will take humanity to paradise! We will live forever in his light!" Keith yelled.

I looked at Joseph and raised my eyebrow in a silent question. He nodded.

"Alrighty then," I said. "So you are in this for the whole life everlasting thing, then?"

Keith shook his head, shrugging off the older man's hand. "No. I don't expect to make it that far." He relaxed his posture and lifted his chin. "I will be part of his army, sacrificing myself for the better world."

I cocked my eyebrow. This was starting to remind me of our talk with Muriel a few days ago.

"And that means no living forever?" Joseph asked. "Why would you choose to do that?"

Keith shrugged. "I get my payment in other ways."

"Such as...?" Joseph pressed.

Keith clenched his jaw. "Such as..." He paused, glancing from the older man to Muriel. He seemed to be wrestling with something.

Muriel caught his look and narrowed her eyes. "Don't worry about pissing me off. We are past that already."

She stood up. "If you can't answer questions around me because of what I might think, that means I won't like the answers. And when those answers are about whether you are a goddamn con man..."

She kicked at the chair she'd been sitting in sending it sliding across the floor. "You know, I don't think I wanna hear this shit anymore. In fact, I'm done with this. You guys fight amongst yourselves."

Muriel strode out the door, flinging off Mercy's hand when she tried to catch Muriel's arm. I shook my head at Joseph's questioning look. I recognized that energy from our childhood, and Muriel wasn't in the mood to listen to anyone right now.

Keith whispered in the older man's ear, and the older man stared at each of us for a moment before following Muriel out the door. A few seconds after they disappeared from view, we heard the door to the back hallway thud twice as it closed.

I exchanged looks with Joseph and Mercy, then turned back to Keith. He crossed his arms over his chest.

"Happy?" he said. "I was helping her get her life together. I was helping her find purpose."

I snorted. "Better living through tithing? Really?"

He narrowed his eyes at me. "What do you want to hear? That I want the power? That I need the money? Is that the kind of person you want me to be? Would it help you deal if I was just a monster?"

I snarled silently. I wasn't here for what I wanted. That ship had long since sailed. What I wanted from Keith was the space to pretend he didn't exist anymore. But his actions were creating a chain reaction right through my life. The only thing left that he could offer me was the truth.

I pulled up the energy of dark goddesses and gave him a look of dominance and power. I felt my eyes shift, becoming ever so slightly more angled and cat-like. I could feel my throat change, too, feeling almost clogged or full. When I spoke, my voice was deeper with a slight vibrato. "I want the truth."

Keith's eyes twitched slightly, but I knew he wouldn't fight the impulse to answer me.

"That is the truth. I need the money. I want the money. And I want what I was promised. I will gladly pay the price for it with my life."

I released the energy and stared down my nose at him for a long moment. He shifted a little, as if he regretted admitting it. To his credit, though, he didn't try to take it back.

I finally sniffed at him in disgust. "Once a schmuck..."

I turned on my heel and walked out the door.

• • •

Mercy gave me directions to be dropped off at an apartment where a friend was letting her couch surf. We drove silently through the dark streets, each lost in our own thoughts. So much so, I made three wrong turns when Mercy's instructions reached through my brain fog a little too late.

I was finally feeling the stress of the confrontations with Detective Ames and with Keith. It bugged me that Keith would be so easily motivated by outright greed. He had never been like that before. Even rejecting his responsibilities with Ella had been more about his insecurities and fears than outright selfishness.

I tried to shrug it off. Obviously, the man had changed. More than I would have thought possible. But my mind kept going back to the holes in his narrative. Keith wasn't telling me everything. I couldn't shake the feeling that I was missing something important about the change from the man I'd loved to the man I'd confronted today.

Mercy leaned over my shoulder from the back seat and pointed to a building. "That's it, Nicola."

I pulled over and she got out. She leaned in through the door to talk.

"I appreciate the lift. And I'm sorry it didn't go as well as you hoped." She sounded genuinely disappointed.

I shrugged. "Yeah, well, maybe we just need to sleep on it or something. We can talk to Muriel again tomorrow and see if she is leaving Keith's legionnaires. If so, we have a mission accomplished, and that's that."

Mercy paused and rolled her shoulders. I got the feeling she was unhappy with what I'd said, but I couldn't figure out why that would be.

She raised her head and peered over the car at the apartment building across the street. "Speaking of Keith..." She jerked her chin towards the entryway. Keith was just walking into the building.

Joseph raised his eyebrows. "Well, well, well. Just like a bad penny, he turns up. What are the chances?"

I shut off the ignition and opened the door.

"Hey!" Joseph called. "What are you doing?"

I leaned down to talk. "I want to clarify something that's been bugging me with Keith. You can stay here, if you don't want to come."

I trotted over to the sidewalk, smacking the head of a statue of an angel with one wing broken off as I passed. Joseph caught up just as I reached the door. I noticed Mercy trailing behind him.

I frowned when I realized that the door was the kind that you needed a code for or to be buzzed in. That could be a problem. I pulled on the door anyways, choosing the obvious but futile attempt first. The door unlatched and opened easily. A quick glance showed us that someone had abused the latch until it had broken.

We walked inside and stopped. None of us knew which of the dozens of apartments on three stories was Keith's.

I looked around the tiny entryway, feeling stupid, until Joseph spotted a list of names on the buzzers outside. I crossed my fingers, since a lot of apartments didn't bother keeping up with the high turnover of tenants. But, there it was, "Ludlow, K" on the tag for apartment 3F.

"Well, aren't we all double-O seven?" Joseph laughed as we walked to the stairs. "Finding the evil mastermind behind the plot to destroy the world."

I snorted. "So now Keith is Dr. No?" I asked as I started up the darkened steps.

I glanced out of the huge window that served as the outer wall of the stairwell. With the lighting in the stairwell out, I could easily make out our car across the street, and a man walking along the sidewalk next to it. I frowned, thinking the way the man walked was somehow familiar.

"Naturally," he said, drawing my attention back with a Sean Connery-esque accent. "And you, my dear, are shaken, not stirred."

Our laughter echoed in the dark stairwell, as I huffed my way up the stairs. In the dim light of the street lamps filtering in through the huge window that served as the outer wall of the stairwell, I saw Joseph breathing heavily. I noticed that Mercy didn't get winded at all. Bitch. The jealous thought that I sent her way had no real animosity to it.

We reached the third floor and began walking down the hallway. I noted the door that I guessed was 3F and kept my eyes on it, locking on to our goal.

The door I was watching burst open, making us jump, and several tough looking men walked out. Their body language screamed aggression and I stopped in my tracks before I even noticed the guns and knives they had in their hands and strapped to their legs.

I grabbed Joseph's arm, pulling him behind me as my mind raced through scenarios. We were only a few feet from the stairwell. The hallway was straight with no corners or side halls. The stairwell had a fire door. The men hadn't turned towards us yet. There was no way to know for sure that they would attack us.

I pulled at my memories for an emotion that I didn't feel often: paranoid alertness. I found it buried in my childhood when I used to go walking in the sparse forests of my grandparent's house in the country. I'd just seen a large paw print and convinced myself that a mountain lion could be in the area. A snapped twig had set my nerves on edge instantly.

I used the emotional energy to see the men's auras. An overlay of colors and vague shapes showed me what kind of people they were. Horns, claws, fangs, rage, blood.

Shit.

Pushing Joseph towards the stairs and hissing at Mercy, I turned and ran for it. A shout behind me told me they'd spotted us, and I cringed when a loud, sharp cracking noise sounded.

We ran through the door, and Mercy and I turned in perfect synchronicity to shut it behind us. Our eyes met and I saw surprised approval in hers.

I filed that away as we turned and stumbled down the stairs as fast as our feet would move. I clutched the banister to keep my balance as we swung around each corner on the stairwell.

The door above us crashed open and the uppermost pane of the huge window shattered as the fire door flew through the glass. I barely noticed the bits of glass falling around us as we hit the front door as fast as we could move.

We burst out of the apartment building and ran for the car. I threw a glance over my shoulder just as we hit the street. I could see the convoluting shadows of the men moving in the stairwell.

A loud crack rang out in the night and another pane of glass shattered. I stumbled over the fire door, now laying across the sidewalk, and lost my balance.

CHAPT 5

Mercy appeared at my side as I struggled to get up. I could hear the men in the building behind us, arguing. Mercy grabbed my arm and pulled me to my feet. We stumbled towards the car, crossing the street as Joseph raced to the passenger side.

"Oh, shit," he said. "The tire. It's gone."

I ran around the car, Mercy on my heels. The car now rested on three rubber tires and one bare rim.

I kicked at the empty tire rim, hitting it at an odd angle and stubbing my toe. This was not the kind of neighborhood where the tires just came up missing. I flashed a memory of a man walking past the car. Or away from the car.

The memories clicked together. "It was that older guy from Keith's group."

A burst of shouts and curses told me that the men had come out of the building.

Mercy looked over her shoulder at me. "They're coming."

"Well, it's not like we can outrun them," I snapped. "Can we?"

Mercy shrugged. "Maybe."

"Better than nothing, which is what else we got," I said.

I pointed at Joseph, then down the street to the left. "Run. That way, half an hour then back this way." A shudder rolled down my spine as the thought crossed my mind that one of us could die tonight. "Good luck."

Joseph nodded and took off.

I pointed at Mercy, then across the street. "You. That way, same thing." Mercy took off the direction I pointed, and I ran to the right, refusing to give in to the urge to check behind me.

It'd been a while since high school track. A long, long while. And I wasn't into running for fun. It's not my idea of it. I set myself an easy pace, then upped the speed a little. I was hoping I could sustain it for more than just a few minutes.

In between the slap-slap of my sneakers on the sidewalk and the la-lump-la-lump of my heartbeat in my ears, I strained to catch any sounds from the men behind me.

The lull made me think they were trying to figure out which way to go. Hope sprung up that they would get lost or give up. Practicality kept my feet pounding the cement.

I threw a glance back at the apartment building. I only caught a glimpse, but it took me several seconds to process it, and all my will to keep running when I did.

I saw the men. But they were changing. The shouts and curses turned into screeches and growls. They grew taller and more... demonic?

I wanted to go back and look again, to prove to myself that what I'd seen wasn't real. But I knew it was real. Whether what I'd seen was physically real or simply a look at the men's true natures, it was real. And I certainly didn't want to go back.

I angled my way down the street, taking my path off of the direct line of sight from Keith's apartment building. I dodged down an alleyway. I picked up my pace when the noises got louder, closer.

Gods, I would kill for a car.

I dodged around a sharp corner and spotted a police car. I stumbled a second, not sure if the men would attack a cop. The growling got closer and I raced towards the officer.

"Help!" I yelled, trying to get his attention, gasp for breath and be quiet about it all at the same time. "They are right behind me! Get your gun out!"

He looked at me like I was nuts, and placed his hands on his hips while standing with his feet slightly apart.

I swear, they teach all cops that stance. It means, "I got this; you are over-reacting." I changed direction slightly to avoid him and his car, and I just kept running. He dropped his arms and took one step towards me, then his gaze shot to a point over my shoulder and his eyes and mouth formed the exact same "O" shape.

That couldn't be a good sign. Crap.

As I passed by the police car, the cop drew his weapon. "S-stop! Hold it right there! Stop or I'll shoot!"

I counted the shots: one, two, three-four, five. Then the cop screamed, high and terrified. The scream cut off, snarls filling the sudden silence. I hoped he didn't suffer too much.

I slid on some gravel as I rounded the next corner. It hit me that the buildings were getting taller. I must be heading downtown. That meant lots of people. Dammit.

I wasn't familiar enough with my surroundings to be able to figure out where to go to avoid high-traffic areas. Funny thing about running for your life. No time to really plan things out.

My lungs started burning and my muscles were getting that not-quite-there, mushy feeling. I was headed a little bit right, overall, so the next corner I went left.

Apparently, the cop's sacrifice had slowed my pursuers down quite a bit. The sound of their chase was much farther back now.

My body was shooting pains in my side and down one leg. I needed to stop, soon. I needed a place to hide.

I nearly ran past the dead-end alley before it clicked. I stopped dead and ducked into the dark passage, stumbling as the sweet-acrid smell of rot and piss hit my nose.

There was a dumpster sitting a little skewed at the end of the alley and I slipped behind it and squatted down, huddling in the shadows. I hoped that the dark, smelly surroundings would throw off my tails.

I closed my eyes and concentrated on slowing my breathing. I ignored the drip-drip to the left of me, just missing my shoulder, and the cool spread of dampness on my right hip. A distinctly moldy scent teased my nose with a sneeze.

It was just like meditation; in – mind goes blank, out – I'm not here. Over and over; in – mind goes blank, out – I'm not here. Mind blank, not here. Mind blank, not here. Mind blank, not here.

I felt my consciousness go to the other, the place of visions and mindfulness. My awareness slipped into that place of there/not-there, where I could hear and see and smell, but as if watching a movie.

I felt a shadow of gratitude that I'd practiced this until it was second nature. It wasn't me present in that stinky darkness; my knowing was completely objective. I held the distant feeling like a shield. My breathing changed from the panting gasps of an out-of-shape runner to the deep, controlled breaths of one just this side of asleep.

I heard my hunters approach the alley with a sound of scraping claws and wet, snuffling growls. Terror played with the edges of my mind.

They went past the mouth of the alley, and a sliver of relief pierced my objectivity. I heard the noises stop just past the alley and my heart tripped over itself. A light pad-click of clawed feet came closer. I could hear the sniffing of creatures searching for me.

I clung to my detached state, willing the darkness around me to cover me like a cloak. Not here, not here, not here. My mind cycled through the mantra, projecting the image of my physical form transforming into just another shadow behind the trash bin.

The padding footsteps stopped in front of me. My eyes opened, slowly. I kept my mind distant, and my feeling was of curiosity and the small anxiety one feels for a beloved fictional character in trouble.

I could see a sliver of the creatures, mostly still hidden by the dumpster. They had oddly colored skin of gray and blue and purple that faded into the shadows of the alley. Their eyes glinted red and yellow when they caught the faint light. Their teeth stuck out prominently, shining with spit.

They were tall, nearly 8 feet, I would guess. And the first thing that came to mind when searching for a label for the creatures was... demon. These were creatures of fire and torture, taken from the imaginings of hundreds of Christian painters and writers.

One of the creatures stepped forward, bringing its head fully into view. Its jutting lower jaw dripped thick saliva and the deep red of blood.

Terror clawed at the edges of my mind, a gibbering panic that tried to take control. I firmly layered more darkness around me, burying my consciousness beneath the shadows of my own mind.

The creature turned its head to look at me, craning its too-long neck to peer around the dumpster. It stared into the corner where I was crouched, sniffing wetly. The sulfuric smell of its breath hit my face as I forced my lungs to breathe, slow and even.

An eternity passed while it searched my hiding spot, as if it sensed that I was really there. I clung to my mental cloak, fighting the horror each time its mouth passed within inches of my nose.

Tires screeched on the road at the mouth of the alley. The creature jerked its head around and snarled.

"Creatures of the desert god, I challenge you to battle!" a female voice cried out, fearless and powerful.

One by one, they vanished from my field of vision, claws scraping on the filth covered cement.

I sat, frozen with the muted shock of how close I'd come to being caught, listening to the sounds of fighting. I struggled to bring my consciousness back from the shadows. Not the terror and fear in my mind, but the part of me that could think and function.

I heard the dull clink of metal striking flesh and bone, and the curiosity of who my savior was finally dragged my consciousness fully back into my body. I blinked a few times and struggled in the muck to stand up. Clinging to the side of the dumpster, I stared at the sight at the mouth of the alley.

A blonde woman in hiking boots and a red flannel shirt held a huge sword in front of her. Two of the three creatures were still standing, bleeding a black bile from cuts on their arms and chests. One creature lay to the side of the battle, the reddish light gone from its eyes.

I tore my gaze from the fallen monster as one of the creatures lunged at the woman. In a blur that told me she wasn't quite human, she parried the creature's attack with her blade and followed with several slashes, drawing blood again and again.

The other creature attacked while the woman was still slicing at the shoulder of the first, and I swallowed a gasp as the woman pivoted mid-stroke to drag the heavy blade across the second creature's throat. It fell to the ground, twitching as its life drained away. The first creature glanced at its fallen comrades before it bolted away down the street.

I staggered out from behind the dumpster and headed towards the woman. As I came near, she shook the sword in her hands and I watched in awe as it shrunk down into a large bowie knife. The blonde woman sheathed the knife at the small of her back and chuckled.

"I guess he didn't like the odds, huh?" she said, turning to face me.

"Mercy." I said, looking her up and down. She nodded. "What the hell."

"Get in the car," she said. I glanced at the tire, which had the too-small look of a donut. "I doubled back and got the tire changed. I'll explain the rest while we get out of here."

I hesitated a moment. "There was a cop..." She shot a questioning look at me. "He was in the street. I ran past him."

She sighed. "He's dead, then."

I nodded.

"There's nothing we can do for him," Mercy pointed out.

I nodded again, reaching for the passenger door handle.

Mercy grabbed my arm and turned me to face her. "Nicola, it wasn't your fault. Those creatures kill and that cop was just in the wrong place. It isn't because of you. It's just a shitty thing that happened."

I pulled away from her grasp and mumbled, "I know. Doesn't make it better, though." I opened the door and got into the car.

Mercy hesitated a moment, like she was going to try to talk to me again, but she just walked around to the driver's side.

We pulled away from the alley, and I stared out the window, not paying attention to where we were going. I wondered what would happen when someone found the creatures' bodies. I wondered how we would find Joseph and if he was alive. I wondered what the police would believe when they found the cop torn apart.

The flashing red and blue lights caught my attention, and I focused on the scene down the street as we rolled past. Mercy was keeping the speed well below the limit, so I had plenty of time to see the medical examiner bent over the dead officer's body and a detective pulling something out of the dead officer's car.

I also saw Ames standing with his arms crossed over his chest, watching the others work with a critical look on his chubby face. And I saw his face turn towards us. His eyes landed on our car and his arms dropped as he stepped towards us. And a building cut off my view of him as we moved past the intersection.

I turned to Mercy. "Ames saw us."

She shot me a worried look.

"I don't know if he could see us," I clarified. "But I'm sure he recognized the car." I turned my head back to the window. "He probably can't prove it was us, but he'll suspect."

Mercy turned back to face the road, nodded once and slowly accelerated. She turned left at the next major intersection and drove several blocks before turning back in the direction that Joseph had headed.

I noted in the back of my mind that she was making a wide arc around back towards Keith's place. I remembered vaguely that I'd said to head back to the building after losing the men... no, monsters.

An image of the dead creatures flashed in my mind and I choked back a laugh. It was probably hysteria after the shock.

A part of my brain kept the running commentary of objective observations about the evening's events. Another part wept and laughed in equal measure. A third part of my mind noted that the others were pretty standard symptoms of psychological shock. And I stared wide-eyed out of the window, counting doorways and tracing neon signs with my eyes.

We came to a stop at the side of the road and I blinked away the blank expression. I focused on the building we'd pulled up to for a long moment before I recognized it as the apartment building we'd left only an hour earlier. Of course, with weird creatures on our tails, I hadn't really paid much attention to the surroundings.

I did recognize the creepy, broken-winged angel statue in the front yard. And, next to the pathetic heavenly host, Joseph sat perched on the edge of a giant, cement planter.

I rolled down the window and called him over. He seemed as shell-shocked as I was, walking towards us in a dazed, almost drunken way. He climbed into the back seat and Mercy drove away. I'd never been so relieved to leave a place in my life.

CHAPT 6

We abandoned the idea of going back to the hotel I been staying at or to Joseph's place. As much as I despised spending so much money on getting a different hotel, I couldn't argue that we were currently in danger from all sides. Going to an obvious safe haven would be less than safe.

We found a cheap but clean motel with stark white, bleach-scented sheets and peeling paint on the edges of the walls. The two full-sized beds were a little too firm and slightly lumpy, but I was pretty sure that wasn't going to matter anymore than the sharp smell on the pillowcases would.

I sat on one of the beds and watched Joseph take off his shoes and climb up on the other. I turned back to Mercy and stared at her as she moved around the room, checking out the little coffee maker, looking out the window, and locking the door.

She was trying to ignore my look, but my current state had given me a kind of emotionless detachment and focus that a small part of me realized had to be a bit uncomfortable. But, being detached, I just kept staring.

Finally, she pulled one of the uncomfortable looking chairs away from the tiny table and set it in front of the dresser, facing the beds.

"Alright," she said with a sigh. "You want some answers."

I nodded. "But first, we need to catch everyone up to speed."

Mercy nodded. She told us that the man-demon creatures had ignored her, and she had only gone a few blocks before turning back.

Joseph cleared his throat. He'd gone farther, but only because the monstrous sounds had driven him to run longer than he needed to. "They didn't follow me at all."

I swallowed the lump that formed around the implications that the creatures had only come after me. I turned to my friend and explained what had happened as I fled. I was still feeling numb, but my voice cracked when I described the creatures' attack on the police officer.

Joseph listened, eyes slightly widened. When I got to the part about Mercy showing up and fighting off the demons, his eyes darted over to the blonde and he shifted nervously on the bed as I finished the story.

Suddenly, I couldn't take the fear energy filling the room. I stood up and pulled Joseph off the bed.

"We need a smoke," I said as I hauled him towards the door.

Mercy stood up as if to block us, but I shook my head in warning. She seemed to get the message and instead led us to the door and checked the dark hallway outside before waving us out.

After a few deep inhales of the cigarette, I took a moment to appreciate the wisdom of so many Native American tribes in using tobacco as a spiritual cleanser. By Joseph's expression, he was feeling much the same.

I focused on the energy swirling around my gut and in my head. The sickly yellow feel of it saddened me, both that it was from and in me, and that what we'd experienced completely justified having such a strong energetic reaction.

I gathered the energy together and pushed it down my body, feeling a tingling, like pins and needles, as it went through my feet and into the cement below. It didn't get rid of all the fear and anxiety, but it took the sharp edges off of it and made the feelings more manageable.

I eyed Joseph and noticed his energy draining away as he grounded himself as well. I smiled at him, trying to convey the friendship and sympathy that I felt for him, especially now, in our unusual circumstance.

We finished our smokes in silence, both of us sensing that the things we would talk about were not appropriate in such a public space, even deserted as it was. When we finished, we silently stubbed out the cigarettes and turned to go back into the hotel room.

Mercy was watching us with a tension that seemed to say she didn't trust us to remain calm. The idea of her being so worried about Joseph and me getting violent struck me as really funny, and I started giggling. We went back to our previous seats, Mercy stopping to throw the deadbolt and chain, while I threw my head back and let the humor drain the rest of the tension from my gut.

I noticed Joseph looking at me with a concerned expression, but I just waved him off and turned to Mercy. "Okay, now spill."

She took a deep breath and began. "I am not human."

Joseph snorted.

Mercy rolled her eyes. "I realize this is a bit obvious now, but I want to be absolutely clear in what I'm telling you."

I exchanged a glance with Joseph. By his expression, he was wondering the same thing I was: alien or paranormal creature? And did we need to invest in silver or wooden stakes?

We turned back to Mercy.

She took a deep breath. "I'm a Valkyrie," she said, pushing the words out in a breathy rush.

That was it? I reached up and scratched an itch on my forehead. I saw Joseph in the corner of my eye rub a spot on his chin. We both kept watching Mercy, who looked back and forth from Joseph to me.

I shifted my seat on the bed. Joseph brought his feet up to sit cross legged. The silence stretched out. I chewed on the inside of my lower lip.

Finally, I broke the silence. "So..." I said, trying to think of something to say. The myths of the Valkyrie were pretty vague, with some saying they were kind of half gods and others saying they were spirits of dead warrior women. Lots of speculation and theory, but little fact, even for myths. "Does that mean you're dead?"

Mercy drew back, horror and disgust showing on her face. "What? No! I'm not dead! Valkyrie are spirit warriors. We are kind of like extensions of Odin's will." She shifted in her chair, still watching us closely. She hesitated another moment before continuing. "That's all? You aren't going to freak out?"

I laughed. "Probably not." I caught her confused look. "You gotta understand something. We get people coming to us all the time claiming to be stuff."

Joseph nodded and ticked off the more common ones, "Dragons, fae, werewolves, aliens, unicorns, ogres..."

I jumped in. "And don't forget the whole I'm the queen of this group or that group. And, yes," I nodded my head at Mercy, "we've heard 'I'm a Valkyrie' a few times."

I paused and rubbed the side of my chin. "Haven't had much in the way of proof for the Valkyrie thing before, though." I shook myself out of the mental wanderings that I felt my mind going towards. "The point is, me and Joseph may not swallow this stuff hook, line and sinker, but we do try to take these claims seriously. A couple of times, we've even gotten proof that the claims were real, or at least as real as can be expected."

"Which means," Joseph said, "we have had deep, dark, long conversations about how likely these things are. And what it would mean if all of these different creatures actually showed up in the physical world."

"Valkyrie may not be human, but we've gotten to know you as an individual," I pointed out. "And you fought off those demons."

"And demons are much scarier than badass warrior women who aren't trying to kill us," Joseph finished.

Mercy gaped at us. I don't think she was expecting the reaction we'd had.

"I thought I'd have to... I don't know. Calm you down. Keep you from running off..." She trailed off.

I frowned. "Running off would be pretty stupid of us, at this point, what with monsters and gun-toting detectives after us."

Joseph snorted. "The gun-toting detective is only after you," he pointed out. "I only have to worry about drooling creatures from the nether realms." He stopped suddenly, as if he realized what he'd just said, and shuddered.

I forced a laugh, trying to break the mood. "You just aren't as lucky as I am," I teased. "Only the really popular kids get dragged into interrogation rooms, don't you know?"

Joseph smiled, but it didn't quite reach his eyes.

Mercy shook her head at us. "You guys are so weird," she said. "Your world is being turned upside down and your reality is being shaken, and you just... deal with it."

I grinned at her. "Well, it helps that we were crazy to begin with."

I turned to Joseph. "Hungry? Let's get a gooey pizza and a lot of really sugary soda. And breadsticks. With garlic. Cause nobody's copped to being a vamp, but I'm not ruling it out."

I eyed Mercy and Joseph up and down playfully as Joseph grabbed the hotel phone book to check out the pizza places.

We found a local pizza dive and ordered a couple of cheesy pizzas with a selection of toppings, though Joseph and I stood strong against Mercy's criticism of adding cream cheese to pepperoni.

Apparently, being a demi-god doesn't mean you have good taste in pizza.

While we waited for our order to be delivered, Joseph and I sprawled on one of the beds while Mercy sat cross legged on the other, and we took turns quizzing her about the Valkyrie and Norse gods.

"What's Odin like? And does Loki look anything like Tom Hiddleston?" I asked. I like to get the important stuff out first.

Mercy smirked. "Loki is blond and bearded, so... No. And Odin is... funny but serious. And so very wise. You can see the weight of understanding on his shoulders, but he still thinks that puns are hilarious."

She shook her head with a soft smile on her lips. I could tell she was thinking of some memory of bad word play or something. "He cares so much, but he doesn't really know how to show it. He's like an old-school father who was never taught how a grown man can play with the kids, but he wants to..."

We were silent for a moment, each lost in our thoughts about that.

Joseph spoke up first. "So, Ragnarok is really a thing, right? It's going to happen, just like in the stories?"

"Or just like Keith says?" I added.

Mercy tilted her head to the side. "Sort of like the stories. Things have gotten lost in translation. And Odin didn't tell the whole story, 'cause he knew there would always be someone trying to start it, or thinking it was happening and trying to stop it, or trying to be a part of it."

Mercy shook her head "So he gave humans the general run-down and he told the gods what would happen to each of them, but he didn't give all the details about the role Midgard would play."

She shrugged. "Also, it's more complicated than that. I mean, the Norse gods are real and the creation story that the myths tell for them is completely true."

I frowned and glanced at Joseph. He had a thoughtful scowl on his face.

"You mean the cow is real?" I asked.

"Yes." Mercy held up her hand. "But..." she said, waiting until she had our complete attention. "The same is true for the Greek gods." She paused.

"And the Orisha," she said, referencing the gods of Yoruba, an African religion, and Santeria, a belief system in the Caribbean similar to Voodoo. "And any other religions or pantheons you can think of, and all the ones that haven't yet been imagined. And several that have been long forgotten."

My face scrunched up as I tried to follow what Mercy was saying. It wasn't something new for me to hold the belief that all religions were equally valid. Of course, that was easier when there really was no proof that ANY of them were any more real than Santa Claus.

At that point, I realized that, before the night was over, I was going to ask if Santa was real. A part of me felt a sense of defeat about that.

"So," I said, drawing out the word as I tried to organize my thoughts into some kind of coherence. "What does that mean for science and the big bang theory and all that?"

Mercy nodded. "That is also completely true."

"But, how?" Joseph asked. "How is that even possible?"

Mercy sighed and looked down at her hands. I could tell she was trying to figure out how to tell us.

I suddenly remembered a few months back when Ella had asked me about some protesters we had driven past on the street. They were across the street from a cemetery holding signs condemning a teenager who had committed suicide after being bullied for being gay. I remembered the feeling of just... understanding so much background about the situation, the social backdrop that had caused it, the complexities and history of the protesters' beliefs... and I had balked at telling her.

Ella had asked why they were holding signs. It had been a simple question, but the answer was anything but simple. I remembered thinking that this was why parents told their kids that babies came from birds or vegetables, and I remembered struggling with my promise to always be truthful with my child.

I pulled my focus back to Mercy, and I sympathized. I drew energy from the memory of love and compassion that my conversation with Ella had brought out. I directed it at Mercy, lifting her energy and encouraging her mind to find the best way to communicate. I held this for several seconds before she raised her head and straightened her shoulders.

She took a deep breath. "You know how a movie works, right? Making a movie isn't just what the actors do. It's also the set built by the crew. It's the sounds added later. It's the CGI and the wires and the explosions. It's the stunt people and the makeup people, too. A movie isn't just a camera following people around, right?"

I nodded.

"That's how the world works," Mercy explained. "What you see – the actors – that's the science. The gods are all the different crews that work behind the scenes, pushing, pulling, correcting and sometimes adding in a CGI thing – and all of that adds up to the end result."

"Whoa," Joseph said. "I kind of understood that."

Mercy continued. "Each pantheon contributes to the whole thing, but instead of the makeup crew working all together, they are actually gods from everywhere working on the same general thing."

I nodded. "Like art or nature or war?"

Mercy smiled. "Exactly. There will be a Norse god working on this over here, and another working on that over there. So the crew isn't divided by job but by pantheon."

I glanced at Joseph. "You realize what this means, don't you?"

Joseph raised his eyebrows in question.

"This means life is like that one movie, and you're Jim Carrey." I grinned, knowing he would understand the reference.

He rolled his eyes at me while I laughed.

"So all these gods - and science, too," Joseph said. "They all work together but kind of not?"

Mercy nodded. "That's why you have things that are just so complex that it's really hard to figure them out."

I nudged Joseph. "Like weather and evolution," I suggested.

Mercy nodded.

I considered this for a minute. "So, pretty much all the stuff that we explain through chaos theory and other really complex mathematics."

"That would also include human interactions," said Joseph.

"Human interactions, god interactions," I said. "Is there much difference, really?"

We looked at each other for a moment, then turned to Mercy.

"Not that I can see," she said, holding up her hands in a shrugging motion.

"What about the Christian god?" Joseph asked. "Is Yahweh, or Jehovah or whatever, real?"

"I'm not sure," she said. She caught our skeptical looks. "It's not like we hold conventions or something. We don't all get together and do headcounts. But most of us run into a god from another pantheon once in a while," she lifted one shoulder in a half-shrug. "It's just that no one I know has ever seen Jehovah. There's a lot of things that happen that we think he's behind, but we just don't know for sure."

"Great," I muttered. "Deity on the down-low. Just what we need to anticipate for a follow-up performance."

Joseph chuckled and I stuck out my tongue at him.

"Wait a minute," Joseph said. "If you are a Valkyrie, how do you know how to drive a car? Aren't you supposed to be an ancient warrior or something?"

I thought back to the sight of Mercy wielding her sword. "Definitely a warrior."

Mercy shook her head. "Driving a car and fighting aren't really mutually exclusive skills," she pointed out. "Most of what was written down about us is from centuries ago, but we've still been here. We lived through all these technological advances. We've learned to use the 'big mechanical wagons' just fine."

She paused and grinned. "Although Rade doesn't really have the patience to pick up computer skills very well."

I exchanged glances with Joseph and considered that idea. If the Valkyrie – and the gods – all stayed involved in the world, just more subtly, they could very easily pick up on any current fashions, lingo or any other trends, and blend in with everyone else. That would explain why they wouldn't be noticed by anyone.

A knock at the door made us all freeze.

"Pizza!"

Mercy sighed in relief and got up to answer.

"Wait!" I said, remembering.

Mercy paused on her way to the door and Joseph jerked his head around to look at me.

I smiled as innocently as I could. "Is Santa Claus real?"

• • •

It had been years since I'd put away so much pizza in one sitting. I never realized that fitting half a pizza into one's stomach was an acquired skill. But I assure you, it is.

"What you're saying is that Santa is real in the same way that spells are real," Joseph asked.

"Yeah," Mercy said. "A manifestation of energy for a specific purpose that comes into existence in a physical but often temporary form."

I wiped my face with a napkin and flopped back down on the bed. "So why don't all our spells manifest in a physical form?"

Joseph nodded. "I get results, but they are subtler. Like doing a prosperity spell and then getting a bonus check from work."

He tossed his napkin at the trash can and missed. "I believe my spell worked, but part of me wonders if it wouldn't have happened anyways." He got up, picked up the napkin and threw it away.

"Well, that's the thing," Mercy said. "If you had done the spell and gotten a bag of money that appeared out of nowhere, you would probably turn it over to the authorities or something, right? You would reject the more obvious result."

She shrugged. "Human spirits are built to make magic, but your brains are built to understand systems. You learn cause and effect from before birth, and that's the only thing you really ever see proof of, particularly in modern times."

Mercy paused and eyed the rest of the pizza in the box beside her, then pushed it away. "Your science is built on finding cause and effect, on statistics, on provability. Science is solid and repeatable. Magic is... less so."

She stood up and walked to the bathroom, still talking as she washed the pizza grease from her hands. "Magic is more provable when you don't require proof. It's more solid and repeatable when you don't look for those qualities. It manifests without any cause when you don't require a cause."

Joseph and I exchanged a glance.

"I've never required a 'cause' from my spells," he pointed out.

I shook my head, agreeing with him.

Mercy chuckled as she sat back down. "Not as a built-in condition of the spell, no. But in your literal, scientifically taught mind, you were looking for a 'how' and a 'why' for the spell to happen." She tapped her head. "Your brain was looking for a cause, even if you weren't doing it consciously."

I nodded, suddenly understanding what she was saying. The idea Mercy was explaining was something I'd talked with Joseph before, just in a different way.

"It's the Easter Bunny Effect," I said to him, reminding him of those conversations. "You can't just decide that you believe in the Easter Bunny as a real being. There's a part of you that calls BS on it, no matter how much you want to believe."

Mercy nodded. "Exactly. That inner scientist, that inner skeptic, calls BS, as you put it. And the more scientific your culture is, the stronger that inner skeptic is."

She shrugged. "So even when you do magic, part of you denies it. And that makes the magic work in a subtler way, which reinforces the inner skeptic. The gods have watched this happen for centuries."

I frowned. "So how do we counter that little spiral downward?"

"It's not easy," Mercy said. "You pretty much have to tap into a strong emotion. Emotions trump logic, most of the time. You see this all the time in disasters, survival situations, and even horror movies."

"Yeah," Joseph said. "Those idiots run through the woods in the dark, running from some guy that never goes faster than a determined walk. Of course they are going to trip over something. And they just make it worse by looking over their shoulder. It's like, watch where you're going ya moron!"

I grinned at Joseph. He loved to yell at movies while he watched them. That was probably why we never went to the movie theater any more. Too much risk of getting kicked out.

Mercy shook her head at us. "Something like that. But emotions like fear and desperation are extremely powerful. They give you the magic manifested to lift cars off of your trapped kid. Or make a jump over a crevice that you never could have done before. Or climb a tree to get away from a wolf, or whatever."

Mercy gave us a look of skepticism. "You excuse it as adrenaline, but, seriously? Ever wonder why they've never come out with a study where those kinds of feats were performed by someone who had gotten adrenaline injected into them?"

I sat up. "Holy shitsicles, batman."

I looked at Joseph. His eyes had gone wide as he came to the same conclusion.

"That's a really good point," he said. "The military should have been all over that, giving epi pens to soldiers in combat or something."

Mercy shrugged. "But it doesn't work that way. No emotion, no magic. Intense love and joy can do the same, but most people with those emotions – the positive ones – aren't looking for something in their situation to change, so the magic doesn't do anything except enhance it."

She reached over and grabbed her cup of soda. "You can store the magic or the emotion to use later. It drains away slowly, though, but can be re-charged, just like the way magical tools work."

I considered this. "You mean, like ritual knives, or stones?"

Mercy nodded. "Or herbs. All of those hold magic. Ritual clothing, jewelry, and even symbols can hold the emotions or magic, too. A symbol is especially powerful."

"How does that work?" asked Joseph. "I can create a symbol out of my memory, or make one up. And it works for me, but not the Joe-schmoe who bought the same symbol on a necklace because it was 'cool'."

"It works because the emotions – the energy – are in your mind," Mercy explained. "The symbol connects your memory of the shape and meaning with the emotions and energy that you put into it. You've essentially assigned that emotional power to that symbol, so it acts as a shortcut. The more you work with a symbol, the better it works, right?"

We nodded.

"That's because you keep reinforcing that mental connection," she pointed out. "You are creating the magical-emotional equivalent of muscle memory."

"That... really makes sense," I said. Then I thought of something. "Can you use magic?"

Mercy smiled. "Yes, the gods and even my sisters and I can use magic. But we don't like to use it in Midgard."

"Why not?"

"Our magic is more obvious and it sticks around longer. But here, it's like walking through tar, because it gets so difficult to fight the mentality of humans."

She shrugged. "You control how Midgard works, you see. And human minds are really kind of delicate. Sensitive to things that don't make sense. You don't really process things that you aren't ready for."

I considered what she was saying, not really grasping it. Then I remembered something I'd heard years ago. "Oh! Like how the Natives couldn't see Columbus' ships because boats like that were so far out of what they had known before. They literally couldn't perceive the ships. Like their brains had nothing to base the perception on. No frame of reference."

"That's a BS story," Joseph pointed out.

"Yeah, but the idea is still there," I said. "And it's a pretty well-known idea, too. Like when you watch the video of the group of people tossing balls back and forth, and you never even notice the guy in the bear costume walking through the group. We ignore things that are too far outside of our expectations of how things should be."

"That's exactly right," Mercy said. "If we were using magic, especially now, after so long of Midgard being more and more magic free, you'd either ignore it, or explain it away, or try to fight it. Even those demons we encountered tonight. The average person who saw those things would run in terror. And 30 minutes later would swear on their own lives that it was a guy in a mask or something. Any rational explanation will do."

"So why don't we do that?" Joseph asked.

Mercy shrugged. "You guys are like the frogs getting boiled. You get a little more and a little more, so it doesn't give you that shock, that denial reaction."

She shifted her sitting position. "I wasn't sure how I was ever going to tell you about me, or even if I would be able to. Even after tonight, I wasn't completely sure that you would be able to accept it. But you've both had experiences in your lives that have prepared you. You embrace the idea of magic, even if you can't get the full effects. And despite your shock over the monsters, you didn't try to explain it away as some sort of costume or misunderstanding." She smiled, wryly. "I think you probably wanted to, though."

I nodded. "Truth." I glanced at the clock next to the bed. "Well, I hate to break up this party. But, if we are going to be functional tomorrow, we better get some shut-eye tonight."

Joseph nodded and Mercy stood up.

"I don't require sleep," she said. "I'll stand watch and you guys can take the beds."

I stretched out under the bed sheets and barely got my head on the pillow before I was out.

• • •

I had the dream again. I was running through a warehouse, digging through piles of grain. I heard the voice, naming me as chosen. And I jerked awake.

Mercy was sitting there, watching me. "Bad dream?"

I sat up and rubbed the sleep from my face. "Not really. Just a weird dream. Probably too much pizza." I got up and went to the bathroom to try to pull myself together.

After a washcloth wipe down and a call to the front desk for a complimentary toothbrush, I was feeling more alive.

Joseph got up and did his own freshening before stepping out for his morning cigarette. We picked up the room and headed for the front desk to raid the pastries and coffee that the cheap motel offered as a breakfast.

I sat at a tiny table, picking at a stale Danish and a mushy muffin, hoping the coffee tasted better than it smelled. Joseph grimaced over his dry bagel, and Mercy just sipped at her coffee with extra creamer, if the color was any indication.

I leaned forward, keeping my voice low. I would bet that the weary-looking people at the other tables wouldn't even pay attention to our conversation, but better safe than sorry.

"Okay, Mercy. Something's been bothering me about you."

Mercy and Joseph both stared at me.

"Why are you here?" I asked. "Did you know those monsters would be after us? Is this some giant set up?"

Mercy shook her head. "Not a set up."

"Then how is it your friend lives right next to Keith?" I hissed. "That is way too coincidental."

Mercy sipped at her coffee and grimaced. "We knew that this situation has to be handled by a human. It was caused by human actions and human actions have to be what stops it. There are non-human players, but we are only pawns. The game is directed by humans."

She sat back and stretched her arms, her shoulders popping. "We figured there were a quite a few ways that some human would take up the part of opposing Keith, and several Valkyrie were put in position to watch and help. Like me at the bridge and Misty across the street from Keith."

Mercy shrugged. "I'm just the lucky one who met up with you two first."

"Did you know that it would be us when we showed up at the bridge?" Joseph asked.

"No," Mercy said. "I was just in position to keep an eye on Muriel, but then she vanished. You guys looking for her was as good a lead as any, so I went with it."

I nodded. "And what, exactly, is the endgame here?"

Mercy hesitated and swallowed the rest of her coffee. She played with the Styrofoam cup for a moment before answering. "Find the Runespells. Keep the other side from getting them."

I frowned. "What are Runespells?"

"They are sigils, pendants or something – I'm not entirely sure what form they have taken this time. They are, in some way, the shape of bind runes."

"Bind runes?" Joseph asked.

I jumped in to explain. "Bind runes are a symbol created out of two or more runes that represent a more complex idea. They are usually used as a talisman or a representation of a spell. Like a spell to help with studying, or a spell to find a house across the country."

Mercy nodded. "And these Runespells are the same bind runes that Odin learned when he gave his eye to Mimir's Well."

I sat up, eyes going wide. "What? Don't tell me you are after *those* spells."

Mercy shrugged and nodded. "In Midgard, they manifest into a physical form. A permanent spell that humans can use and take, but that gods cannot."

I thought about the lines of the Eddas telling about those spells. They were pretty hefty spells, though they were also extremely specific. There was one for deflecting arrows, healing, raising the dead, and...

"Shit!" I dropped my head into my hands.

"What is it?" Joseph asked.

I muttered at the table top. "Two of those spells are for stopping fire from burning you and being immune to blades."

Joseph flinched back. "Oh, crap. So Keith does have them."

"That's the only reasonable explanation."

Mercy leaned forward. "Keith has several of them, but we don't know which ones or how many. And we don't know what he intends to do with them. Whatever it is, it probably won't be for the greater good."

I rolled my eyes at her. "He's got spells that make him immune to a bunch of shit and he's building an army to initiate Ragnarok, the Norse equivalent of Armageddon. I think we can safely say that what he's got in mind is the opposite of the greater good."

Joseph chewed his lip. "If Keith starts Ragnarok, and all the gods and pantheons are real, would that also start the end of the world scenarios for all the other religions, as well?" He looked from Mercy to me, then back to Mercy. "Wouldn't he actually be starting Armageddon, too?"

Mercy shifted uncomfortably. "Well, we've never tested the theory. But, that's the most likely result, yes."

•　　•　　•

We went out to the car just in time to see a familiar-looking, twenty-year-old sedan pull up next to it. The driver's door opened and Detective Ames huffed his way out of the driver's seat.

We slowed but kept walking. Mercy had the car keys jingling in her hand, and I figured she was about ready to take him down and make a run for it. I was seriously tempted to let it happen, too. Damn my sense of honor.

I smiled at the man. "Good morning, Detective," I said, forcing a cheerful tone. "What can I do for you today?"

He scowled at me, eyed Mercy and Joseph up and down, then slowly walked around the car, looking it over. He flashed a brief smile when his eyes fell on the donut tire. He walked back around to the rear of the car and crossed his arms over his chest. "You were up just north of Downtown last night."

I cocked my head to the side and made a show of considering his words. I shrugged, "Sounds about right. And? Was there a curfew I was unaware of?"

Ames dropped his arms and took a single step forward. "No, there was a cop torn to damn shreds!"

I let myself feel the full effects of the news. I'd known that that was probably what had happened, but hearing it for certain still hit me in the gut.

I gasped, "That's horrible." I let my words hang for a moment. "But, why are you asking me if I was up that way?"

Detective Ames let out a snarl. He raised his finger to point at me. "I know you had something to do with it. And you are going to pay!"

I straightened my spine and looked him in the eye. "The fact that I was in the area doesn't mean I had anything to do with the cop's death. It's just a coincidence." I lifted my chin. "Since you haven't tried to arrest me, I'm going to assume that you haven't found any evidence that you think you can pin on me. If I can be of any further help, please call me."

I stepped around him to move to the passenger door. Then I paused and turned back to him. "However, I suggest you try a different tactic next time. Your accusatory tone and complete lack of proof, or anything at all other than a minor coincidence and an unsubstantiated tip could drive me to doing something outside my comfort zone, something drastic."

He sneered at me. "Like what? Running? Killing... again?"

I pulled the energy around me, envisioning strong women characters, like Maleficent, or Galadriel. I could feel the strength and charisma filling me up and making subtle changes to my face and eyes.

"No," I said, my voice changing subtly with the power, growing deeper and more vibrant. "Like a harassment lawsuit."

I turned away and slid into the passenger seat. I knew that the mundane words combined with the feeling that the power would project would be just a little jarring. After all, you don't expect a powerful sorceress to threaten to take you to court. It's just weird.

The thought of how Detective Ames must be reacting made me smile as Mercy and Joseph joined me in the car.

"He isn't going to stop coming after you," Joseph said, as we drove away.

I kept the smile on my face, though I knew it was now tinged with sorrow.

"I know." I sighed. "And I'll deal with it each time he comes at me."

CHAPT 7

Mercy decided that all we could really do about the Runespells was to find Keith and demand answers. But first, I insisted on finishing what I had started. I had to save Muriel.

We pulled in to the parking lot of the convenience store just before noon. We'd slept pretty late after our crazy night and we figured Muriel was working the 7 - 3 shift. At least we hoped so.

I walked into the store on the heels of Joseph and Mercy, caught up in the idea of getting an iced cappuccino from the pre-mixed dispenser. Joseph's sudden stop sent me bouncing off his back and landing on my butt. Joseph spun around to help me up, which he could have done a better job at if he'd stopped looking over his shoulder.

Then I heard the sound of someone slowly clapping. I stood up with Joseph's help and peered around his tall form.

Theo, once again in a long black trench coat and round sunglasses, leaned against the counter. His smug expression as he clapped his hands infuriated me for no other reason then I'd had a really bad day.

I'll just stick to that story.

Next to him, a thin woman in her late 50s stood, posing regally and staring down her small nose at me with a disgusted look. With her bright orange-red hair and long baby blue robe, she stood out in a crowd, which was just how Rowan liked it.

I rolled my eyes, not trying to be subtle, and glanced behind Theo at the cashier. It was Muriel, all right, and she looked pissed. Her lips were pressed tightly together, and she had her arms crossed with her shoulders tensed.

I mentally pulled myself together and tried to piece together the situation we'd walked into. I sent out energy to guide me to what I needed to see, then I followed the tendrils.

Rowan was standing as if she'd turned towards us from facing Muriel. She was in her full, non-ritual regalia: light blue robe with white and gold sun-and-stars printed scarf as a belt, an un-dyed wool shawl, and a metric ton of necklaces which looked somewhat tangled and messy. Some people could pull off the multiple necklace look, but Rowan was not one of them.

Her watery blue eyes were narrowed, but I couldn't tell if she had been glaring at Muriel or if I was the target. Her hands were on her hips, long nails painted a dark color and rings glinting from every finger.

Theo was leaning against the counter, but the tension in his shoulders and the way his feet were planted was anything but relaxed. He had gone with a dark gray button-down shirt today, and the color accented his pale complexion in a very attractive way.

When Theo looked good, it was because Theo wanted to look good.

I frowned. If Rowan was aggressive, and Theo was attractive, they wanted something. From Muriel.

I glanced at Muriel, noticing her hair was messy and standing up, giving her the appearance of a scared cat. I could see that her hazel-eyed glare was darting from Rowan to Theo... to me!

Crap. They had to have been talking about me. And there was only one reason Rowan would talk about me.

I put my weight on one hip, resting my hand on it, and turned to examine the finger nails of the other hand. I straightened my spine and raised my eyebrow.

"Well, well, well," I said, using my most pretentious East Coast voice. "Look what the cat dragged in." I threw a look at Rowan, raking her from head to toe with heavy-lidded eyes and a slight pursing of my lips. "I appreciate the gift from Kitteh, but... I think I should throw it out." I sniffed loudly.

I watched Rowan out of the corner of my eye as she bristled at my attitude. She struggled silently for a moment, trying to maintain her posturing.

While I waited for her response, I noted that most conflicts in the local Pagan community ended up being elaborate games of posturing.

It was ridiculous and usually more effort than I was willing to put in. But, since Rowan was apparently trying to get to me through Muriel, this was game on.

Rowan recovered her calm and cocked her head to one side. "I'm surprised at you, Nicola," she spat out my name. "I wouldn't have guessed that you would have the courage to return after you were so completely disgraced."

I dropped my fingernail hand and pivoted on my heel to face Rowan.

"There's only one disgrace in this building, Rowan," I said, emphasizing her name. "Pretending you could banish me, and for such a juvenile reason, only showed you to be nothing more than a toddler throwing a tantrum on the floor of the local Shop N Save." I flicked my hand out in a shooing motion towards her, throwing a good amount of power behind the movement.

Theo stood up quickly and Rowan's eyes widened.

I considered for a brief moment that I had moved too quickly in escalating the situation, but... dammit, I had shit to do! I was never very patient about these games. I swallowed my doubt and struck a pose, challenging the older witch with my eyes.

Rowan stood tall, chin raised, staring me down. It was a common tactic, since it required a pretty good amount of power and mental control to win a staring contest. Blinking or letting your eyes glance away meant losing face, and I wasn't very good with the intense eye focus.

There was a way to win without winning, though. I deliberately turned my head, raised my hand and covered my mouth as I faked a huge yawn.

Rowan glared at me, tensing up. Theo quietly cleared his throat. Rowan's eyes flicked towards him and I noticed the look the two exchanged.

Rowan's stance relaxed. This did not look good.

"Speaking of children," she said.

My eyes narrowed. She was not going to go there. She wouldn't dare.

Rowan smirked as she continued. "How is your little one? Raising her all alone must be so hard."

I pressed my lips together.

"You lost her father. You had to leave your home and friends, your spiritual community." Rowan shook her head with a tsking sound. "You must stay up nights worrying about her."

She locked her gaze on me. "You must worry that you aren't enough for her." She punctuated each word, "You just... aren't... enough."

I struggled to keep my composure as the words found their way into my soul.

Rowan must have remembered how I had confessed my greatest fear to her when I was pregnant, just days before we had our falling out. And now she used it to undermine my confidence.

Damn her! I hated that the fear of inadequacy still hit me like a punch in the gut.

I stood, hands clenched into fists at my sides, lips pressed tightly together, not knowing how to react. If I attacked her physically, I would lose the game simply because I had resorted to physical means.

I tried to focus on my breathing, knowing the black and red going through my vision was a result of my anger and fear. I reached for my most treasured memories of my daughter – her joy, praising her successes. And my vision cleared.

I relaxed my hands and smiled. "My dear Rowan, most people worry, at some point, that they aren't enough. That's called 'having standards'. You should try it sometime."

Rowan sputtered for a moment before she grabbed Theo and muttered something that sounded like "This isn't over."

Muriel glared at me as Rowan and Theo swept out of the store, and I heaved a sigh. Her look was a big neon sign that I still had another battle to fight.

Joseph came up behind me, and I could feel a small energy boost as he channeled some of his mojo to me.

"Are you trying to get me fired?" Muriel said through clenched teeth.

I raised my eyebrow. "No. I didn't exactly start this, you know."

Muriel crossed her arms over her chest. "So. She came here because she was desperate for cheap nachos? You just happened to come in and you saw her and you decided to just go ahead and finish what she'd started. That was ten goddamn years ago! And you can't let it go any more than that... Toucan Samantha!"

It took me a second to get the Bewitched reference. Joseph got it sooner, based on his snickering laugh.

I smiled and opened my mouth to defend myself, but Muriel cut me off. "I don't care. I don't want to hear your excuses."

Joseph broke in. "Muriel, we need to talk to you."

Muriel turned to him. "Well, isn't that a surprise?"

Joseph gaped at her. He'd never been around Muriel when she was like this.

She looked back at me. "You come in here – to my place of employment! – acting all high and mighty, pretending I need fucking saving just so you can feel all heroic and important. But, every time I turn around, you need me." She waved her finger at all of us.

Mercy stepped forward. "Muriel, now just calm down..."

I winced. Telling someone to calm down usually had the opposite effect.

Muriel screamed and brought her fists down on the counter. "No, dammit! I won't calm down. You people have gone too far this time. I don't need this crap in my life. I don't need you pulling this shit into my life."

She bent down and came up with a heavy looking wooden pole about five feet long. "I'm sick of it! From you. From Joseph. From Keith. From everyone!"

She tried to point the pole at me, but it was too long and it bounced off of the plastic barrier. My eyes widened as I watched her fury grow as she looked from me to the pole, to Joseph and Mercy, and back to me. The brick red cloud around her was pulsing like a heartbeat, growing larger with each beat.

"Muriel..." I began, holding up my hand to stop her.

With a wild cry, she pulled the pole back in a batter's pose and hit the barrier. She paused a second, as if absorbing what she had done.

Then it was like a dam had broken. She hit the barrier again and again, shrieking wordlessly. She swung wildly, knocking over displays and equipment and hitting the barrier.

The dull crack of shattering plastic brought her up short. The Plexiglas broke open with a hole over a foot wide and at least two foot tall. Pieces of sharded plastic fell onto the potato chip display in front of the counter and onto the floor.

We all stared in shock at what she'd done.

"Muriel, sweetie..." I took a step forward.

"No!" she cried, holding the pole up with one hand as if to fend me off. "You stay the hell away from me!"

She looked at the broken barrier and slowly shook her head in disbelief. "I have to call my supervisor." Her breath caught and her face went pale. "I'm going to lose my job..." She dropped the pole with a loud clacking and stood silently staring.

I glanced at Joseph. His eyes were wide and he seemed to be just as much at a loss as I was.

Mercy stepped up to the broken barrier, her shoes crunching on the plastic. "Muriel, why don't you come with us. We can take you home..."

Muriel jerked her eyes up to Mercy's face. "You don't get it, do you. I just lost my home. Without my job, we can't keep our house." She looked around at the damage she'd done. "We will be back on the streets in a few weeks."

I bit my lower lip. I could see the panic taking Muriel over. She'd worked so hard to get her life together, and then I showed up, throwing everything off. All because I'd come rushing to save her from herself without really considering her needs.

It hit me, then, what I'd done. Muriel was a grown woman. She had her failures, that's for sure. But no one really talked about her like she could make her own decisions. We had to save her, whether she asked for help or not.

We stole her autonomy and called it "for her own good". We took away her right to make mistakes and learn from them.

I felt horrible about the way I'd been treating her. I'd made myself her protector, but locked her in a tower to do so.

She needed to be away. Away from me, and away from everyone who couldn't see past her fumbles to believe in her ability to succeed.

I swallowed my pride, nearly choking on the lump it made. "Hop the train."

Muriel looked at me. Mercy and Joseph turned to shoot me confused looks, as well.

I shrugged and repeated myself. "Take your family and hop the train. Head down to Kentucky or Louisiana for the winter. Or longer. Whatever you need."

Mercy hesitated, then nodded. "That's a great idea."

She turned to Muriel. "Get away from this shit and get your head cleared. Get some distance. From Keith, from Nicola. Hell, even from me." She offered Muriel a half-smile.

I bit my tongue and stayed quiet while Muriel thought about this. Lots of street kids hopped trains to warmer places during the winter months. It reduced the strain on resources for the homeless during the harsher seasons and gave them a semblance of a fresh start.

I knew Muriel would agree when her mouth relaxed from her frown.

"I'll give you some cash," I offered. "To make up for screwing up your life." I hesitated. Even to my ears, that reasoning sounded really lame. "I know it won't make up for jumping in all the time, but it'll give you a chance to start fresh without me."

I pulled out my wallet, counting out my cash. From the corner of my eye, I saw Joseph pull out his ATM card and head over to the machine. We came up with a little more than $400 while Muriel quietly called her supervisor. She locked the door and removed her smock. She stood holding the worn orange fabric, staring at nothing, while we waited with her.

It actually went a lot better than I'd thought. The supervisor, a middle-aged woman with tired eyes, showed up, took a look around, and held out her hand for Muriel's smock.

"You can pick up your final check next Tuesday," she said. "And, Muriel..."

Muriel looked at her.

"I..." The woman looked around.

Muriel nodded. "I'm disappointed in me, too." She walked out the door without another word.

The woman looked at us. "You had something to do with this?"

Joseph shook his head. "Not directly, no." He glanced at me. "We... well. We may have set her off. It wasn't really her fault, you know."

The woman nodded with an aura of defeat. "You need to leave.

And don't come back."

We walked out of the store, a feeling of mourning around us. Muriel was already out of sight.

I felt frustration building up. It seemed like every time we did anything or went anywhere, things were getting out of control. Drastically, weirdly out of control. I mean, we went into a damn convenience store to talk, and look at what happened!

"Dammit!" I cried. "Why does the world hate me?"

Joseph and Mercy looked at me.

I scowled at them. "All I wanted was a fucking iced cappuccino!"

•　•　•

Once we got in the car, we decide that we could use some lunch. Breakfast had been forgettable, at best, after all. We went to a local cafe-style eatery and soon sat down with food that looked like it might be following in the footsteps of the stale danish.

"So what do we do now?" asked Joseph, picking at a baked potato that looked really dry despite the funky-smelling chili and fake cheese shreds.

I swallowed a bit of over-cooked chicken strips. "What do you mean?"

"We came here to find Muriel and get her out of trouble," Joseph pointed out. "Despite the shitty turn of events, we did technically accomplish that goal."

"Yeah," I mumbled, eyeing the french fries with concern. They were soggy and oily, and the thought of eating them was not sitting well. My on-the-road diet of fast food and greasy spoons always gave me a bad case of travel-tummy. The stress wasn't helping either.

Mercy watched us as we talked back and forth. Her brow wrinkled in concern. "You aren't going to leave, are you?" she asked.

I shrugged. "I did what I needed to do. I've been the good sister, now I need to get back to being the good mother."

Mercy frowned. "But what about the Runespells?"

"You can get them..."

"No, I can't," Mercy reminded me. "I'm technically a divine, so I can't 'take' them. I can transport them at the request of a mortal. I can keep them if they are given to me. But I can't retrieve them or steal them."

I rolled my shoulders and slumped back in my seat. "So find someone else to 'retrieve them or steal them'."

Mercy sighed and shook her head. "It took nearly a month before you two showed up. I don't know how much more time we have."

"Why don't you just get one of the Bridge Kids to do it?" Joseph asked.

I thought of petit, nervous Jade being chased by the demons and shuddered. I clenched my jaw and pushed the thought away. I had to do what was best for me and for Ella. Sometimes that meant I didn't run into the fire.

Mercy shook her head again. "I can't just tap someone on the shoulder and make them a hero," she said. "Heroes are chosen by destiny."

I jerked my head up and sat upright in my chair. "Whoa! Wait a second!" I said. "Who said anything about heroes, here?"

Mercy looked at me like I was crazy. "Nicola, is there anything about this situation that does NOT scream 'epic quest'? And epic quests are completed by heroes. This is one of those universal laws that the gods must abide by."

She held up one hand, palm up. "Epic quest." She held up the other hand, also palm up. "Hero."

"Well, then," I said. "It's a good thing I'm not trying to complete this quest, because I am NOT a hero."

"Heroes are chosen by destiny."

"You said that already," I pointed out. I sat back and considered what Mercy had said. "If heroes are chosen by destiny, how do you know who's a hero?"

"Heroes complete the epic quest," Mercy said.

I raised an eyebrow at her. "So, heroes complete the epic quest that can only be completed by heroes?" I paused a moment. "Is that all you've got?"

Mercy rolled her eyes. "That's an oversimplification. There's more nuance than that."

I stared at her, waiting for her to give me something.

She sighed, puffing out her cheeks. "Okay, a hero is in the right place at the right time."

"Coincidence."

"A hero survives the first encounter with the enemy, in this case, the demons." She ticked off another finger.

"Luck," I said. "And you showed up with your sword."

"Regardless. A hero has a relationship to other players in the quest that gives them the potential to complete the quest. In your case, your relationship to Muriel, and former relationship to Keith."

I rolled my eyes. "That's a pretty big stretch."

"A hero has a crisis of faith," Mercy said quietly. "During which she questions if she is really the hero."

I narrowed my eyes. "Low blow, there."

"Well, heroes also get called to the quest."

I sneered. "My phone must be off the hook."

Mercy glared at me. "The call is usually one of two things. The classic, mythic way, is an old sage – or witch or wizard or wise man or woman or something – tells the hero to go on the quest."

Joseph slapped the table. "Nicola, you must take the ring into Mordor!"

I snorted.

"Something like that," Mercy muttered.

"Yeah," I said. "That didn't happen. Try again, 'cause this little hobbit is staying home."

Joseph broke in. "So if Nicola is the hero, am I free to go?"

I reached over and smacked his arm. "Seriously?"

Joseph shrugged. "Hey, one of us has to make it out alive in order to get the book deal afterwards."

Mercy shook her head. "Sorry. The hero has someone who helps her through the quest, right up until the end. That person is often a servant..."

I barked a laugh, pointing my finger at Joseph.

Mercy glared and continued. "Or a best friend."

Joseph stuck his tongue out at me. I returned the gesture.

"It doesn't matter," I said, slouching in my chair and chomping on a french fry before I remembered how awful they were. "I didn't get any calls on the batphone."

Mercy sat back. "The more common way for a hero to be called these days is that the hero has dreams."

Joseph started laughing.

I thought about the dream I'd had the night Joseph had shown up at my door. Nearly a week had passed and I'd had that dream every single night since.

I noticed Mercy staring at me. I knew she knew, but I just clenched my jaw and stared right back.

Joseph caught the tension between us and stopped laughing.

"There's a lot of coincidence and just plain chance in those hero characteristics," I pointed out. "I mean, it could literally be anyone."

Mercy sat back in her chair. "It could. Heroes - true heroes - tend to be everyday people until their quest begins."

She looked around the restaurant. I followed her gaze. Around a dozen tables were filled with customers, chatting and clanking silverware.

She gestured at the people. "But, how many of these people got themselves involved with a cult determined to start the end of the world? How many would be able to watch Keith's show, objectively, without being affected? Swayed?"

Mercy shook her head. "How many of these people would be able to see—" she tapped her forehead "—what people's motivations are? How many of these people could squat in a dirty alley in the middle of the night, inches away from a demon intent on hunting them down and ripping them apart — how many of these people would survive that?"

She turned back to look me in the eye. "But, Nicola, you did all of that."

• • •

I sucked on the cigarette as a chill wind cooled my cheeks. Joseph and I stood on the curb separating the parking lot from a large grassy ditch.

I considered the idea that I was tempting cancer. Between the shit I'd seen and my recent brush with death, it was almost... logical.

Perhaps that was the reason for extreme sports - when a person survives one death-teasing feat, they just can't stop trying for it. Maybe a brush with death leaves a little death-y residue on your soul, and so you get the urge to revisit death over and over again.

Mercy walked up and I shook myself out of my thoughts.

She eyed Joseph, then me. "Well?"

I stared up at the white-gray sky, blowing out smoke in small billowing clouds. "Demons and detectives. Detectives and demons. I'm completely out-gunned here." I turned to face Mercy.

"So will you finish what you've started?" She asked.

I exchanged looks with Joseph. The shrug was written on his face, and I knew he would back me up, whatever my decision.

I considered for a moment. "Let's just take this one step at a time. First, we tell Keith that Muriel is out of bounds, now."

Joseph nodded. "This calls for some classic Bowie." We walked to the car as he broke into an intentionally off-key song. "We could be heroes! Forevuh and evuh!"

CHAPT 8

Joseph and I stood back as Mercy reached up to knock at Keith's door, but it opened before her hand hit the faux wood panel.

The older man from Keith's entourage stepped out. He paused, staring all of us up and down before he stalked towards the stairs. I shivered when his eyes met mine, and I quickly looked away.

Mercy pushed her way into the apartment before the door could close, giving us entry in her wake.

"What the..." Keith stopped as his eyes fell on me. "What are you doing here? You can't be here."

I walked down the short narrow entry hall, noting the worn but clean carpets and outdated fake-wood wall paneling. I brushed past Keith and shrugged. "Yet, here I am.

I walked into the small open space of the kitchen just off the hallway and turned to lean against the counter next to the stove. "What are you up to?"

Keith glanced at Mercy and Joseph who made an impressive show just standing there with their arms crossed over their chests. Joseph towered over Mercy by nearly a foot, but the blonde woman managed to be more imposing. I made a mental note to talk to her about her super-powers leaking through her secret identity.

"I was just finishing up some business before bed," Keith said.

I gave him a big smile that never reached my eyes. "Oh, really? What kind of business? Counting tithes? Planning your next big recruitment?"

Keith sputtered over my verbal dig. "Gods, Nicola! Why don't you just lay off?"

Joseph glanced towards the living room furnished with several mismatched chairs and two loveseats. I could tell by the look of concentration on his face that he was scanning the apartment. I threw out some energy feelers for myself, focusing on the hallway outside.

"Just trying to protect my sister," I said. I put my hands on my hips. "She's leaving town, by the way, so you need to leave her alone and let her go."

I frowned when Keith's expression seemed to be relief. It reminded me of all the inconsistencies in Keith's behavior. I decided to push him.

"You owe me answers, you know. And I'm not gonna drop this until I'm satisfied." I hesitated about reminding him of how close we'd once been. "You know how determined I can be."

Keith stared at me for a moment before his shoulders slumped and he walked over to the nearest loveseat. "Sure. Why not? But you have no idea what you are doing. There will be consequences for this." He dropped onto the cushions and gestured to the other furniture. "Let's get this over with. Quickly." He glanced at the clock on the wall.

Joseph moved to one of the chairs while I took the other loveseat. Mercy refused to move from her position at the end of the entry hall.

Keith sat forward in his seat. "What do you want to know?"

"Where did you get the idea for the cult?" I asked, coloring my voice with light curiosity. Intensity could scare him off of answering more truthfully.

Keith scowled. "We call it an army." He shrugged. "You could say I'm on a mission from god."

Joseph rolled his eyes. "Which one?"

"Jehovah," Keith said. He held up his hands defensively. "Yeah, I know. I'm still not Christian, per se, but Jehovah came to me. He gave me..."

"Gave you what, Keith?" I pressed him when he hesitated.

"Only what I needed," he waved my question off. He glanced up at the clock again. "Jehovah shows up and gives me this mission and... some stuff to help. Then he tells me what needs to be done. So I ask, what's in it for me, and he says he'd give me the one thing I want. So I agreed."

I rubbed the bridge of my nose, trying to process what Keith was saying. Jehovah? Seriously? The one god who pretty much never shows up, showed up for Keith, who didn't even believe in the guy. There was definitely something off about the whole thing. "So, Jehovah wants to start Ragnarok?"

He huffed a laugh. "Yeah, I questioned it, too. Apparently, Ragnarok is part of the whole Armageddon, Revelations thing. He's ready to get the party started." He shrugged. "Or ended, as the case may be."

I nodded. "And he gave you... things? Lemme guess," I said. "He gave you some amulets or sigils or whatever that you use to work the miracles for your recruiting, right?"

Keith's eyes went wide. He nodded. "Yeah. That's pretty much it."

"Okay, well, we need those sigils. Where are they?"

Keith snorted and shook his head. "I don't think so." He leaned forward. "I need them."

"Why?"

"It's the only way I stay in control of this thing. I need the power in my hands or..." He hesitated. "I'm not backing off of this, Nicola. You've always been so damn... strong. But this is mine."

I shook my head. "Ragnarok will destroy the world and take most of the people with it," I said, fighting a sudden queasy feeling in my gut. "There is no guarantee that you or me or Ella will survive."

Keith paused. "You and Ella will survive." He shook his head sadly. "I've made sure of that."

I frowned. What did he mean by that?

Keith glanced at the clock again and stood up suddenly. "You have to leave now. They know you're here, and they will be here soon. Very soon. I've given you as much time as I can. Maybe too much."

"What do you mean?" Mercy asked. "Who are they?"

Keith shook his head, trying to pull me up from the loveseat. "No time. They came last night when someone showed up. They'll be here any minute. You don't want to meet them, I promise you."

I shot a look at Joseph and Mercy. We all made the connection.

"Shit!" Joseph exclaimed as he jumped up and took a step towards me.

"We already met them," I told Keith. "Last night."

Time slowed down. I saw Joseph stop in his tracks and touch his head like he had a headache. I saw Mercy flex her shoulders. I felt the queasiness in my stomach and knew it for what it was.

The energy feelers were picking up something. Something I'd encountered before. I felt the world drop out from beneath me as my reality roiled against the sudden fear that crashed over me in waves.

And then time returned to normal.

"Shit!" I pulled away from Keith's grasp.

Mercy reached for her knife as I turned to Keith. "We need a back way out."

Keith stared at me. "You know what they are?"

Mercy took a long sniff of the air. "Demons," she said.

I nodded. "Those monsters from last night. They are here. Now."

Keith hesitated another second before nodding. He grabbed my arm and pulled me towards one of the rooms in the back. "This way."

"Too late!" Mercy called out the warning a split second before the gunfire began.

I'd never been in a gunfight before. Aside from last night, I'd never even been shot at before, but being shot at in the confined space of Keith's apartment was different, more intense. It was fast and confusing and very noisy. Things seemed to just pop in little explosions all around: the walls, the loveseat where I'd been sitting, the window behind us.

I grabbed at Joseph and Keith, and we ran for the back room.

Joseph clung to me and Keith as hard as I was holding them both, so when Keith stumbled, we both just kept pulling him with us. I looked back to see Mercy whirling her huge sword around right behind us, holding back humanoid shapes that seemed too large for the space they were in.

We burst through the door, and Mercy darted inside and slammed it shut behind us. I pulled my hands free as Keith fell to the floor, taking Joseph with him.

I turned to see Mercy moving a large filing cabinet. I'd seen enough movies to understand what she was doing and I rushed to help her shove the metal cabinet in front of the door. The pinging sound didn't register in my mind, but when the door above the filing cabinet exploded in two mini-bursts, I dropped low into a crouch.

The pinging and popping stopped, replaced by growling and scratching. I found myself missing the gunfire noises.

I turned to find Joseph crouched over Keith, a wet, red splotch growing on Keith's shirt.

"Ohmigod!" I dropped to my knees beside Keith, pushing Joseph away. Keith's breath was coming in short, painful-sounding gasps.

"Nicola," he whispered.

I grabbed his hand and held in both of mine. His eyes met mine, then fluttered shut.

"Oh, Keith. Why did you get involved in this crap?" I begged him with my eyes to tell me, to not make me dig for it.

He rasped a cough, wincing as he did so. "I wanted..." He looked away, squeezing his eyes shut. "I wanted to help you... and Ella. I wanted to be what you saw in me."

"What?" I whispered. "What do you mean?"

Keith focused on my face, the glassiness in his eyes clearing up for a moment. He struggled to get the words out. "You told me... while we were together. You saw me... potential."

"Oh, gods," I breathed. I could feel the cold shock sweeping through my body. I fought the darkness that pressed on my vision. Too much, too much, too much! "You remembered that?"

I'd always been able to cut through the fluff of people, to see the truth underneath. With an ironic thread of optimism, I had always seen the best that people could be. Joseph had once told me that my sarcasm was because so many people failed to live up to their potential, and it was an expression of my bitter disappointment.

He nodded. "I had to try... to be that... for you... Ella."

"For Ella? You did all this for Ella?" Tears welled up and I squeezed my eyes shut to clear them from my vision. "That wasn't necessary. We didn't need the perfect you. Just you would have been fine."

"Not... for you... my girls," he gasped painfully. "I had... to save Ella. And you." He coughed. "That was... the deal. Armageddon... you will... survive."

"Oh Keith, no," I moaned. I could see his struggle to keep breathing.

Keith tried to smile. "Take... sigils. He... betrayed..." He struggled to drag in a breath. "Don't let... him have... the power... Under... my desk... small... file cabinet... bottom drawer... There's... a pouch. And take... envelope, too."

I caught Joseph's eye. He nodded in understanding and moved around to the desk, checking underneath. He came back up with a cheap velvet bag and manila envelope in hand. "Got it!"

I touched Keith's face with one hand, gripping his hand tightly in the other. "You didn't have to do that."

He tried to smile again, but winced in pain. "Go out... the window... fire escape..."

I nodded. "Thank you."

Keith took a rattling breath. I flinched from the sound.

"And Nicola... Ella..."

I tried to speak through my tears. I cleared my throat and sniffed before I could get any words out. "She will know about you, I promise. I'll tell her about her father, and how you tried to save us. I'll tell her you were a hero, in the end." I felt his hand squeeze mine, then go limp. "But Keith..."

His eyes refocused for just a second.

I smoothed his hair back from his face. "Next time, don't try so hard. You were just fine as you were."

Keith's mouth twitched into a smile as his hand fell from mine. And I broke down, sobbing.

I let my thoughts shut down as the pain washed through me. The unfairness of his death, the possibilities lost, the love I'd had.

After only a few seconds, Mercy touched my shoulder. "We have to get going."

I let her pull me to my feet and push me towards the window. My entire body felt numb, like I'd sat on all of my limbs for too long.

The window had been shattered and a piece of fabric had been laid over the sill, allowing me to slide out the window onto the fire escape without getting cut up.

Joseph, standing on the fire escape, helped me out. I made my way to the steps going down and began climbing as quickly as my deadened limbs would allow.

As I made my way down, I mentally reviewed my body's reactions against the half-remembered list of the symptoms of shock. It had seemed clearer last night, but then the emotional shock was much worse this time around.

By the time I got to the ladder at the bottom, the numbness had started to fade away, replaced by muscle shakes going through my arms and legs. I forced my hands to lower the ladder and began going down it.

I noticed that Joseph was right above me, speaking softly to encourage me. Mercy was above him, standing on the fire escape with her eyes on the window above. I finally reached the ground, slipping on the last step and falling onto my back.

Joseph clambered down and rushed to my side. I was only winded, struggling to catch my breath while Joseph pulled me to my feet on shaking legs. I glanced up at Mercy just in time to see her vault over the railing and drop the 20 feet to the ground.

"Let's go!" she called, motioning us towards the mouth of the alley.

I shook off Joseph's grip and pushed him ahead. I staggered just a few steps behind him.

A huge shadow suddenly blocked my view of the street. A familiar, repulsive smell hit my nose and I heard a low growl.

I followed my gut and dropped to my knees. A gust of air hit my neck as I covered my head with my arms. I held the fetal position for a long moment before my brain identified the sounds I heard as fighting.

I peeked up and saw Mercy standing between me and three of the monsters. I didn't wait for her to speak before I scrambled to my feet and ran down the alley in the only direction that was not blocked – the opposite way from the car and Joseph.

This run was nothing like the night before. I had the memories of last night's experience feeding my fears. Panic drove my feet as fast as I could make them move. I skittered on the gravel at the mouth of the alley as I made a turn onto the street. I headed towards the sounds of traffic, my lizard brain screaming for the safety of the herd.

The streets became blindingly bright as I entered an area filled with nighttime activity. Lights blinked from well-maintained signs, cars moved quickly along streets lined with sidewalks, people gathered in groups, walking or standing near the doors to clubs, restaurants and bars.

I flinched in the sudden light and noise, then skidded to a halt, nearly body checking a parked car. I glanced back, but the streetlights and neon signs kept me from being able to see anything in the darker streets behind me.

I headed down the sidewalk, walking quickly. I dodged around a group of people and darted across the two-lane, one-way street before the light changed. I now had a large, well-lit street full of people and vehicles between me and the monsters. But that wasn't enough. They would follow me.

I turned and looked with my second sight for my scent and energy trail. The fog-like wake I'd left showed up to me as my favorite color, turquoise, streaked with a sickly greenish yellow, the color I associate with fear.

I reached out my active energy to grasp the end of the trail and considered for a moment. Changing energy to mask it required a good mental and emotional image of who to change the energy to. I dismissed Mercy, Joseph and Keith. Those three would be unlikely to throw off the creatures, being either likely targets or so obviously out of the game.

I winced at the fresh reminder of Keith's death.

I also dismissed my family. It was unlikely that the creatures would be able to hunt my daughter down, but I certainly didn't want to give them any hint of her in case they could use it against me.

I finally latched on to the idea of former co-workers and immediately knew who it would be. Cathy was the most mundane, least magical person I'd ever known. Her narrow-minded perception of reality and restrictive belief systems would be so completely opposite to myself that I was sure the demons wouldn't be able to find any hint of me in that energy.

I pulled the memories of Cathy over me, wallowing in the emotions I recalled from time spent with her. I let the feeling and energy leak down my active energy grasp on to the smoky trail, letting it overwhelm my scent-energy up to the point where it nearly collided with the parked car.

At first nothing happened. Then, like a mood ring when it warms up, the color began to change, slowly at first, then more quickly, to a rather bland amber color, warm but with little depth. I fed the emotion into my scent-trail until I was sure it had taken completely.

I carefully disconnected the trail before the parked car from the modified trail after the parked car. The whole process was difficult, but still much easier than trying to dissipate or erase the energy completely.

Finally, I gently released the trail from where I was standing and let it go from my energy grasp. I breathed a sigh of relief and stopped a moment to consider my options.

If Joseph hadn't made it to the car, there wasn't much I could do but mourn him. I brushed that thought away quickly.

If Mercy hadn't successfully fought off the monsters, I needed to keep moving. I needed to find safety. If Joseph or Mercy, or both, had made it out alive, they would come looking for me.

That meant I needed to find a place to lay low, but it needed to be a place where either of the two would be able to find me. It would have to be further away - the thought of the demons still coming for me made me itch to run.

But where would both Joseph and Mercy think to look for me? I took off walking quickly down the sidewalk without a destination in mind. I just needed to keep moving. But I chewed on the question while my feet marked off the yards.

• • •

I plopped down in the cracked maroon vinyl seat of the booth and rasped out a request for coffee and water to the server. It wasn't the same lady who had waited on us just a few days ago. After we had seen Keith's little performance.

I dropped my head on my arms.

Keith. He was dead.

A few days ago, we were watching him with suspicion, trying to figure out his game. And now he was dead. He'd given us the sigils. He'd entered into a devil's bargain. For Ella, our daughter.

The server set down the drinks and gave me a funny look. I blinked and felt the tears fall down my cheeks. I sat up and wiped them off.

I shot a weary half-smile at the woman. "Bad day," I offered.

She nodded, sympathetically, and walked away.

I began pouring creamer and sugar into my coffee. I stirred it after each addition until it was the right color and a lick of the spoon told me that the sugar had overcome the bitterness of cheap, stale grounds.

I thought back to when I'd met Keith, seven years earlier. I'd been crazy about his Irish good looks, but too timid back then to make the first move. We'd met through a mutual friend at a Pagan open ritual. I'd never been to a ritual open to the public before, and I'd had no idea who to talk to. So I'd stayed near Graham and Keith the whole time.

At the end of the event, Graham had decided to take off with another friend from out of town. Since I'd ridden with him, I was stranded. Keith had given me a ride home. Then he tried to kiss me.

Months later, we'd become an unofficial item. We'd attend groups and rituals together, and he'd spend the night once in a while. Soon people just assumed we were together. Only he and I had known that we'd never talked about a relationship, or where we were going with it. We'd just let it become what it would become.

I had been on birth control, but nothing was guaranteed, and I had gotten a little plus sign on a pregnancy test. I'd informed him of the news. He had said he wasn't ready to be a father. I took off for my mother's the next day.

Keith had never shown interest in Ella, in knowing her at all. Joseph had told me that he and some other mutual friends had taken it upon themselves to keep Keith updated whether he wanted it or not. I wondered now if he'd been trying to protect himself, emotionally.

I played Keith's final words over and over in my mind, trying to decode them. Maybe he had wanted fatherhood after all. Maybe I hadn't let him in.

"Nicola! Thank the All-father!"

I looked up at the sound of my name. Mercy stood a few feet from the table, looking like she'd been in a fight.

I choked back a laugh at the thought. "I hope you have money," I said, gesturing to my coffee. "I'm out of cash."

CHAPT 9

We drove the car Mercy had borrowed from her sister-Valkyrie, Misty, through the darkened streets of the residential areas near Keith's apartment. We hadn't talked about what we were going to do. There was no discussion. We just needed to find Joseph.

Hopefully, he was also driving through the streets, looking for us. Maybe he was walking for some reason. He might be near the apartment, or as far away as he could run or drive. There was no way to know.

Or, he might be...

My thoughts skittered away again, like drops of water on a hot skillet.

"Can I ask you some questions?" Mercy asked.

I sighed. I really just wanted to retreat into my own mind. Mercy seemed determined to invade my mental space, though, and I couldn't think of a reason to avoid it.

"Sure," I said, shrugging.

"You said that you use chemicals to dull your psychic abilities," Mercy said. "Like smoking or alcohol. I just don't get that. I don't see why you would have this wonderful gift and mute it all the time."

"You call it a gift," I said, slouching into the seat. "I call it a pain in the ass. Or a complication, depending on the day."

I glanced at her pointedly. "In case you're not sure, this is not a great day."

Mercy glanced at me, frowning. "You treat your gifts with disrespect and irreverence."

I shrugged.

"You can go through all the worlds and the astral plane," Mercy pressed forward. She seemed a little awestruck by the idea. "We can travel to the worlds, through the bifrost, but you can just... be there."

She shifted in her seat. "The gods need gateways to even enter the bifrost. But humans are part of all the worlds. Humans exist in all the worlds. You can just move into the astral or into the bifrost, or any other world, with enough skill."

Mercy looked over at me. "You humans have such capacity for knowledge and intuition because of this, not that you ever use it. You could be as powerful as the gods in your own right."

I smirked. "Oh what fun that would be."

I caught her look of surprise, so I elaborated. The subject was at least keeping my mind from going over the possibilities of what had happened to Joseph. "Yeah, sure, great cosmic power. But everyone forgets the downside."

Mercy raised an eyebrow. "Itty bitty living space?"

I snorted a laugh. "I wish. Power. Knowledge. Even intuition. In this world, especially now, that just sucks. It doesn't help. Not very often. It's... a burden. A weight on your heart and soul."

Mercy shook her head. "No, that can't be right. Too many of you crave power. Even you have embraced some portion of the ability you could have."

"Yeah," I snapped. "And. It. Sucks."

I sat up in my seat. "It hurts me. It hurts my friends and family." I flinched from the words as I said them. "It hurts my frickin' theoretical career. I get nothing good out of it."

I flung my hand out to gesture into the night. "Look at what's happened just today!"

"But you... know things," Mercy said. "You use that knowledge to help yourself and your companions."

"But they wouldn't even need the help if it wasn't for the little blips and beeps of power and such that people have gotten."

I shook my head. "Besides, plain old knowledge doesn't usually change much. I could tell people what I know, what I've seen, but even those who believe in my 'gifts' wouldn't change their lives based on that. Knowledge demands experience. If you don't get the knowledge from the experience, you won't truly get the knowledge until you have the experience."

I glanced over to make sure Mercy had understood my play on

words. She nodded, thinking about what I'd said.

I sighed. "If I could wave my hand and take away all the power, I would. I would even do it to just myself if I could."

Mercy turned to look at me with her piercing gaze. "But... why?"

I struggled to find the words to explain. "I could be... normal. I could have been a scientist, or a teacher, or a nurse, or a flippin' accountant," I ticked off the list on my fingers. "I could have a husband in a mediocre marriage with two point three kids. I could have money and spend all of my time shopping. Or have affairs to keep things interesting. I could go on business trips. In a plane. Not just trippin' off to the astral to get a little change in scenery. And I would be happier."

"That doesn't sound happier."

"Of course it doesn't," I said. "Because we know better. And that's what sucks. We know there's better than that."

"So, you know that there is better out there, and that's a bad thing?" Mercy looked like I'd just tried to smack her with a flounder, confused and a little WTF.

"Yeah," I said, rubbing my hand over my face. "My entire life could have been mediocre and met low standards. But now? Now, I have knowledge of great awesomeness, ecstatic love that destroys and rebuilds your heart and lasts forever, and I've seen the power and beauty of the universe inside my own head. The bar has been raised for my life experiences, and I can't keep THIS life at THAT level. That just sucks."

I looked over at her. "And that's why so many of us seek the additional power. To reach an impossible, unachievable level where it doesn't suck so much. Where life is more like what we have learned is possible. Or at least theoretically possible."

"Why do you say it's a burden, though?" Mercy asked.

I sighed. "With great power comes great responsibility," I quoted. "We get these gifts, then we get all these mixed messages. Do you know how many people cannot bring themselves to accept compensation for their magic because it comes in the form of money?"

Mercy shook her head.

"Most of them," I explained. "It's taught to be sacrilege to take money. To make enough to be able to afford to eat or pay rent."

"Back when the gods were worshipped throughout the northern world," Mercy said, slowly, "my sisters and I would come to earth and watch those of you with gifts. They were called völva, women of the seidre. They revered their gifts. They didn't call them a pain in the ass. They were provided for, with shelter and food wherever they went."

I smiled. "Yeah, the völva. Honored and respected in their communities. So, they weren't called crazy? Or sinful? The devil's whores? Baby-eaters?"

Mercy stared at me for a long moment. "You mean the witch hunts? The inquisitions? Those are over."

"Not really," I said. "It's not as obvious, or as deadly, sure. But the feeling is still there in a lot of people and communities. It permeates our culture."

Mercy frowned. "Not everyone sees these powers as anti-Christian, though. Atheists...

"Atheists and other people who take the path of extreme logic can sometimes be worse," I bit out. "They aren't looking for a spiritual reason that our powers are bad. They are looking for a psychological cause for our delusions."

I shook my head. "Those völva didn't have the threat of psychological condemnation hanging over their heads. Or the dismissal of 'mere superstitious behavior'. We are lumped in with people who have actual and sometimes serious problems, and it's not fair to either group."

I shifted my position, turning towards Mercy in my seat. "Back in the time of the völva, there hadn't been a couple hundred years' history of people getting tortured, electrocuted, drugged, raped and even killed."

I caught Mercy's look of disbelief. "That's what has happened in the past if you displayed symptoms of mental disorders, most of which are very similar to full-on but untrained psychic abilities. Some of those things still happen."

I ticked them off on my fingers. "Those symptoms can include feelings of depression and feeling overwhelmed or helpless, or out of control. Confusion. Unexplained feelings of worry and guilt, 'cause you try so hard to help everyone and you can't. Lack of concentration, usually 'cause spirits have really shitty interpersonal skills and interrupt all the time."

I sighed. "Mood changes, low energy or insomnia. How about physical problems that have no 'real world' explanation, from empathic sensing or getting into trouble on the astral plane? That must be hypochondria or some psychosomatic illness."

"Oh, wow," Mercy said.

I continued. "Seeing other worlds or spirits, which is labeled as hallucinations. Trouble relating to how people present themselves because of the insights to their energy or spirit."

"I never considered that," Mercy said, shaking her head. "Such knowledge was just accepted. People feared the völva for what they might know, but no one blamed the völva for it."

"These are things that can get you locked up," I pointed out. "And they are common in people who are learning or adapting to their gifts, either for the first time or because some power has developed to be stronger or a variation has come out."

I shrugged. "Plus, you gotta get food and pay rent and crap. If you can't find a way to do that with your 'gifts', you have to pile a 'real life' job on top of all of it. No tribal care of the local shaman, nowadays. That's commie socialism, right there."

Mercy stared out the window for a moment. "I never thought about it before, but you're implying that the growth of psychological problems might be connected to the lower number of magic-users in the world."

"Yeah, well, think about it now. We are still here; it's just that we have to hide our abilities behind metaphors, dismissal of the true depth of the power, or just plain suppression." I turned away to stare out the window, feeling a bit sorry for myself.

Mercy just kept driving in silence, letting me dwell on my thoughts in silence.

We continued cris-crossing through the streets. I stared at the cars and people on my side as we passed, glancing at faces, searching for my friend.

I'd known Joseph for years, since our sophomoric year in the University of Indianapolis. I'd been majoring in Psychology; he'd taken Civil Engineering and Business. We had shared some sociology classes and, after a few in-class discussions, we realized we'd had a lot in common and started hanging out after classes.

We helped each other study and carpooled in the snowy winter months. After the first semester, we'd pretty much become inseparable. We joined and started campus clubs together, including a Pagan group and a spiritual discussion group.

"Nicola," Mercy said softly into the silence. "We may have to consider..."

"Nope," I cut her off without taking my eyes off the sidewalk. "I'm not having that conversation. We will find him if we have to go over every street in Indy and beyond. Twice."

I turned to her. "Did we check that crap hotel we crashed in last night?" It was only last night? It seemed like a year had passed since the lumpy bed and cheesy pizza.

Mercy shook her head. "I'll swing over and go past the apartment, then head that direction. We might get lucky and find him on the way."

She turned at the next block and headed towards Keith's place. I continued my searching, and my self-indulgent reminiscing.

Joseph had been there for emotional support during my pregnancy, even helping me pack and say my goodbyes when I'd moved away. He'd been the one I had missed the most.

Not that he'd been perfect. He had a tendency to fence-sit on issues where he didn't want to piss people off, while I considered such consideration for those who were wrong to be rather weak. He was definitely more diplomatic than I was.

He had always been willing to point out when I was being overly sensitive to people's behavior. He'd been the one to help me learn how to brush off insignificant slights and unintentional insults. Our emotional support for each other had gotten us through more than one break-up with friends and significant others.

We'd had fights, too. Massive blow-ups that ended up just this side of coming to physical blows. I couldn't remember what any of them were about now, but we'd always worked through it. Our friendship was more valuable than any of the issues that had tried to pull us apart.

I sat up, spotting a tall, leggy man next to a familiar-looking four-door sedan. "There he is." We pulled up next to the stalled rental and a frightened, weary looking Joseph.

I leaned out the window, my mood lifting immediately. "Hey, sexy, wanna ride?"

He jumped at the sound of my voice, but broke into a grin when he recognized me. He grabbed a few things from the car and got into the back seat, and we pulled away.

CHAPT 10

We never did find a hotel or any room like that. Every time we pulled into a parking lot, either Joseph or I got a creepy feeling, something we weren't willing to dismiss so easily at this time, or we saw something that scared us off.

The first place was a moderately priced, three-floor hotel with the look of superficial maintenance. Looking around, I saw a looming, demon-shaped shadow lurking in the dark corner at the end of the hotel. The others didn't see anything until two reddish pinpoints appeared to lock on our car. We backed out of the drive in front of the lobby doors and left quickly, pulling out in front of a semi and crossing two lanes of fairly busy traffic.

Another place had a car that Joseph said was the sedan that Detective Ames had been driving the day we met him outside of the mall. I wasn't up for that confrontation, so we left that hotel less dramatically.

Several of the hotels were just too filthy, had flimsy doors that wouldn't hold up against cop or demon for more than a few seconds, or were out of the price-range of our pooled cash.

We also considered leaving the city, but we had no idea where we would go. Going home wasn't an option for me. I wasn't going to lead the creatures to my daughter or mother.

On the road, we would be more obvious targets, possibly endangering people in any small town that we stopped in for gas or food. After much discussion, we decided our gut reaction against leaving was probably a warning. We needed to play this out in the city.

Finally Mercy offered to just drive around while Joseph and I slept.

• • •

I jerked awake at the sound of my phone's shrill ring. Barely conscious, I scrambled in my pocket, wriggling around the reclined passenger seat and getting caught twice in the seat belt.

I pulled out the phone and peered at the number. I didn't recognize it.

I took a deep breath and mumbled sleepily. "Hello?" I shrugged at Mercy, who kept glancing at me.

"Nicola Crandall?" A deep male voice came out of the earpiece.

"Yes?" I fumbled for the latch on the side of the seat to put it upright.

"My name is Robert Hersey, Bob," the voice said. "I can help you."

I scowled. "I'm sorry," I said. "Who are you?"

The voice hesitated. "I was a friend of Keith's," he said. "I know what happened last night."

I paused. What did he know? That Keith... My mind still danced away from those thoughts. Did he know about the demons? The sigils?

"I don't know what you're talking about," I said, hoping he would clarify.

"I know Keith is dead."

His blunt statement made me flinch. I closed my eyes against the feelings of grief and pain that washed over me.

Bob continued. "I also know what he gave you. And I know what killed him."

I focused on breathing for a moment. What to do? What approach should I take? Trust was not coming for this guy, but we were floundering like a trio of fish on dry land.

"And?" I asked, forcing him to carry the conversation.

"I can help you get rid of the sigils," he said. "I know what to do with them."

I rubbed the sleep from my eyes. "And how do I know we can trust you?" I pointed out. "Why should I believe you?"

Bob hesitated. "Did you take the envelope, too?" he asked.

I glanced back at Joseph, who was now sitting up. He had the pouch with the sigils in his lap. The envelope was under them, a bit wrinkled from the night on the run.

"Maybe," I said.

"It's Keith's will," he said. "And a life insurance policy. You'll find my name as the witness. Meet me in an hour at Suite 243B at the Eaglepoint Village mall." He hung up.

I turned in my seat and snatched the envelope out of Joseph's lap, ignoring his yelped protest. I carefully ripped the tab open and pulled out the papers. I scanned through the documents.

Bob was right; they were Keith's will and a life insurance policy. My eye fell on a section of the policy declaring that it would be void if the death was by suicide. I barked out a bitter laugh. I didn't think that there would be any question about that.

I turned back to the front page and read through a little deeper. Then I blinked and went back to the first line to read through it a third time.

"Shit!" I muttered. I flipped to the second page.

"What is it?" Joseph asked, leaning forward.

I flipped to the last page, reading each line. There, at the end, was Keith's signature. And the witness was Robert Hersey.

I turned to Joseph. "This is Keith's will," I explained. "He left everything, including the corporation that he created to hold the money from the cult tithing... he left it all to Ella."

Joseph sat back in shock. "And that's how much?"

I shrugged. "It doesn't list exact amounts," I said. "But it looks like it may be several thousand."

I shuffled the will to the back and looked through the insurance policy. I quickly found the beneficiary and the pay-out amount.

"Sweet Genesha!" I said, invoking the Hindu god of wealth. "The policy is for Ella, as well, with me as the secondary."

I paused, rereading the amount to be sure. "This is a goddamn million-dollar policy."

Joseph whistled. "Man, when Keith redeems himself, he doesn't do it half-assed."

I pressed a hand to my stomach. "Mercy, find me a post office."

Mercy nodded and changed lanes.

• • •

I repackaged and mailed the papers to my mother, in case my series of bad days ended even more badly. At least Ella would be taken care of.

While I worked on that, I explained to Joseph and Mercy about the phone call from Bob. We talked over the pros and cons, but decided that we had to try something, even if none of us really trusted Bob.

After the post office, we drove to Eaglepoint Village, a fancy new-looking mini mall in the suburbs. The mall was a collection of smaller buildings around a stretch of storefronts. Most of the space was taken up with eye doctors, chiropractors, lawyers, and hair and nail salons.

A high-cost grocery store dominated the line of storefronts. We drove around the smaller buildings, peering at addresses above the doors. We finally located the building labeled 243, a longer building that, based on the blank signs, was mostly empty.

We parked across the lot and got out of the car. We stayed silent as we walked across the parking lot and into the building.

Halfway down the hallway, I stopped and caught Joseph and Mercy's attention. "We don't trust this guy, right?"

They shook their heads.

I held my hand out to Joseph. "Give me the pouch," I said. "I'm going to hide it."

I stuffed the pouch into my pants. I undid the button and put the loops around one side before rebuttoning it. The button held the bag onto my pants for extra security.

I looked up to see Joseph and Mercy staring at me. "What? It's about as secure as I can make it for now."

Mercy nodded, but Joseph threw back his head and laughed. "You look like you switched sexes and got your first hard on!"

I scowled and adjusted the bag. The sigils inside were digging into my crotch and left thigh. "No wonder you guys are always readjusting."

Our bickering was cut short by a sudden loud roar. We spun around towards the sound and saw five... people?... running towards the door we'd just come through.

As I stared at them, the man in front, a decent looking, well-built guy, pulled open the door and flickered into a giant humanoid demon creature. I noticed the others doing the same. The man's giant form shouldn't have been able to fit into the doorway, it was so big, but the spirit world doesn't pay much attention to "should".

"Run!" Mercy shrieked. I took off down the hallway with Joseph and Mercy on my heels.

I embraced my spirit vision, sent out a generic prayer and tried to look around while I ran. A few steps later, a plain metal door flashed colors. I veered over, grabbed the handle and used my grip on it to crash myself into the wall as a make-shift brake. I yanked the door open, hoping I'd read the signs correctly.

The door swung open and I barely got in before Joseph and Mercy were crowding through the door, pushing past me. Still gripping the handle, I checked on our pursuers in the brief second as I slammed the door closed and fumbled the lock into place.

"Thank the All-Father for dead bolting doors," Mercy gasped.

"Amen!" I responded.

"Hallelujah!" Joseph echoed.

Joseph and I exchanged a look before we each barked out a nervous laugh.

I glanced around at the small room. It was probably meant for a general storage area, but it was currently empty. It had no windows, only the one door, and a few electrical outlets.

Mercy grabbed each of us by the arm and pulled us back from the door. It shook from the impact of a body on the other side.

"We have to get these sigils away from here," Joseph shouted.

"How would you suggest we do that?" I demanded. "Magic?"

Joseph and Mercy both stopped and looked at me.

I rolled my eyes. "I'm getting really sick of this magic crap. It's causing way more trouble than it's worth."

Mercy stared at me.

"Fine," I said. "Let's see what we can do."

I grabbed Joseph's arm and pulled him down into a crouch with me in one corner. I looked him in the eye and we both took several deep breaths. Our hands touched briefly as we aligned our magics and we flung out our arms to create a sacred space.

I pulled the pouch with the sigils out of my pants and set them between us. I began humming a song we were both familiar with.

Joseph quickly joined in, finding the rhythm from the song.

I reached out with my mind, searching for the spell to sing. I could tell by the way Joseph closed his eyes that he was doing the same.

"Sigils hiding," I began. "Where monsters can't find." We repeated the line a few times.

"Seek them only in Nicola's mind," Joseph added the second line. I glared at him, but we repeated the two lines together.

"Beyond the world, outside the tree," I said, giving the third line.

Joseph didn't even pause to repeat the whole thing before he added the last line. "Past all the boundaries, so mote it be."

We sang the chant again, repeating it over and over, embracing the beat of the words, visualizing the sigils disappearing.

Joseph picked up a melody in his chanting. After a few repetitions, I began a counterpoint.

My eyes closed and my body swayed to the rhythm. We could feel the power building up. Our song picked up speed, but kept the rhythm.

"Sigils hiding..." My body moved in a circle, swaying counterclockwise. I could feel the power getting closer to the point of release, like the feeling of an orgasm approaching. "Beyond the world..." The energy was nearly at the peak.

"So mote it be!" We shouted the final words, releasing the spell.

Joseph fell forward, catching himself with his hands. I fell sideways and caught myself on shaky arms. The release of the magic had drained us both, and we struggled to catch our breath.

The door burst open, drawing our attention.

Mercy backed up, keeping herself between the creatures and Joseph and I. We scrambled on hands and knees to back farther into the corner.

The creatures spilled into the room, filling it up. Their faces flashed between a generic gangster human and monsters with jutting lower jaws, scattered horns projecting from cheeks and brows. Their skin faded between shades of tan and brown, and deep oranges, blues and greens.

I ducked my head, trying to protect my throat from the attack I was sure would come any minute. My eyes fell on one of the creatures' knees. I stared in fascinated horror as they flashed between the backwards bending joint of a human knee to the forward bending joint of a four-legged animal.

I could hear Joseph's panicked breathing at my back, and the high-pitched singing of Mercy's sword moving through the air.

The creatures moved away from the door, surrounding us and I braced myself for vicious claws digging into my back. I visualized Ella's face, laughing as I tickled her. I held on to that image, wanting it to be the last thing in my mind.

"Stop!" cried a vaguely familiar voice.

Bob? My head jerked up and I saw the older man from Keith's entourage. The creepy one.

I didn't need the sinking feeling in my stomach to tell me that it had been a mistake to trust this guy.

The man looked over the three of us with hard eyes. He seemed to smirk at the sight of Joseph and me huddled in the corner. His eyes scanned over us and along the floor.

I could see his expression turn to one of satisfaction when he spotted the pouch. I cursed myself for leaving it out in the open, and I lurched toward it.

I felt the impact of my body on the wall before my brain processed the feel of a huge arm impacting against my face and chest. I couldn't breathe or move and, even though my eyes worked, I couldn't understand what I was seeing.

I heard a noise, but struggled to understand it. It was like someone had taken the loudest single second from the sound of waves crashing and looped it into a deafening rush.

The pain showed up, late to the experience, slipping in quickly under the numbness. My muscles suddenly ached so badly I couldn't move them. Sharp pains radiated along my chest and spine as I struggled to take a first shuddering breath.

I could feel the spasms in my arms and legs as I struggled to come back to myself. I gasped in short breaths and strained to focus my mind on comprehending the shapes in my vision. It seems dramatic to say that a demon knocked my spirit from my body, but it certainly felt like that was the case.

The first thing I was able to lock my eyes and mind onto was the ceiling. It was white. Not beige, not ecru or eggshell. White. Nearly blue. It had those little speckley bumps on it that many ceilings have. I wondered for a second what they were for.

The next thing that I was able to grasp was a deep male voice screaming curses and obscenities. As I focused my eyes on Joseph's face above mine, I noticed his lips were moving. It took another second for me to realize that he wasn't the one yelling, though.

Joseph was murmuring assurances that I would be okay. I began to believe him as my breaths got deeper and the sharpness of the pains lessened a little. I tried moving my legs and felt them shift under Joseph's weight. He was covering my body with his own.

I tried to speak but only managed a slight wheezing. I gulped a breath and swallowed dryly.

I tried again. "Over-protective macho," I gasped out in Joseph's face.

He broke into a grin and hugged me. I squeaked my discomfort, but let him help me sit up slowly. I looked around.

Mercy was on her stomach, held in place by one of the creatures. She looked at me and smiled, blood trickling down from the corner of her mouth. A bloody cut parted her shirt just below her shoulder. Her arms were wrenched behind her back with the creature holding them with a bird-like clawed foot.

The demon leaned over her, growling and drooling over her neck.

Bob stood in the middle of the room, one foot on the pouch. He looked like he was about to pop a blood vessel. His face was a dark red with veins standing out against his forehead. He held his hands clenched in fists, elbows slightly bent as if he was ready to throw a punch. His eyes darted from Mercy to Joseph to me.

Hope bloomed suddenly in my chest as I pieced together the possibilities. I glanced down at the pouch again. The pouch lying flat under Bob's foot.

I realized that the cold on my cheeks was from tears running down my cheeks, and I burst out laughing.

CHAPT 11

I leaned my aching head against the wall, listening to sounds in the darkness. There was murmuring from conversations outside our tiny room, and the clicking thumps of demon feet walking overhead. A tiny drip seemed to dominate my ears.

Next to me, I heard Joseph shift, no doubt trying to get comfortable. We were sitting on a cold, cement floor in a basement somewhere. I was pretty sure that comfort was not possible. The thought, however, didn't keep me from shifting my weight around as well.

There was a window above our heads. Based on the speckled look of the light seeping in around the edges, it had been spray painted over. The tiny light only gave us shades of darkness to distinguish our surroundings.

A darker shape moved back and forth in front of us. Mercy was pacing again. She'd been walking around like a caged lion since I had regained consciousness. Probably before, too.

I probably shouldn't have laughed at Bob. But his expression and the relief I'd felt when I realized the sigils had vanished... well, it was just too much to hold in.

Bob had snarled out a few words, and the demons had grabbed us and knocked us out before we could do more than yelp in surprise. I supposed I should feel grateful that we weren't dead, but our current situation wasn't really inspiring gratitude at the moment.

I reached out and touched Joseph, both seeking and giving reassurance. Just knowing he and Mercy were here gave me some small hope.

Footsteps approached, and the shadow that was Mercy stopped and moved to the side of the door, distinguishable only by the small line of dim gray light along the floor. The gray light disappeared as the footsteps stopped outside the door.

There was a sound of metallic fumbling, then a click and the door swung open. The sudden increase in light made me blink and raise a hand to block it from my eyes, so I only heard a scuffle that ended with Mercy's sharp cry.

My eyes adjusted to the light and I saw Bob in the doorway, surrounded by the demon creatures. Mercy was shoved face-first into the door jam, held by a demon who had her arms twisted behind her back.

I considered the irony that the last time I'd actually seen Mercy clearly, she'd been in the same position, but on the ground. A part of me recognized that I was mentally avoiding facing the bigger issue here. I wrestled my thoughts under control and dragged my attention to Bob.

Good ol' Bob. He stood, feet apart, hands fisted on his hips, sneering down at us.

I cleared my throat and squinted up at him. "Come to join the party?" I asked.

He huffed at my comment and gestured towards me and Joseph. Two of the creatures stepped forward, reaching for us. I couldn't help but shrink away.

One grabbed me by the upper arms and picked me up like I weighed nothing. Out of the corner of my eye, I could see Joseph being hauled up the same way. We were placed on our feet and guided by the creatures towards the door.

I swayed on my feet, stumbling as I felt the pricks and pins of circulation returning to my numb legs. We only took a few steps before we were dragged to a stop in front of Bob, who was still in the doorway, like some kind of guard dog. Or a gargoyle.

I suppressed a smile as I visualized good ol' Bob with huge lower fangs and a lolling tongue, like the rain spouts on Notre Dame.

Good ol' Bob - I was really starting to like thinking of him like that - looked from me to Joseph and back to me. "We can do this the easy way..."

"Or the easier way?" I asked, intentionally making my tone hopeful.

Good ol' Bob stared at me. His face slowly curved into an unpleasant grin. "Sure. Easy or easier... for me."

He turned to Joseph. "Tell me where the sigils are."

Joseph shot a glance at me.

"Don't tell him," I said.

Good ol' Bob backhanded him. I seriously reconsidered his new nickname.

"Tell me!" he shouted into Joseph's face.

Mercy snarled and struggled in the grasp of her demon.

Joseph sagged in the grasp of the creature and coughed weakly.

Not-so-good ol' Bob pulled back his hand and turned. His next blow was aimed at my face. I raised my chin and glared at him, daring him to do it.

"I don't know!" cried Joseph.

Bob grabbed Joseph by the throat. "You know. And you'll tell me."

He shot a glance at me. "Or I will have my minions peel the skin from your friend, here."

Joseph struggled and gasped against Bob's grip. Bob let him go and Joseph fell back against the creature holding him up.

"I can't!" Joseph said, coughing.

Bob took a step towards him.

I strained against the grip of the demon holding me. "Stop it! Damn you, stop!"

Mercy fought to free herself and cried out as the demon twisted her arm harder.

Bob took another step.

I let out a frustrated sob. My mind raced through scenario after scenario. But I could only think of one that wouldn't get Joseph killed.

"He doesn't know where they are!" I cried.

Bob lifted his arm to deliver another blow.

I took a deep breath and met Mercy's eyes. I hoped the look she was sending me really meant she approved of my next step.

"Only I know where they are," I said.

Bob froze. He slowly turned his head towards me. "Is that so?" he said in a quiet, deadly voice.

I nodded. "It was a condition of the spell that sent them away," I admitted.

Bob moved towards me. "And you will tell me," he commanded.

I shrugged. "It isn't that simple," I said.

Bob raised an eyebrow.

"I don't actually know where they are right now," I explained. "But I'm the only one who will be able to find them."

Bob turned slightly and gestured at Joseph. The demon holding him began twisting Joseph's arms. Joseph let out a high-pitched scream of pain.

I lunged at Bob, but was held in place by the creature gripping my arms. "Stop it!" I shrieked. "Or I will never help you! I swear on his life!"

Bob gestured a halt to the torture. He looked me up and down, as if seeing me for the first time. A muscle in his temple twitched. "Is that so?"

I snarled. "If you hurt either of them again, you had better be willing to kill us all, because that will be your only choice."

Bob leaned back on his heels, considering my words.

My eyes were drawn towards Joseph, wanting to check on him, wanting to see if he approved. I dragged my gaze back to Bob, leaving my eyelid twitching. I wrestled my fear and doubt into submission, drawing what little power I had left after all I'd been through. I lifted my chin another notch and pushed the power forward, projecting stubborn determination.

"If you don't hurt us, I will find the sigils," I promised. "But if any of us feels even a scratch more..." I narrowed my eyes at good ol' Bob. "Game over. And you will never find them without me."

Bob stared at me for a long moment. "How do I know what you say is true?" he asked.

I shrugged my shoulders despite the demon's grip on my arms. "We cast a spell to hide the sigils. They were in the pouch when we went into the room."

I tilted my head. "Part of the spell was that only I would be able to find where they were hidden. The sigils are gone. The spell worked."

Bob frowned. "I don't know. Maybe you are just saying you hid them with a spell in order to distract me from finding them."

He leaned forward. I could smell the staleness of his breath. "Prove it."

I rolled my eyes. "How would you like me to do that?"

Bob smiled. "Do a spell. Now."

I barked out a laugh.

The smile fell from Bob's face, replaced by an angry scowl. "What's so funny about that?"

I shook my head. "You just don't get how magic works, do you?" I asked. "It's not like we just say a stupid rhyme and whatever we say happens. We need energy to do magic."

Bob frowned, his face a mask of doubt and confusion.

I sighed. "We are tired, hungry and beaten up. We can barely walk. And you want us to twist reality in this condition?" I paused, staring at him. "Seriously?"

Bob looked around at the creatures. He looked uncomfortable. "Well, what would you suggest?"

I pulled my arms free from the demon. "Keep us in here, if it makes you feel better," I said. "But we need food, water, bedding and time to rest."

Bob's expression hardened.

I realized I was about to lose him, so I finished in a rush, "Give us 24 hours to get our energy up and we can get to work."

His face relaxed. I could almost read his thoughts: one day wasn't such a long time; still time to do what he needed to do.

He gave a short nod. "Fine," he said. "But if you don't follow through, it'll be worse for you."

I nodded. "Yeah, yeah, pain, suffering, torment. I'm aware of the consequences," I assured him.

The creatures pushed past us as they left with Bob, leaving the three of us alone, again, in the dark. The footsteps had barely faded away before Mercy and Joseph turned on me.

"What the hell!" Joseph said. The shadow that was him stepped forward.

I gasped, feeling the hope that had begun to grow wither away.

Shadow Mercy nudged him aside. "What were you thinking?" she demanded. "You can't help him find the sigils!"

I backed up until I hit the wall. "I know that," I said. I flinched at the whine in my voice, and I struggled to hold myself together. "But..."

Mercy cut me off, closing in on me. "You are supposed to keep them from getting the Runespells, not hand them over!"

I felt smothered, claustrophobic. I felt the anger and desperation pressing up against me. I struggled for breath.

Joseph jumped in, stepping closer. "You just gave him carte blanche to kill us all!" he pointed out.

I pressed myself against the wall, my protests dying in my throat. My hands grasped at the wall behind me, searching for a lifeline.

"What happens when you don't find them? What happens to us?" Joseph asked.

A dark red filled my vision, covering the shadows in a bloody hue. A rushing roar filled my ears, muffling the sounds of Joseph and Mercy yelling at me. I was about to have a full-blown panic attack.

"What happens when you do find them? The whole world is at stake," Mercy demanded in a muted voice.

"I don't know!" I screamed, throwing my arms out to drive them away. "I don't know, I don't know, I don't know!"

I stepped forward and shoved one of them back with both hands. The shadow - Mercy? - staggered away.

I snarled at them both. "I don't know if I can find them. I don't know what happens if I do. I don't know how to stop this. I don't know how I'm going make this work. I don't know!"

I rounded on the other shadow. It backed away from me, stumbling and falling in the darkness. I didn't care. My self-control was gone. I swung out with my fists and words.

"I know he was hurting you," I choked out. I could feel the tears streaming down my face. "I know he won't stop. I know he wants the sigils. I know he will kill us all. And I know," I gagged on the words, swallowed convulsively and forced them out. "I know that I won't be able to handle another death on MY hands."

I turned to the only acceptable target I could find and hit the wall with my fists over and over, screaming wordlessly until my voice gave out. Each strike was a desperate plea for forgiveness through suffering or a strike against those who would hurt those I loved. Who *had* hurt those I loved.

I kept pounding at the wall, screaming a hoarse, voiceless cry. A thick ache built up in my throat. In my mind's eye, I saw Keith lying in a pool of his own blood. I saw Joseph's head snap with the impact of a fist. I saw Mercy cry out in pain from wrenched arms. I saw the unnamed police officer torn apart. I saw a crowd of strangers ripped limb from limb. I saw the pained, screaming face of my baby, Ella, surrounded by the flames of Armageddon.

My fists gave out, numb from the pain, falling unfeeling to my sides. I stepped back to kick at the wall, tripped and fell with a jolt that sent shocks of pain up my spine. I paused a moment before I launched my body at the hated wall, beating at it with palms, arms, legs and even my head.

The jolts of pain radiating up my arms and through my head were the only lifeline I had to feeling... anything. There was only desperation, and it filled me. I had to do something, but the only thing I could do was beat myself against this wall. So I did.

Time ceased to exist. The only measure of life was the rhythmic thumping of my body against paneling. My ears were filled with the roar of waves that never quite crashed. My eyes didn't see darkness, just a dull blood-red. Too soon, my body wore out and the flailing slowed to an occasional thump.

I felt myself being dragged across the floor away from the wall. My arms no long struck anything solid, so they dropped limply to my sides. My head lolled back as my muscles turned to jelly, and I felt my torso being held up.

I collapsed against the thing holding me, struggling for breath between the barking sobs and wheezing croaks. I don't know how much time passed while I lay there, weaker than I'd ever felt in my life. I only lay there and wept until the tears stopped falling. Then I wept without tears.

Slowly, the roar in my ears faded away, and I could hear the sounds of Joseph chanting a healing song and Mercy murmuring over and over, "It's okay. You're okay."

I latched on to their voices, letting them draw my soul back from the terrible darkness and lust for violence that had overtaken me.

The feeling came back into my body. I felt the deep, agonizing ache in my head, and the lesser aches in the bones of my arms and hands. I could feel my fingers start to twitch with the pain, spasming uncontrollably. I felt the pains along the back of my throat from sobbing and screaming, and the periodic jerking of my legs, working out the abuse I'd put them through.

I drew a shuddering breath, rolled over and vomited a glob of mucus, drained from my sinuses into my stomach. I rolled back into Mercy's arms and closed my aching eyes. The sweet sounds of my friends' voices lulled me into a deep, dreamless sleep.

•   •   •

I first became aware of being warm, toasty warm, except for my nose and the toes of my right foot. I was lying on my side on something that could only be described as trying to be cushiony.

My hands felt muffled and I noticed a stale smell from under my head. The cover over my shoulders was slightly rough and scratchy.

As I became more conscious, I realized that someone was lying behind me, snuggled against my back with a hand resting on my waist. I blinked my eyes open and struggled to focus on the wall a mere inch from my nose.

Cold radiated from the wall, chilling my nostrils. I shifted slightly, not quite rolling over. The person behind me moved and I felt them sit up. I rolled over onto my back and saw Joseph shrugging out of the cheap, synthetic fabric blanket that had been covering us.

"What happened?" I asked. I remembered being captured, and I vaguely recalled Bob's visit, but everything else had faded to incoherent images and muted feelings.

Mercy shifted her position and her movement drew my attention to her. She stood near the door, in a posture that indicated she'd been guarding the entry for us for hours.

"You don't remember?" she asked.

I sat up on the thin mattress - that's where the stale smell had come from - and shook my head. "Not... Nothing that I can make any sense of," I said.

Joseph had gotten to his feet and he pointed to the wall at the foot of the mattress. I looked at where he'd pointed, a sinking feeling coming over me.

The wall paneling looked like it had been hit with a baseball bat. Several times. There were dents and scuffs covering a good section of it. Dark brownish stains scattered over the area.

My eyes widened. Then I felt it on the side of my forehead. The tight feel of a bandage. I raised my hand and touched it, confirming the cotton and paper-tape over several inches of my head.

Out of the corner of my eye, I caught a glimpse of white on my hand. I held my hands out and saw that they were completely wrapped in bandages, giving them a mummy-like appearance.

I raised my head to look at Joseph and Mercy. I knew there was confusion written on my face.

"What is this?" I said, panic rising in my voice.

Mercy nodded, as if I'd confirmed something. "You beat the wall. Then you passed out. When they brought us blankets and the mattress, we asked for bandages and got you fixed up."

I opened my mouth to speak, but I had no idea what to say, so I closed it again.

Joseph squatted down on the mattress next to me. He had some granola bars and a juice box in his hands, which he handed to me.

I took them gratefully and quickly opened the juice box and gulped it down. I tore into a granola bar next, taking the bottle of water that Mercy held out to me and swallowed half of that.

I chewed and swallowed my way through four granola bars, two juice boxes and two bottles of water before I finally slowed down. I had fully woken up and my brain had kick-started its way to functional, once more.

I sighed and glanced sideways at Joseph. "I did that, didn't I," I said, gesturing to the damaged wall. I swallowed hard as it hit me that the brown spots were likely my blood.

He nodded. "Scared the shit out of us, too."

I looked down, staring at a rip in my jeans at the knee to keep from looking at my hands. "I don't remember much after the office building at the mall."

I looked up at Mercy. "What happened here?"

In a brisk tone, Mercy laid out what I'd done during the meeting with Bob. And after. To her credit, she looked a little ashamed when she described how she and Joseph had ripped into me before I lost it.

I stared at a crack in the floor, tracing it over and over with my eyes, as she spoke. When she finished, I frowned. I looked at the floor, then at the wall. I glanced at Joseph and Mercy.

"There's light," I said. Mercy gestured to the wall behind and above me. I craned my still-sore neck around to look. The window had been broken out. It was too small to get out of, but it provided enough light to see by. "Did I do that, too?"

Joseph laughed. "No, that was Mercy."

I huffed. "Great. I go ape-shit on a wall and it's the wrong spot to valiantly provide illumination to our intrepid, would-be heroes." I flinched when the "H" word left my mouth.

Joseph smiled. "Figures your aim sucks."

I stuck my tongue out at him, glad to see his mood lifting despite the situation we faced.

I noticed Mercy was staring at me. "What is it?" I asked. "Afraid I'm gonna flip out again?"

Mercy shook her head slightly. "I was just wondering..."

She hesitated and I waved at her to continue.

"I was wondering if anything like that," she gestured at the beaten wall, "has ever happened to you before."

I frowned. "What? Me going to town on a random bit of building?"

Mercy shook her head and rolled her eyes. "Not that, specifically. I mean the losing control. The anger, the fear." She looked me in the eye. "The red vision and roar in your ears. And even the throwing up and passing out afterwards."

I frowned. "It happened once when I was a teen, around 15 or 16," I said. "But how did you know about..."

We all jumped as a crashing noise interrupted, the sound of breaking wood and shattering glass sounding above us. Joseph and I leapt to our feet. We stood, tensely, staring at the ceiling. Thumps and crashes moved around the upper floor, interspersed with growls, roars and yells.

Mercy shook off the surprise first, pulling us to the side of the room and shooting orders at us to tie our shoes and grab the remaining granola bars and waters. I obeyed, bending over to check my shoelaces and grabbing granola bars to shove into my pants pockets.

Joseph shoved a bottle of water into each of my hands and held another two in his own. We stood with Mercy between us and the door - I was shoved into the corner - waiting as the sounds of fighting got closer.

Time stretched out as we waiting, trying to decipher the muffled sounds that rattled the walls of our prison. I shifted on my feet, drawing a quick glance from Mercy. I could see the tension in Joseph's shoulders, the muscles knotted under his shirt.

Several minutes passed and the initial adrenaline began to ease out of my system. I muffled a yawn, and my muscles began to feel weak again.

I jumped when the door burst open, swinging in and towards us, temporarily blocking our view of the entry. Mercy's hands clenched into fists, and Joseph raised the bottles of water, threateningly.

I held my breath as the seconds passed, the door hitting Mercy's foot and swinging back. I saw that the latch had been broken, and I noted that it was just like when a door was kicked open in the movies. I wondered briefly if that's what had been done.

Then the door stopped swinging shut, apparently caught by the person who'd opened it. I caught a glimpse of a human-looking hand on the edge of the door, then a woman stepped into the room.

She looked enough like Mercy that they could have been related. But where Mercy's face had an edge of compassion, this woman's expression was alive with pure energy, like she couldn't wait to get back to doing... something, anything at all.

She looked around and spotted us, her eyes flashing with... not humor, not satisfaction. I couldn't quite place it. Her blonde hair was pulled back into a braid, but wisps of it stood out and floated on the air, as if it was full of static. Her eyes were blue-gray and flashed expressively, unlike Mercy's calm pale blue ones.

The woman stepped towards us, causing Joseph to draw back an arm, water bottle ready to fly. She stopped and flashed him a patronizing smile, then turned to Mercy.

"The creatures are on the retreat," she announced. "We are planning to route them completely."

Mercy nodded. "Thank you, Kara," she said. "And thank our sisters for us, too."

Mercy glanced back at Joseph and me. "We will find a safe-haven and search out the Runespells. I'll send word to... our father... when we have them again."

The woman, Kara, nodded briskly, turned on her heel and left. Joseph slowly lowered his arms. I nearly collapsed against the wall in relief. Mercy turned to us.

"What now?" Joseph asked.

"Now," Mercy said. "We get out of here."

We found my bag, Mercy's knife and the empty pouch lying in a pile on the floor near the front door. Our cell phones had been turned off and dumped in my bag. A quick check showed that my phone was dead, but Joseph's phone still worked. And we still had our little bit of cash.

Joseph and I were careful to keep our heads turned away from the two demons lying dead nearby.

We headed out the door, walking quickly away from the house. It looked like it was abandoned, sitting on the end of a road in a sparsely populated residential area. We walked along the side of the road, keeping an eye out for cars or any other signs of life. The street was completely deserted and the handful of houses we passed seemed to be empty.

After about 30 minutes, we reached a street that showed signs of life, including a gas station. I frowned at the street signs, trying to figure out where we were.

"I think we're on the East side of Indy," Joseph said beside me, looking up at the signs. "He took us all the way across the city."

I whistled. That was quite a drive, and with all those demonic creatures and three prisoners, it was risky of him. That meant he was either willing to take out anyone who might see him, or absolutely confident that he could pull it off. Probably a little of both.

Joseph got on his phone and called for a taxi to pick us up. I went into the gas station and picked up a couple drinks. Joseph came in and threw a pack of menthols on my tab.

We sat outside, munching on the remaining granola bars and smoking while we waiting for the taxi to show. Mercy stood in front of us as though she was still guarding us from the demons.

"So," I said, breaking the silence. "We are heading back to the mall to see if we can get the car back?"

Joseph hesitated and looked at Mercy. She shrugged and nodded.

"Then what?" I asked.

Mercy stared down a couple of teenagers who were walking into the gas station. "We need a place to work," she said. She turned to look at me. "We need to figure out a way for you to find the sigils. Some place safe. Not a hotel and not someone's house. Someplace off the grid..." She trailed off.

I glanced at Joseph, who frowned, thinking. I looked back at Mercy and nodded.

"We need Hound Dog," I said.

• • •

We rode in silence as the taxi took us back to the Eaglepoint Village mall. There was a tangible feeling of relief when we found the car exactly how we had left it in the nearly deserted parking lot. I paid the taxi driver while Mercy and Joseph checked the car and transferred our stuff into it.

As the cab pulled away, another car pulled up. My shoulders sagged as I recognized the sedan. The window rolled down.

"Good morning, Detective Ames," I said, pushing as much cheerfulness into my voice as I could manage. "What can I do for you this fine day?"

The detective looked me up and down. With my torn jeans, dirty shirt, bandaged hands and head, and undoubtedly messy hair, I'm sure I looked like I'd been through some kind of hell.

Ames grinned, showing coffee-stained teeth. "You haven't been answering my calls," he accused.

I shrugged and pulled out my phone, making my movements a little slower than normal so I wouldn't get the gun treatment again. I made a show of looking at it and turned it to show him.

"Dead battery," I said. I nodded towards the car. "Power cord is in the car, so I'll be charging it up here soon. I've been a little distracted recently."

I put the phone back in my pocket and propped my sore hands on my hips. "What did you need?"

Detective Ames opened the door and hefted himself out of the car. "We have more dead bodies, Ms. Crandall," he said, staring out across the parking lot, his voice light. "A couple of nights ago, an officer was killed in the street, and yesterday, Keith Ludlow was found, shot dead in his apartment."

I grimaced, remembering Keith and the cop. I briefly wondered why no one was bringing up the demon bodies Mercy had left scattered in our wake.

The detective turned to stare at me. "Keith was your daughter's father, according to the records we found. And we have some footage from the cop's dash cam that shows someone looking a lot like you running towards the cop before his death."

His eyes narrowed. "Too much of this points to you."

"Tell me about it," I muttered under my breath. I took a deep breath and set my shoulders. "Detective Ames, I understand that there is a lot of extremely circumstantial evidence pointing towards my involvement. And I wish I could explain this away easily, but frankly, I have more important issues to deal with right now."

I turned to find Mercy and Joseph leaning against the car. The set of their shoulders indicated they were more than willing to get involved in the discussion. I headed towards them.

"I will find out what has been going on!" Detective Ames shouted behind me.

I paused and turned around. "Gods, Detective, I sincerely hope not," I said, reaching up to rub the ache under the bandage on my forehead. "For your sake."

Detective Ames stared after us as we drove away, well below the posted speed limit.

•   •   •

It hadn't been more than a handful of days since we'd first come to the Rainbow Bridge looking for Muriel, but my entire life had been shaken up.

I hoped that Muriel had successfully made it out of town. Discovering that I had failed to get her to safety would probably push me right off the crazy cliff. Again.

I scanned the kids sitting along the bank on each side. No Muriel, but I jerked my head up in a silent greeting to Big Ralph, who was sitting next to a couple of younger boys, talking and eating sandwiches. He waved back.

We spotted Hound Dog and walked over to meet him. When we got closer, he hesitated, eyes going over our disheveled appearance. I realized that even street living wouldn't explain how badly we looked.

"Hey, rich girl," he called with forced cheerfulness in his voice. "What brings you here?"

I considered pretending things were better than they really were, but shook my head at that. Hound Dog didn't deserve being played, especially since so many of the kids he kept an eye on were involved.

"The end of the world," I said with a heavy voice.

He forced a laugh, then paused. He stared at me, eyes flicking over my bandages and dirty clothes. Then he turned to examine Joseph and, finally, Mercy. He peered closely at Joseph's tired eyes and Mercy's serious expression.

"No shit?" he asked.

I shook my head. "This is serious," I said. "Keith's dead and his little cult is way more big a deal than we thought. More people could die before we are done."

I held up a hand to stop him from interrupting. "And no, there's not much that you guys can do. Except..."

I paused and exchanged looks with Mercy and Joseph before turning back to Hound Dog. "We need somewhere that we can drop off the face. Where no one will be able to track us. And that won't be traced to anyone else. We don't want to be leadin' this shit-storm to innocent people."

Hound Dog rubbed his hand over his face. "Look, I trust you guys, but there's only so far that can go. If I'm gonna help you, you gotta know there's a line that I won't cross for you."

I nodded my understanding.

He turned to Mercy. "And how the hell did you end up so involved in this? A couple days ago, you were just going to help them find Muriel."

Mercy shrugged her shoulders. "I suppose you could say I was waiting for this," she said.

Hound Dog gave her a hard look. "Undercover?" Mercy nodded. "We trusted you. We told you our secrets. And you're a cop?"

Mercy shook her head. "I'm not a cop," she corrected him. "I'm more like... special ops."

I barked out a laugh at her understatement. Joseph grinned.

Mercy rolled her eyes at us. "Point is, Hound Dog, I got no reason to tell anyone about you, or your secrets, or the rest of the kids."

She glanced at a group of girls laughing under a tree near the bank. "I was told to protect you and help if the opportunity arose. That's it. We don't deal with petty theft or runaways or anything like that."

Hound Dog stared at her for a long moment before he nodded. "I guess I got no reason to think you'd sell us out." He turned to me. "I can hide you all. And no one would ever be able to figure out where you are."

• • •

We pulled up in front of Keith's apartment half an hour later. Joseph and I stared silently out the window at the apartment, remembering the events of that night. Mercy got out of the car.

I glanced at Hound Dog, who shrugged, then followed her out.

"Why are we here?" I asked.

Mercy glanced up at the apartment building. "Remember when we first found Keith here?" I nodded. "We were here because you were dropping me off across the street at my friend's house."

I turned to look at the apartments on the other side of the street. I slowly nodded, remembering the weird coincidence. As I watched, a woman who looked a lot like Mercy and the other one - Kara? - walked out of the apartment and trotted across the street.

Mercy greeted her and explained that we needed a ride, but we couldn't keep the car with us. The woman nodded.

I climbed into the back seat with Joseph and Hound Dog, and Mercy got into the passenger seat with the other woman driving. As we pulled away, Mercy turned around.

"This is Misty, one of my sisters," she explained. She glanced at Hound Dog and hesitated. "We were working undercover together. She was watching Keith."

I nodded. That made sense that one of the Valkyrie would be keeping an eye on the guy with the sigils, though I wondered about her absence the night he had died.

Mercy looked at me, reading the expressions on my face. "She was making sure Muriel left the city safely. She wasn't here to be able to help us that night."

I stared at Mercy, processing what she said. Muriel was safe and gone. I finally nodded, accepting the situation for what it was.

Mercy turned back around and sat silently while Hound Dog provided Misty with the address.

We headed into the downtown area where traffic was much heavier. Misty navigated the streets with confidence, eventually pulling up beside a huge cathedral. We spilled out of the car and watched it drive away before we turned to the building.

The rectangular building sprawled across an entire city block. It had a huge square shape on the east side, with rounded columns climbing the walls. Round towers stood guard at each corner, and a peaked archway rose up several stories above the huge wooden double door. A single tower, twice the height of the rest of the building, stretched up to dominate the western side of the building, with huge arched windows on each side.

The entire building gleamed with the sunlight reflecting off of the light tan brick. There was no fancy color on the building, but the architectural details stood out against the bright neutral material. Overall, it was stunning.

Joseph laughed. "You have got to be kidding, Hound Dog."

Hound Dog just grinned and nodded.

I turned to shoot Joseph a questioning look. He shook his head in disbelief.

"This is the Scottish Rite temple," Joseph explained. "Freemasons. Hound Dog wants to hide us in a place just this side of the Illuminati."

I grinned and turned back to the grand building. "It's perfect!"

•   •   •

We walked around to one of the side doors. Hound Dog dug through a pocket of the backpack he'd brought while he explained that he had a key, thanks to a Mason whose kid Hound Dog had helped out a few years back. The runaway had gotten home safely, and when Hound Dog asked for a key to access the temple basement, the Mason had hesitated only a little before agreeing.

"I bet you didn't know that Indianapolis has a network of catacombs, did you?" Hound Dog asked. He grinned at my look of disbelief. "It's true. The City Market does tours of a small section of them."

He led us up to the door, taking steps two at a time with his long legs. "But the catacombs extend out much farther than what is on the tour, connecting to old sewer lines that are big enough to drive a car through." He hesitated. "Don't ask how I know that."

He bent to work the lock with a key on the keychain he pulled from his pocket. "They also connect to the quarry roads – these giant underground transport tunnels that they drive semis through to haul rocks. Lots of street kids know where a few access points are, so we can get out of the weather or hide from the cops, if we need to."

The lock clicked and Hound Dog grinned as he pushed open the door. He gestured us through, holding a finger to his lips to indicate we should keep quiet.

I nodded my understanding as I slipped past him and through the door. Then I stopped and stared.

I couldn't help it. I was blown away by the gorgeous architecture and details, even in this side area. The huge hallway was lined with columns and plaques, pictures of Masonic officers, and huge double doors that no doubt led to equally huge ballrooms, auditoriums and other meeting and performance areas.

The energy filling the building was old and dignified and powerful. And secretive.

Hound Dog closed the door behind him and gestured us to follow him through a small door to the side. The door opened into a staircase going down.

We shuffled in a silent row through the dark stairwell. Hound Dog carefully opened the door at the bottom of the stairs and peered out into the hallway. Satisfied, he pulled the door open and we filed into the hall. This part of the building felt more like administrative offices, with halls and rooms that were more normal, person sized.

Hound Dog glanced around and I worried for a moment that he didn't know where he was leading us. Then he seemed to get his bearings and heading down the hallway with confidence. We stopped outside a room marked "Archives" and Hound Dog reached out to turn the handle.

"What are you people doing in here?" The strange voice rang out, and we froze.

CHAPT 12

We slowly turned towards the voice. An older man in a brown coverall stood in a defensive posture, holding a broom in both hands like a quarterstaff. He stared at us with narrowed eyes, his gaze sweeping over each of us.

I grimaced as I realized that we looked horrible and probably like we were up to no good.

The man suddenly did a double-take as Joseph took a step forward.

"Brother Andress?" the man said, confusion written in his expression. "Is that you?"

Joseph nodded. "Yeah. Fred, right?"

The man nodded.

"As you can see," Joseph continued, "we've had a rough couple of days. I just need to pick some things up from the archives." He held up his hand to stop the man's protests. "I'll sign it all out."

Fred looked pointedly at Mercy, Hound Dog and me. Joseph turned to follow his gaze.

"And these folks?" Fred asked.

Joseph turned back to face Fred and shrugged. "They're friends. I'll keep them away from the oath-bound texts."

I could see his grin flash and he shrugged his shoulders. "They found out I needed to come here and they pestered me for a mini-tour. You know how people get about the Masons."

Fred relaxed visibly and huffed. "Don't I ever. I had to chase away three groups of kids this week alone. Damn goths think we got the secret to eternal youth or something."

He looked me right in the eyes. "Do I look like I got the secret to eternal youth?"

I blinked at the man whose tanned and weathered face was lined with small wrinkles, and whose head was topped with a thinning mop of hair more gray than brown.

"Ummm..." I shot a look at Joseph, silently begging for help.

Joseph laughed. "No, Fred, you don't," he said. "And if my joints keep up the way they are, I'll be wheelchair bound by the time I'm your age."

Joseph lifted a hand in a farewell gesture and turned back to the "Archives". Before Fred could say another word, Joseph had ushered us inside.

I turned on him as soon as the door closed. "What... the actual..." I began.

Joseph rolled his eyes. "I'm a member of this chapter," he said in a rush, keeping his voice just above a whisper. "I'm sort of in charge of the archives and cataloguing the texts."

I realized my mouth was hanging open and I snapped it shut. "Sort of... Sweet baby Baldur, Joseph!" I cursed in a muted squeak. "How long were you going to let us stumble around before you let us know that?"

Joseph shook his head. "Look," he said. "I applied for membership back when you were pregnant. I told you then, but you had your own shit to deal with, so I just never bothered you with it after that."

He shrugged, looking a little uncomfortable. "By the time I got in and everything, it just seemed like it wasn't important enough to bring up. Then, when we pulled up outside, I wasn't sure how to just up and say 'Oh, by the way, guess what I did'." He sighed.

"Plus Hound Dog was doing great," he said, gesturing to our friend. "So you didn't even need me to step in. Well, until Fred showed up."

I slowly walked towards Joseph, taking measured steps as I spoke. "You have access to what is considered one of the greatest occult libraries outside the Vatican City, and you didn't think I should be bothered with it?"

My eyes narrowed as I positioned myself nose-to-nose with him. "Is that what you are trying to tell me?"

Joseph looked down at me. We stared at each other for a long moment, glaring at each other.

Then Joseph broke into a huge grin, winked and said, "Yup!"

I raised an eyebrow, put my hands on my hips and gave a contemptuous sniff. "Well, alrighty then."

I turned on my heel and walked over to Hound Dog. "So, where's this secret entrance of yours?"

Hound Dog looked back and forth from me to Joseph a few times.

Mercy rolled her eyes. "By the All-Father, you two are just too much," she said, nudging Hound Dog to move as Joseph and I chuckled.

He hesitated another minute before moving to a built-in bookshelf on one of the inner walls of the large room. I caught Joseph's slight nod out of the corner of my eye and I wondered if he had known about the entrance or just suspected.

Hound Dog ran his hand along the left side of the bookshelf and I heard a soft click. He pulled on one of the shelves and the entire bookshelf swung away from the wall, revealing an opening just large enough for a full-grown man to squeeze through.

Hound Dog reached into a side pocket of his backpack again, and brought out an electric lantern with a solar panel and hand-crank. He handed it to Joseph, but Mercy grabbed it and went through the passage first.

I shrugged at Hound Dog and followed her with Joseph on my heels. The passageway was cramped for the first few steps, then the tunnels opened up into a huge hallway.

It was about 20 feet across and 10 feet high at the center of the slight arch in the ceiling. There were large, arched doorways every couple of yards leading to crisscrossing passages. The tunnels were built, not carved, with faded pinkish brick laid in the typical, overlapping brick pattern.

I turned to look at the passageway we'd come in from. It was in a wall of larger cut river rock in shades of greenish-gray. The opening was a squat rectangle and smaller than the doorways lining the passage.

I let out a whistle, impressed by the size and craftsmanship of the catacombs.

Mercy stopped several feet from the entryway and waited, holding the lantern high for the rest of us to see our way. Hound Dog emerged from the dark passage and looked around, getting his bearings. He nodded sharply and gestured us to follow him as he took one of the side passages.

As we walked, I saw more signs of wear in the brickwork. We passed several arches that had collapsed into huge piles of brick, mortar and dirt from the ceiling. A few of the arches appeared to be reinforced with cobbled-together two-by-fours. I shivered at the thought of being buried under one of those piles.

After several minutes, Hound Dog took us through another small, squarish doorway and into a large room. It was bare and had the same dirt floor as the rest of the catacombs, but it was quiet and dry.

"This is it," he said. He pointed out the small circle of bricks around slightly blackened dirt.

"We've used this place a few times, but it isn't as easy to get to as some of the other areas," he explained. "It is further away from the nicer parts of the catacombs, where they do the tours, so no one comes around here unless there's a maintenance problem, or they are hiding."

"This is great," I said. "It'll be perfect for what we need."

Hound Dog shrugged off his backpack and handed it to me. It was heavy and felt full.

"I got you a few blankets, some jerky and granola bars," he said. "There's a few bottles of water in there, too. It should last you about a day before you need to come out to get more. You'll be able to find your way back out?"

"Not a problem," Mercy said.

Joseph and I shrugged and nodded. If Mercy was confident, I was pretty sure we could be out of the catacombs in a matter of minutes.

He pointed to a dark corner, farthest from the door. "Courtesy is that you pee in the corner and throw some dirt over it. Clean up after yourselves. If any maintenance crews find too much evidence of squatting, they'll lock this area down and no one will be able to use it."

We nodded our understanding and thanked him. He brushed off our attempts to shake his hand and hugged us instead, before he took off back down the passageway.

I turned to face Joseph and Mercy. We stared at each other for a long moment before I heaved a sigh.

"Time to get to work," I said.

Joseph nodded. "No rest for the wicked."

I grinned and let loose with a perfect witch's cackle that echoed through the tunnels.

• • •

I sat with my head in my hands. I struggled to get myself centered through the frustration of trying to force an idea. I avoided looking at Joseph, knowing that he was just as much at a loss as I was. Brainstorming under stress was a generally futile process, and the events of the past few days would definitely fall under the stress category.

I thought about the stress chart taught in every Psych class, with the numerical values assigned to different scenarios. Death in the family was the most stressful at 100. I wondered if Keith would be considered family. Probably.

I didn't remember anything about being chased by demons on the chart. It figured that my life would fall so far outside the norm that something like a chart would come nowhere near to touching it.

I pulled my thoughts from the track that they were on. I needed to focus on finding the sigils. Based on the line Joseph had thrown into the spell, I was the only one who could find them. I sat back leaning on my arms with my legs stretched out in front of me and tried to organized the available information.

"Either I am the only one who would be given access to the sigils," I said, speaking my thoughts aloud. "Or I am the only one with the ability to access the sigils."

Joseph nodded.

I shook my head. "I don't buy the idea that I'm the only one with the ability. I don't think I have some special and unique superpower. That's too ridiculous."

"That leaves the idea that you are the only one who would be given access to the sigils," Joseph pointed out.

I nodded. "That means that there would be some sort of way for the sigils, or the knowledge of where they are, to be keyed to me." I smiled to myself, thinking of some kind of magical thumbprint or retinal scanning.

Unless...

I sat up. Energy signatures were unique to each person in the same way as fingerprints, retinas and DNA. So the sigils or the information about them could be coded energetically. Since the sigils weren't just popping out at us, or in a place where they could easily be found, it was far more likely that the knowledge of their location was what only I could access.

I explained my thinking to Joseph. He slowly nodded. When energy and knowledge combined, there was only one place to go.

"The Akashic Records," he said, confirming my thought.

Mercy, watching us go back and forth, sat up. "You are going to access the Great Library? You can do that?"

I nodded. An infinite library of information, the Records were accessible through various portals, but most easily, for me at least, through the Astral plane.

Some said that everything that ever happened or ever could was recorded in the Akashic library. Many considered it to be another world, a world in the mind or collective unconscious, which was solely a giant library filled with books and scrolls or a divine master server.

I personally felt that the Akashic Records took the form of what was most appropriate to the user.

The sheer amount of information in the Akashic Records was daunting, and tantalizing. People were always trying to figure out a way to access it and bring the information back. I'm sure that some considered the Records to hold the key to power, fame or wealth, and my own experiences didn't contradict that idea.

Yes, I'd been to the Akashic Records before. Many times. And I'd quickly realized that one of the characteristics of the library was that it gave you the information you needed, not the information you wanted. Most of the time, that was the same thing, if your intentions were pure. And I don't mean the whole innocent, pure of heart BS tossed around in fairy tales.

The Records were information. They responded best to motives of information.

If you found the Akashic Records and were motivated by world domination or fame and fortune, the Records would be likely to give you historical information, not the key to your own success.

They don't function well as a short-cut to enlightenment either.

The Records seem to understand, as much as information can understand, that experience is a key factor in knowledge and growth, that short-cutting the process also short-circuited the process.

The Records could be incredibly frustrating when you are looking to jump levels of spiritual knowledge.

With that in mind, you would assume that facts would be pretty straight forward in the library, but no. You couldn't go to the Akashic Records and find lottery numbers, safe combinations or that kind of thing. Well, you could, but you wouldn't be able to bring the information back.

Like the electronic security at a big box store, trying to leave with information that would let you steal from or even know the thoughts or feelings of another person would result in a noisy, embarrassing and sometimes painful experience. Headaches happen, and the energetic ripping of information from the mind was never pleasant.

I always felt that the Records were connected to a person's dharma, the path that a person was meant to take in life to have the most satisfying version of that life. Now a dharma didn't mean that people didn't have choices.

You could choose against your dharma, and most people did. Often. But most of the big coincidences of life were to bring you back to the path that would fulfill you. And the Records would not give you information that went against your dharma.

I had found the Akashic Records pretty quickly in my spiritual journey, but not before I had come to the conclusion that world domination would suck, and enlightenment shortcuts would cheat me out of the experience of growth. My learning curve at the library had been pretty smooth.

Yeah, I'd occasionally tried to bring back information that I shouldn't have, mostly for fun and to see if I could, so the attempts resulted in less painful consequences than some others I'd heard about. In the Akashic Library, I was considered a good patron, which was a good sign of how any attempts I would make to find the sigils through the Records would go.

I sat quietly feeling out the rightness of my decision. "I think I'm going to have to go through the astral plane to search for the Records," I said.

• • •

Joseph knew as much as I did about astral travel. We both had had plenty of experience there, and we often talked about the differences in individual experiences and what that could mean.

Thankfully, he also knew that I wouldn't come back to or take care of my physical body unless I had to. When you go astral, you go in spirit. Your body stays put and, usually, gets ignored.

He helped me get comfortable and covered me with one of the blankets after making sure I'd had some water and food, in case my trip took longer than expected. It sucks coming back to a dehydrated body, I can tell you for sure. The headache alone follows you for days.

I smiled at him, giving and seeking reassurance, and took a deep breath and closed my eyes. I'd done this a million times and it always surprised me how easy and hard it was to do.

I focused my thoughts on the feeling of being embraced, full body, by Mother, by the arms of love and acceptance and protection. I allowed the child inside to get her fix of being not-in-charge for a brief moment.

Once I felt the batteries recharged on that, I dragged my mind into my place of clarity: the night sky. I focused on the pure blackness speckled with the lights from a hundred thousand distant suns. I dove into that sky and swam the Milky Way, feeling the constant barrage of life energies fade into the background. The clean, uncomplicated energy of the stars and the emptiness washed my mind free of distractions.

I took another deep breath and focused on the other world. I thought about the things from the other side that I'd seen over the last few days. Things that had barely registered in my conscious mind, I was so used to it. Things that helped me read the emotions of others. Things that told me the story of other people's lives, past and present.

I remembered the gold Prius in the middle of the fast-moving traffic of downtown; then, it was a bay courser carrying a knight in full plate with a long sword, drawn and ready.

A brick-covered plaza had briefly become a grass and rock landscape around a twenty-foot waterfall with graceful black and white swans hissing territorially in the pool at the bottom.

There was the park that had suddenly come alive with lusty, dancing satyrs and the dryads who ran from them.

A glance down at the sidewalk to watch where my feet were landing had revealed a black, yellow and lime green snake followed by a spotted skunk, spirit animals keeping pace with the people they were meant to give guidance to.

Then there were the people flashing images of their souls. Whether the images were symbols or relevant pieces of past lives, they told me about the person.

A red-headed, male police officer who had held the door for me at the police station flashed with the image of a Hispanic nun: he had an innate sense of morality.

The stylish woman in a business suit who had cut me off on the sidewalk outside the Circle Centre Mall flashed the image of a starving Mongolian child: she had a deep fear of being without.

A young Asian man straightening his tie in front of a building that we had driven by flashed to an African farmer: he was more comfortable with hard, physical work than with his office job.

This was the world that told me people's secrets. This was the world that no one else could see, at least not in the same way. This was the world of second sight, lost paradise, and the path of the future.

I knew this world. It was comfortable in the way that the same job for five years is comfortable; it didn't matter if I liked it or not.

And I didn't.

I hated this world, the visions, the flashes. I hated it in a way that stinks of fear. And I admitted freely that I feared it. Because there is no way to validate it.

I had long ago admitted to myself that I knew, deep down, in my most secret thoughts, that I could really be just seeing things. I could be having full-on hallucinations that were not a spiritual message, but the ramblings of a broken mind. And that broken mind could break further. If I was crazy, and this was the first step, what if I became dangerous to my friends, to my daughter?

I would rip the third eye from my mind in a second if I could just know for sure. But I couldn't. I just had to keep working with the reality I knew, and hope. Hope that my insanity was not as real as my second sight.

I felt the shift as I moved easily into the astral plane, using the memories of visions as a guide. My inner eye opened and I could feel my body go slack in the back of my consciousness.

I moved quickly through the veils until I had immersed myself fully in the astral and looked around to get my bearings. It was an odd habit that I still looked, even though it was easier to find your way if you just used your gut and your emotions. I supposed I was more practical than I should be in dealing with the other worlds.

The amorphous background jumped into clarity when I focused on it. I could see the reflections of several worlds: buildings, meadows, forests. It was all there at the same time like triple-exposed photographs, perfectly mashed together and yet I could see them as different places.

I knew where I was, but I still wasn't sure where I was going.

I glanced at the silver-blue ribbon that was always in view in the astral plane, no matter where you were. It functioned rather like an expressway throughout the astral, moving travelers quickly in a more physical-like fashion.

It was easily accessible, but I'd never had much luck finding what I needed by using it. I figured it had a specific purpose, but I hadn't found out what yet. And my own method of travel was just as fast, but more accurate.

I thought for a moment about the bag of sigils, trying to pull the emotions for it. I brought back the fear of running from the monsters with the bag bulging in my pants. I thought of the sorrow of Keith's death just after he told us where to find them.

I brought up the helplessness and desperation of running through the city before Mercy found me. I thought about the shock and joy of seeing the spell had worked when we made them disappear.

I closed my inner eye and concentrated on feeling all of those feelings while visualizing the worn black velvet bag.

I pushed on those feelings, directing them through the memories of libraries, card catalogues, online searches, and huge musty books sitting on hardwood tables in huge, dimly lit rooms lined with even more books.

I projected out a feeling of anticipation overlaying a memory of a book being brought to me. I infused the memory with confidence that the book would contain the information I needed.

I opened my eyes and waited for the book to appear.

Nothing happened. I frowned. After a few seconds, I looked around.

Still nothing.

I closed my eyes and repeated the process. It had always worked, even if it wasn't always how I wanted it to. I latched on to that knowledge and faith in what I'd done before.

My eyes popped open and darted around, searching for the sought information.

More big fat nothing. I sighed.

What could it mean that this wasn't working? Was I being denied the information? That couldn't be it. According to the spell, I was meant to find the sigils.

I briefly considered a more literal interpretation of the spell and wondered if the sigils had been hidden inside my brain.

I shook my head. That kind of non-subtlety was pretty much against the way magic worked, even if spells did seem to have a wicked sense of humor at times.

The only other explanation was that the Akashic Library was not the path that I needed to take to get the sigils back. Though it wasn't usually so blunt about things, if the Library was following my dharma - and this whole situation was a pretty huge life path and experiences kind of thing - then maybe it was just not even going to tease me with the usual hints that indicated it wouldn't tell me.

I sighed. It looked like I was going to be sleuthing through the astral plane the old-fashioned way. I closed my inner eye and went back to the feelings surrounding the sigils, this time, pulling on them directly.

I opened my inner eye and looked around. The layers of worlds had changed. They now showed a forest with a castle in the distance, a field of wheat, a horse-like creature grazing in a grassy plain.

I was in a different place, that was certain, but there was still no sign of the sigils. I frowned.

This kind of travel in this place always worked, but it could very quickly become symbolic. Even though the sigils weren't here, I knew there was a clue for them somewhere here.

I looked more closely at the castle. It was white, with turrets and towers at each of the four corners and a drawbridge in the center of the wall facing me, much like the castle in every history book. A triangular blue flag flew above the towers, flapping in a breeze I didn't feel. A white circle filled the center of the flag with some kind of blue lettering that I couldn't make out.

I turned my attention to the field. The shades of pale green, gold and tan melded together in my eyes, until I looked closer. I frowned. There were different plants in the field.

I noted the shapes of the leaves, the size of the stems, the flowers and grain heads. It took me a while, but I noted seven different types of plants before I couldn't find any other differences.

I shook my head. This was getting me nowhere.

I refocused, this time on the horse-like creature. It looked a little like a cross between a standard ranch horse and a Holstein, the typical black and white splotched cow. Its head was that of a horse, but it had the bald, broad nose of a cow. Its body was horse-like and a dark tan, but the udders between its back legs were definitely cow-like, and I could see the shadow of a splotched pattern in its coat.

As it walked, grazing in the grass, I could see its front feet were cloven like a cow's, but its back feet had the single hoof of a horse. It had a mane down its long narrow neck, but the tail was tufted with the long hair only at the end of it.

I drew back my attention, confused. If this was symbolic, I was at a total loss as to what it could mean.

This wasn't working. I ground my teeth together and let the frustration flow through my body, fueling my search. I hunted through the layers of world and energy, jumping from layer to layer while standing in place.

I looked under bushes and dug in the dirt, searched within stone walls and inside giant oaks. When I had exhausted every hiding place I could think of, I stepped back and looked at the whole picture, viewing all the worlds and the astral plane together.

Nothing. I could see nothing.

"Shit!" I screamed. "Why is this so damn hard? Just... where are they? I'm here. I'm doing the work. I'm making the energetic effort.

I'm the person who has to do it. I didn't want to, but I'm here and I'm trying and why the hell isn't this working?"

I stopped and closed my eyes, trying to stop the frustration that wasn't working anymore than my earlier calm logic had. I stood with the heels of my hands pressed against my eyes, keeping back the tears of frustration.

Then I felt the world tilt.

His scent surrounded me, warm vanilla with the spice of cinnamon and nutmeg. It overwhelmed my nostrils, immediately calming my anger.

I let my head fall back on my neck. The deliciousness of his smell trickled through my nose and down my throat until I could taste him on my tongue.

I went numb. Not the kind of numb where you can't feel, but the kind where you don't have the will or desire to move.

"You don't deserve this, Nicola," his voice rumbled in my ear. His warm, sweet breath tickled my ear and brushed against my neck. "You had a good life, a simple life."

His deep voice lulled me, filling my head, pushing away all thoughts.

"This was forced upon you."

"Forced," I murmured in agreement.

"You deserve peace."

"Peace," I whispered. Longing bloomed in my chest for my child, for a single peaceful moment with Ella.

"Happiness," his voice rumbled. "With your daughter."

I could see Ella in my mind, laughing, dancing.

"Leave this chaos for someone else to take care of," the voice continued. "For someone who wants to be a hero."

I smiled at the memory of Ella's smile. So much like her father.

I felt a jolt in my gut, and the smile faded from my lips. Keith had wanted to be a hero. He was dead now. He'd been killed.

A tear fell from my eye. I could feel his finger touch my cheek. My eyes fluttered open and I glimpsed a strong hand. The tip of one perfect finger held a tiny piece of amber.

My eyelids were too heavy and I let them drift shut.

I felt his arm around my waist. Who was he that held me? I

couldn't remember. I couldn't think.

"You don't want to be a hero," his voice said, tantalizing me, drawing me in.

His lips moved against my neck, right on the sensitive spot under my ear. I tilted my head to allow him access.

My limbs felt heavy, impossible to move. Like the moments after the demon threw me against the wall.

The jolt ran through my gut again. I lifted my head and struggled to open my eyes.

"No," I murmured.

"No, you don't want to be a hero," his voice affirmed.

I relaxed into the surety of his comment.

His arm tightened around my waist, holding me securely. His other hand was at my breast. He gently pinched my nipple and pleasure arced through my body.

My thoughts fled and my awareness narrowed to the skill in his fingers. His lips brushed against mine.

But that wasn't right.

I struggled to stand upright. I reached for my thoughts. I grasped for the logic that was my confidence, my skill.

My "no" wasn't an agreement with him. My "no" was for him.

His arms and hands and lips tried to draw me back in.

I struggled to block out the sensations in my reaction to him, the reaction of my body. I was a creature of the mind, of thought.

And I had told him "no."

Because I had not given him permission to touch me with such familiarity.

I latched on to this thought, grasping at it to keep my wits. Reaching for more thoughts that weren't put there by him. I found another one, small, tickling my mind, and I grabbed it.

Skill or not, this man was groping me. And I had no idea who he was.

My eyes popped open and I bent the world around me to transport my body away from his grasp.

•　　•　　•

I stared at the beautiful man in shock. His face slowly curved into a smile and he clapped his hands approvingly.

"I had heard you were strong of mind," he said in his voice of melted chocolate. "Not many can break free of my temptations."

I tried to speak, but my throat was still tight. I cleared it and tried again. "Who are you?"

He smiled smugly, his perfect expressive eyebrows arching into an inverted "V" as he shot me a look of pure sin. "Can't you guess my name?" he asked.

I shook my head, trying to clear it.

This was a game, and one of symbolism. I could feel the brush of the double-entendre in his words on my mind. I mentally reviewed the conversation and his actions. A look of sin. Break free of temptations. Can't you guess my name...

I rolled my eyes as the answer hit me. "Seriously?" I asked. "Isn't quoting Sympathy for the Devil a little trite?"

He threw back his head on his perfect neck and laughed, a deep harmonic sound. He clapped his hands together like a child.

"You, my dearest Nicola," he said, running his gaze down my body suggestively, "are a perfect delight!"

He bowed, his movements as graceful as water flowing. "I am he. Lucifer, Satan, the Devil, Father of Lies, Prince of the Devils, any number of names."

He waved his hand dismissively at the list of titles. His gaze locked on me, a smile teasing his lips. "I much prefer 'Tempter'."

I narrowed my eyes. "I'm sure you do," I said. "What do you want with me?"

He laughed. "You are not as fearless as you act, my dear," he said. "But you do act the part well."

He straightened and became serious. "I am here to tempt you into my... bed." His eyes gleamed with lust and desire.

I snorted. "Not gonna happen, Lucy," I snapped.

He shrugged and turned away. "It matters little to me, but I can help you get out of this little pickle you are in."

I considered his words.

No doubt he was going to offer me an easy way to renege on my unwanted mantle of hero. And it was tempting, without question. But it was also against every moral and honorable fiber in my body.

I wanted to abandon my quest, but I would never be able to go through with it. I had some ethics, such as they were.

"I don't want anything to do with your little pickle, thanks," I told him, smirking at my play on his words.

His face contorted beautifully with a momentary rage before he regained his poise. He stared at me for a moment, then broke into an unpleasant smile.

"You will regret your choice," he warned.

"And my little dog, too," I said, with a sneer.

The world tilted again throwing me to the ground and blurring the scenery, and he was gone.

I sat where I'd fallen, considering my situation. The unfairness of it all overwhelmed me. Muriel's ridiculous knack for getting into trouble. Keith's stupid, yet heroic attempt to save Ella while simultaneously trying to destroy the world. Mercy's spouting on about heroes and quests and rules. And, of course, my arrogance in jumping in to save everyone else from themselves.

Then, Satan just shows up, big as life, for little old me. He wanted to tempt me off of my quest. And to think, a week ago, he probably didn't know me from any other schmuck in the world.

I frowned. If Satan wanted me off the case, then he didn't want me to stop the sigils from being used to start Ragnarok. But Keith had said that Jehovah had given him the sigils to use. So... were Satan and Jehovah working together? That made no sense.

I replayed the conversation with Keith in his apartment over and over in my mind, but I kept seeing his blood leaking onto the floor.

I felt a thickness in my throat and tried to figure out if I was fighting back tears or trying not to scream. The dry, clogged feeling grew with my frustration, so I breathed deeply to try to calm myself down and distract my mind from the painful memories.

I lay back and stared up into the void of space, letting my thoughts drift in meditation. I watched the blackness, letting the white specks slowly pull my attention. I focused on one star, then another, using that focus to clear my head of my frustrated emotions.

That star had a yellow tint. That one a bluish tint. That group over there made a cloud. Those twin stars were... moving?

I sat up and stared hard at the two stars, a reddish one and a bluish one, spinning around each other, getting bigger. Coming closer?

I scrambled to my feet, watching the stars. They were definitely coming towards me. I braced myself for another encounter, wondering if this would be a helpful one but afraid it might be another attempt to derail my quest.

As I watched, the stars began to take shape, not of twinkling lights or gaseous balls, but of some sort of winged creature.

I wondered if they were dragons, which were common in the astral plane. People liked to take the shape of the creatures when they traveled in the astral and I often met others in the form of dragons or wolves.

No, they weren't dragons. As they got closer, I could see that they didn't have the typical long neck and long tail shape of the flying reptiles. They appeared to be more bird shaped. Eagles or hawks, perhaps.

Their color seemed to change subtly from bright blue and red into a deep black with blue and red highlights, like a colored aura around the dark feathers.

Crows, then. Or ravens.

The black birds made a final circling swoop and landed on a fallen log nearby, staring at me with intelligent eyes. That wasn't unusual. Most creatures in the astral plane were intelligent, whether they were spirit guides or people in an animal form.

"Hello, Nicola," a gravelly voice croaked out.

I jumped at the sound and stared at the birds. Their beaks were still closed, but I knew that the voice had come from the bluish one.

"Who are you?" I demanded. "Speak in truth!" I invoked the words that made most creatures honest, though more trickster-like creatures would play word games until you couldn't tell what was fact and what wasn't, despite them only speaking truths.

The reddish bird chuckled. "We are the Ravens called Thought and Memory," it said.

"We are Huginn" said the bluish one, shaking its feathers, "and Muninn," the reddish bird ruffled its feathers. "Servants of the Alfodr."

The two birds bowed, spreading their wings and bobbing their heads down, as I stared at them. I vaguely recognized the name, Alfodr, as meaning all-father.

"You are Odin's Ravens?" I asked, disbelief leaking into my tone. I remembered what Mercy had told me in the car when we'd talked about astral travel. "I thought the gods and their creatures couldn't go into the astral plane."

Muninn opened its beak and croaked a laugh. "True, true!" it called. "But not entirely true."

Huginn bobbed its head. "Gods and creatures travel the astral," it said. "But only through the bifrost."

The two birds turned and flicked their beaks at the silver-blue ribbon weaving through the astral plane. I stared at it a moment before turning back to the ravens.

"You mean that thing," I gestured at the ribbon, "is the bifrost? The way to travel to Asgard?"

Huginn bobbed its head again. "To Asgard. To Midgard. To Helheim. To Alfheim. To the root of the tree. To the Nine Worlds."

Muninn flapped its wings, getting my attention. "And beyond!"

"Beyond?" I asked. "Beyond what? The Nine Worlds?"

Huginn croaked a laugh. "To infinity...

Muninn bobbed. "To beyond," it said. "Beyond the Nine Worlds. Beyond the samsara."

"Samsara is the cycle of life and death," I interrupted, remembering the term from my studies of Eastern religions.

"Beyond the Dreaming," Muninn said, pecking at the log under its feet. I recognized the reference to Australian aboriginal beliefs.

"Beyond all you know," Huginn added. "To Olympus and Hades. To Nirvana. To Heaven. To Valhalla!" Both ravens flapped their wings and cawed loudly, as if cheering Odin's Hall.

I glanced at the ribbon, the bifrost, and considered what the ravens had said. My assumption that it was an expressway wasn't very far off point, but I had seriously underestimated how far it extended. If I could control my travel in it, I could literally travel to every world and afterlife I'd ever heard of.

I thought about what Huginn had said, gods traveling the astral only through the bifrost.

"Wait a minute," I said. "So the gods and their creatures can travel by the bifrost, but they can't get out into the rest of the astral plane?"

The ravens flapped and cawed again, and I got the impression they were applauding me.

"Good, good!" cried Muninn. "You remember so well what we've taught you."

"Good, good!" called Huginn. "Your thoughts are sharp to cut through misunderstanding."

I narrowed my eyes at the birds. Were they testing me? And if so, was it for their own amusement or as part of some kind of verification?

"But you are in the astral plane and not the bifrost," I pointed out.

Huginn bobbed its head. "We are of a special nature."

"Our nature is specific." Muninn bobbed its head in synchronous rhythm with its twin.

"We travel the worlds," Huginn said.

"We travel everywhere," Muninn added.

"We seek knowledge wherever it is found," Huginn said.

"We bring it back to Odin," Muninn finished, as the birds stopped bobbing.

I rubbed at my chin, trying to decode their back-and-forth speech. "You can travel the astral because you, by your very natures, travel everywhere?" I asked.

The ravens applauded me again.

"But tell not the gods," Huginn said. "They are sometimes jealous of what others can do."

Muninn flicked its beak upwards in agreement. "And nothing can be done to change it," it said. "Though some gods may try."

I nodded in understanding. "I get it," I said. "Sometimes, what they don't know, can't hurt you."

The ravens cawed in delight at my words, and I felt like they approved of the humorous slant I'd given them. I grinned. I was beginning to like the ravens.

I put my hands on my hips as a thought hit me. "So what are you doing here?" I asked. "Did you seek me out?"

Muninn bobbed and tossed its head, affirming. "We sought you out," it said, rasping in its gravelly voice. "We sought you here."

Huginn cawed once. "You sought us, which called us to you."

I blinked and considered that. "You mean, when I was looking for the sigils?" I asked. "That called you to me?"

The ravens bobbed their heads, and a thought crept into my head.

"Wait a minute... do you know where the sigils are?" I asked, hope blooming.

The ravens tilted their heads to the side, first both tilting left, then both tilting right.

Huginn pecked at the log. "We do not know where to find, but we know where to look," it said.

Muninn pecked at the same spot. "We can't tell you where to look, but we can tell you how to see."

I frowned. "You mean, you can give me... clues, or something?"

Muninn bobbed its head and chanted in a croaking sing-song, "Clues to look for where to look for what you seek but cannot find."

Huginn added, "But they are sights and sounds and smells, not words."

It switched to the same croaking sing-song as its twin had just used. "We cannot tell you, only show you. Show you things that can't be seen."

I considered what they said for a long moment. It dawned on me that the ravens were talking about telepathic memories, where they would literally insert the memories of sights, sounds and smells into my mind. It was a pretty invasive process and I, as the recipient, could have some negative side effects from it.

I considered my other options, which didn't take long. I didn't have any other options.

I nodded slowly, agreeing to the procedure. "I understand," I said quietly. "Let's do this."

Huginn flapped its wings. "Lie down," it said in its raspy voice. "Open your mouth."

"Lie back," Muninn added. "Open wide."

I lay down on the astral grass, wriggling a little to get comfortable. I took a deep breath and opened my mouth.

"Wider!" Muninn cried. It flapped down from the log and hopped over to me, jumping up on my stomach.

Huginn tilted its head to watch me closely out of one eye. "You must open wider."

I swallowed my nerves and tilted my head back, opening up wide. I felt a little ridiculous and exposed, but it was just like going to the dentist.

I didn't quite convince myself of that.

Muninn craned its head around and used its beak to dig into the feathers under its wing. It came back up with a small white sphere in its beak. It glowed like an opalescent pearl with a soft white-blue light and my nervousness hit me full force in the gut.

Huginn cawed and flapped its wings as Muninn hopped up to my chest and reached into my mouth with its large, wicked-looking beak. My eyes rolled in my head, as I struggled with the feeling of alarm that washed over me.

I felt the sharp peck as Muninn jabbed the pearl into the very back of my soft palate at the top of the back of my throat. I felt a burning sensation in the space between my throat and my sinuses, and I fought back the urge to vomit.

Vaguely, I felt the slight push of Muninn taking flight off of my stomach before the memories hit me.

They were little more than flashes in my mind. Hundreds of sensations flickering through my body.

The sensations of touch: soft velvet, sandpaper, fur, cool water, hot rock, cold slime. A dozen textures and temperatures covered my skin, so I felt them all at once. My nerves screamed for release, but they kept coming. I could feel myself twitching away from the tactile sensations, writhing in a desperate attempt to escape.

My nose twitched at the assault of smells and my tongue pushed against my teeth, trying to rid itself of the barrage of tastes. I gagged over and over, heaving against the force-feeding of the sensations. It was as if everything I'd ever tasted and smelled in my whole life was being re-experienced in one unending moment.

With the more visceral senses of touch, smell and taste on overload, I barely registered the sights and sounds, quickly tuning them out as my brain made a desperate bid for holding onto sanity.

With my mind being pulled in so many directions, I was unprepared for the first wave of emotions.

My eyes, already leaking tears from dry-heaving, gushed with the sudden, disconcerting joy. I'd barely wrestled with that when deep despair washed over me, and my mind begged for death as a release from the agony.

Fear choked me as I tried to scream around my abused tongue and throat. And my heart leapt to a gallop at the first jolt of surprise.

The memories just kept coming, flash after flash of sensation, each jarring my body anew so I never had a chance to get used to the overload. All the brain's defenses were geared towards handling a single change or a long-term discomfort, so it could block out that which it had already processed.

But all of this was new, and it all demanded attention from the brain. Each sensation demanded that my mind identify, categorize and connect it to other memories.

But they were coming in too fast.

My back arched, lifting my torso off the ground in a grotesque bridge. My eyes rolled back in my head until they ached. My throat clenched until I couldn't breathe.

A gravelly voice rose above the cacophony, though my brain could not process the words. And the greatest computer ever created, the human brain, crashed.

CHAPT 13

The first thing I became aware of was the gentle roar of waves. As I focused on the sound, I realized I was surrounded by white. It was like cotton wrapping me up, but without the feeling of anything on my skin. I felt the pressure of it, but not the texture.

I sighed.

I was probably dead. They were embalming me, wrapping my body into a mummy form. Never mind that I didn't follow the Egyptian gods. I briefly wondered if I would one day be resurrected to stumble around seeking out and killing those who had disturbed my eternal rest.

The roar was fading into the background and I could hear a high-tinny sound, like a bell ring that never wavered or stopped. I remembered that sound and I held onto that thought, trying to find the place in my mind where the memory came from.

I flashed back to a night when I was in college. I'd gone to a concert and stood in the area just outside the heaving mosh pit. The speakers had been blasting in my ears so loudly that I'd actually covered them. When I left the concert venue with my friends, my ears had felt full and I'd heard that same ringing sound due to the temporary damage in my ears.

Damage. My ear canals were wounded. My tympanic membrane was stretched like an overused rubber band. My little snail-like cochlea was cooked like an escargot.

I giggled inside my mind at where my thoughts were leading me. I mentally placed the back of my hand on my forehead and fainted into the not-cotton mummy wrappings. No. Not fainted. Swooned.

I giggled inside my mind again. This was no big deal. After all, I was dead, being prepared for the other side. I had no use for my ears.

They wouldn't even go into those cool jars with the organs.

I noticed that the ringing was fading, along with the white-out in my vision. I could hear something else now. Something that wasn't roaring or ringing. It sounded like music. Or speech.

I frowned. What was a word for speech that started with the letter "R"? Roaring, ringing... rambling? Reticulation? No that was a lattice pattern. But I liked the word.

Roaring, ringing, reticulation.

I repeated the words in my mind, like a chant. Roaring, ringing, reticulation. Repeat.

I tried to laugh, and my chest heaved with the effort, but nothing happened. I considered this for a brief moment.

Repeat! Roaring, ringing, reticulation.

My chest heaved again, and I felt the air force its way past my vocal chords, but still no sound.

I felt some disappointment. I loved to laugh and I loved to laugh loud. With joy, with surprise. If I was dead, I still wanted to be able to laugh.

I heaved my breath against my voice box. Love laughing loud. Heave. Love laughing loud. Heave. This time I felt a rasping cough, and the sound of music-voices paused.

That's right. Dead girl gonna laugh in her grave. Hear my amusement and despair!

Suddenly, I felt my body being turned as a hand grabbed my shoulder, reaching through the no-longer-white, not-cotton wrappings as if – no, because – they weren't really there. The light around me grew less warm and the feeling of pressure on my body began to lighten.

I frowned. This wasn't better. This was much less better.

"Nicola! Can you hear me?"

Yeah, I can hear you, annoying voice from beyond the not-cotton illusion. Put me back in the warm light!

"Nicola, try to wake up. You have to wake up."

Do not! I'm dead and done for. I get to sleep now. Until my eternal rest is disturbed. Then I have to stumble and kill.

I frowned. I felt quite disturbed now. Should I do the stumbly-mummy thing?

I opened my mouth and went for a moan. It came out raspy and weak, but it was a start.

"That's it, Nicola. You can do it."

My eyes fluttered open and I blinked at Joseph staring down at me. I was a little saddened by that. I didn't want to stumble after Joseph and kill him. But them's the rules.

I groaned, getting louder this time. I struggled to lift my arms, straight-elbowed. Joseph pushed them down.

"Don't try to get up, Nicola. Not just yet."

I licked my lips and a water bottle appeared at my mouth. I swallowed some, swishing it around my parched mouth first.

I groaned again. That was great volume, this time. I lifted my arms again.

Joseph watched my arms go up, straight out in front of me. He looked confused. "Nicola, what are you trying to do? Can you talk?"

"Not s'posed to talk," I mumbled. "S'posed to stumble."

Joseph stared at me. "You are supposed to stumble? Is that what you said?"

I nodded and cleared my throat. I noticed Mercy behind Joseph, leaning close to hear us.

Joseph pushed my arms down and held the water to my lips again. I swallowed twice, then put my arms back up.

Joseph leaned back. "What are you doing, Nicola?"

I blinked at him. "Mummy," I said, my tongue feeling thick in my mouth. "You disturbed me."

Joseph frowned. I could tell he wasn't getting it.

"You disturbed me," I said, getting it out more clearly this time. "I'm a mummy. I have to stumble after you and kill you."

Joseph burst out laughing, right in my face. Mercy looked very confused and not at all frightened by my words.

I began to reconsider the mummy life.

•   •   •

It took a good 15 minutes before I was able to sit up without help, though I suppose my recovery was pretty fast, considering. Joseph kept helping me drink from the water bottles Hound Dog had left us.

Mercy went to stand outside the room. I think she felt better pretending that guard duty was necessary.

Soon I was able to stand up, though I was grateful that Joseph never asked about what happened. Every time I thought about the astral plane, my brain started jumping around like an old cartoon character after they'd sat on a fire.

First, physical recovery, then work on the mind and remembering.

I was walking slowly around the room, getting my legs to work together without pretending they were pudding, when Mercy rushed in.

"Someone's coming!" she hissed.

I looked at Joseph and he looked at me. I shrugged and went back to walking.

Joseph turned to Mercy. "Well, we'll have to deal with them," he said. He nodded at me. "Nicola isn't in any condition to run or fight."

Mercy stared at us, then slowly nodded. She pulled out her knife and I watched it grow into a full-sized sword, still awed by it. Mercy headed back out the door.

Joseph walked up beside me, ready to help if I lost my balance. We reached the end of the room and turned around to head back across the room with my shuffling, unsteady steps.

I nearly ran head-first into a chest.

"Ah, shit!" Joseph bit out, holding his hand to his chest in a gesture of shock. "Who the hell are you?"

Mercy rushed back in.

I looked up to find myself seeing double. The men were identical in appearance, with black hair and dark, dark eyes. They had the same sharp, narrow faces with a nose too long to be considered handsome. They were dressed in black from head to toe and watching me with a curious, familiar gaze, heads cocked slightly to one side.

Joseph grabbed the lantern and held it up to get a better look at the two men. I caught a glimpse of a blue tint in their hair.

No, I corrected myself. Not both of them. The one on the left had a bluish tint to his black hair. The one on the right had a reddish tint. Memory crashed down on me and I staggered.

When my head cleared, I could recall the conversation with the Ravens, and Joseph was holding me up. Mercy was looking at the men in disbelief and they were just standing, heads tilted to one side.

"What are you two doing here?" Mercy demanded. She stopped short and threw a glance at Joseph and me. I guess she didn't think we knew who they were. And she was half right.

I caught Muninn's eye and he shook his head slightly. I realized that if I let on that I knew them, I would have to reveal that I'd met them in the astral plane, which they specifically didn't want anyone to know.

I winked at him and stood up straight.

"Who are you?" I demanded. "And why are you here?"

Huginn smiled. "We are here to help."

Muninn flashed an identical smile. "You were followed."

Mercy narrowed her eyes. "What do you mean, followed?"

Huginn turned to look at Mercy. "The creatures you fight..."

Muninn mirrored his twin. "They know where you are."

Huginn turned back to look at me. "They followed their master."

Muninn turned towards me as well. "Their master is the deceiver."

"The deceiver?" I asked. "What...?"

I trailed off as it hit me. The Prince of Lies. The Deceiver. Satan. Lord of Demons. Who I'd encountered during my search. And if he'd could follow me back...

"Crap!" I said. "We gotta go."

Mercy looked at the twins. "Is it safe to go back through the temple?"

Huginn grinned. "Safe from the monsters."

Muninn smiled. "Safe enough for you." He nodded to Joseph and me.

The twins turned away from each other and faded away.

"The hell!" Joseph exclaimed.

I ignored Joseph's shock and stumbled over to the backpack, grabbing at the things lying around to shove inside. Mercy appeared at my side and pushed me up at Joseph. She took over cleaning up as Joseph helped me out the doorway and back down the hall.

Mercy caught up a few moments later, taking the lead. I couldn't be sure, over the sound of my own panting, but I thought I heard a faint snarling behind us.

We found the doorway for the passage back up to the temple, and a quick feel up along the door frame showed us the latch.

Mercy cracked open the bookshelf to check for anyone in the room, then pushed it open all the way. We tumbled into the archives room and closed the opening behind us. I headed for the door with Mercy on my heels. Joseph didn't move.

We stopped to look back at Joseph, staring at the bookshelf.

"They might come through," he said in a low, sad voice. "People could get hurt."

Mercy stared at him for a moment before nodding once and pushing him aside to go back through. "Get a move on," she said, just before the bookshelf clicked into place.

Joseph and I stared at each other with horror dawning on our faces. He took a step towards the bookshelf.

"No!" I said. "She made the choice. We must honor it. We have to finish what we've started here."

I stepped forward, reaching a hand out to my friend. "I need you to help me figure out what I learned so we can recover the Runespells and stop all of this."

"Save the world," Joseph muttered, bitterness coloring his tone. He turned and grabbed my arm, nearly pulling me along as we rushed out of the archives room, up the stairs and out of the temple.

It was dark outside and we paused a moment on the steps as Joseph locked the door behind us. I stared up at the night sky, only a few stars visible in the city lights. Nothing like the millions I could see at home.

Joseph came up beside me and looked up, as well. We stood a moment in silence, soaking in the brief peace and quiet before we started down the steps.

A bright light clicked on with a shhnk noise. It blinded us and we froze, blinking away the tracers that appeared from the sudden light. We flinched at the whine of a megaphone and a too-loud voice announced they were police and ordered us to put our hands up and get on our knees.

Joseph and I exchanged glanced and did as we were told. I briefly toyed with the idea that the creatures were pretending to be cops so they could get us easily. But then I saw the familiar rotund form of Detective Ames ordering four deputies to handcuff us and get us into two separate cruisers.

The detective swaggered up to me as I was pushed into the back seat of a police sedan. He shot me a smug smile as he leaned down to talk to me.

"Here I thought I was just going to bust a couple trespassing gang-bangers. Looks like I got enough on you now. Enjoy your night in lockup. I'll pay you a visit in the morning." He stood up as the police cruiser pulled away.

Trespassing. I smiled at that. Joseph would be able to prove we weren't trespassing and get us out quickly. Then we would...

The smile fell from my lips. What would we do then? Where would we go?

We had gotten out of the catacombs, but we didn't have a car and I didn't want to go to Hound Dog or the other street kids when the demons were so hot on our tails. We could hole up in a hotel again, but how would we know it was secure?

I thought about the police station. Lots of cops and other people. Lots of guns and stuff.

We could be pretty safe there, locked up. Safe enough for me to go over what had happened in the astral plane. Maybe safe enough for Mercy and her sisters to find us again.

I stubbornly held the belief that Mercy would come for us, that she wasn't gone.

The memory of the cop who'd been killed by the demons flashed in my mind. I pushed it away. He'd been alone, on an empty street. Surely attacking an entire precinct was too direct.

I supposed that depended on how desperate Bob, or Satan, or Jehovah, or whoever else, was to get to me right away.

I heaved a sigh. We didn't have many options, not that that was something new in recent events. I just hoped I could get the message across to Joseph before he pulled out his proof that we hadn't been intruding on the Mason's temple after all.

We pulled into the parking lot at the police station and I was pulled from the cruiser. I saw the other car pull in, Joseph's face staring at me from the backseat window. I flashed him a grin and a wink, hoping he'd understand I had a plan.

I'd never been booked before, but it was pretty boring. We were seated separately in a small area for several minutes, then fingerprinted. We were taken to another small area where we waited another half hour, a burly officer staring at us the whole time.

We finally got our mug shots taken, and I wondered if mine would qualify for one of those online sites where you could look at horrible mug shots of people. Considering I'd been sleeping in cars and on a dirt floor, and I hadn't seen a shower or hair brush in days, I probably looked like crap. Warmed up in the microwave. After sitting in the fridge for a week.

We got moved to yet another small seating area, this time seated side by side. I guessed we were waiting to have our statements taken or be interviewed or something.

I caught Joseph's eye and muttered under my breath, "Don't get us out."

He raised an eyebrow.

"Probably safe in here," I mumbled. "Stay until morning. Buy time."

Joseph hesitated a moment, then gave a slight nod.

I sighed. He understood, though I got the feeling that he wasn't happy about drawing this experience out. We hadn't exactly lived a life of crime, even in our youth.

We were placed in our holding cells which were small individual rooms with a wide plastic bench covered with a pad that couldn't have been more than an inch thick. Next to the door, out of direct view of the windows, was a stainless steel toilet with a sink on the back of it.

I asked the monitoring officers for food and water, and they brought me lunch meat and fake cheese on white bread. I shrugged and ate it. At this point, I wasn't going to be picky about getting food into my stomach.

I also requested a blanket and got a scratchy, cheap wool piece of cloth that barely covered me from feet to shoulders. I tried not to think about poor, so very tall Joseph under one of the blankets, as I lay down on the thin pad and pulled the blanket over me. Obviously, I really needed sleep because I was out instantly.

"Nicola Crandall!"

I jerked awake, jack knifing my body into a sitting position. I looked wildly around until I located the source of the voice. A smug-looking officer stood in the doorway of my cell, hands on his hips.

"You are wanted in interrogation," he said. He turned to the officer standing behind him and took a tray from his hands. Officer Smug turned back and held out the tray for me. "You have 10 minutes to eat and clean up."

He ran his eyes up and down my body with an expression that said he wasn't sure any amount of cleaning up would be enough.

I stumbled to my feet and took the tray, half afraid he would take it back if I waited too long. I called after him to bring me a towel, but I didn't get a response.

I glanced down at the box of corn flakes and carton of milk. A Styrofoam bowl and tan plastic spoon sat next to the cereal. It looked very blah. My stomach growled its disagreement.

I'd just finished up when a knock sounded at the door and a voice demanded to know if I was "decent." I bit back a snarky response and told him I was.

The officer handed me a small hand towel and left. I used a corner of the towel to scrub my face and hands, and briefly wished for a shower and a change of clothes. I tried finger-combing my hair, still pulling knots apart when Officer Smug returned.

"Time's up," he bit out. "Put your hands out in front of you."

I complied, holding out my arms. Officer Smug handcuffed me while another officer stood, hand on his gun holster, outside my cell. Once I was cuffed, Officer Smug – his name badge said "B. Gilpen" – grabbed a hold of my arm and pulled me along.

Officer Smug took me through several doors where we had to wait to be buzzed through and sat me down at the table in an interrogation room much like the one I'd been in - gods, was it only 4 or 5 days ago?

"Hey," I called to Officer Smug as he turned to leave. "What day is it?"

He looked at me like I was crazy.

I shrugged. "It's been a long, fucked up week."

"It's Monday," he growled as he left, shutting the door behind him.

Monday. I'd gotten into town on a Monday, and here it was Monday again. I shook my head. How had I gotten into this mess?

The door opened to show my favorite Detective Ames. He stopped just inside the door to stare at me before he turned and close it.

"I was hoping I'd just seen wrong last night," he said. "But, no, you look like hell. Even worse than when I saw you yesterday morning."

I shot him a grin. "Thanks."

He dropped the folder he'd carried in on the table and sat down heavily in the other chair. "You've had quite the week," he said.

I huffed a laugh. "You have no idea."

"Wednesday I got a tip that you were involved in a homicide," he said, flipping open his folder. "Thursday, I see your car drive by the scene of a cop killing. And Saturday, your ex, Keith Ludlow, shows up dead. Yesterday, your rental car was towed from a spot within a few blocks of your ex's home, where he'd been shot and killed."

I grimaced at his summary.

"Now, you get busted trespassing and looking like you been sleeping under a bridge." He looked up from the folder. "You wanna explain this?"

I leaned back in my chair and let my head roll to one side. Explain it? I would love to explain it to the ambitious detective.

Maybe I should start with the demons chasing me through the streets of Indianapolis. Or maybe I could describe watching my daughter's father die in my arms. I could let him in on the whole Valkyrie and gods thing - I bet he'd really appreciate that information.

I wasn't sure if he'd be sympathetic to my seduction by the devil, though. I'm sure he'd totally understand my having a conversation with a pair of birds about clues to sigils made from god-created spells that had been hidden by Joseph and me through spell-singing while demons were beating down our door.

I sucked on my teeth and consciously relaxed the muscles in my forehead which had gone tense.

Then again, maybe dear Detective Ames wouldn't understand at all. So I kept my mouth shut and shrugged my shoulders.

Detective Ames glared at me across the table. "Why was your car so close to two" he held up two fingers, waving them a few inches from my face, "homicides? And not just any homicides, either."

He grabbed up the folder and flipped to one of the back pages. "There's some weird shit about these cases."

I raised an eyebrow, pressing my lips together. If only he knew.

"Did you know that the officer killed was," he read from the page, "'torn apart by a large wild animal'? What kind of 'large wild animal' gets into the middle of Indianapolis?"

He stared at me for a moment, as if he expected a reaction. Finally, I shrugged.

Detective Ames flipped to another page. "Mr. Ludlow was hit by a bullet. But his apartment was nearly destroyed by gunfire. And forensics is saying only the attackers were shooting! Ludlow managed to make it into another room and barricade himself in before dying from blood loss. That's not very likely. Someone had to be helping him."

He glared at me. "Someone who did not bother to call 911 and report his death. That could be seen as accessory to murder, or interfering with a criminal investigation."

I frowned. I was no legal expert, but I was pretty sure none of those laws applied to the situation. Either way, he still had given me no indication that he knew I had actually been there when Keith died. And I wasn't going to give him that information.

The detective stared at me. I could feel the pressure of him willing me to talk, but I let it wash over me and clenched my teeth.

"Dammit!" he yelled, slapping his palm against the table with a loud crack. "What are you hiding?"

I took a slow, calming breath and simply looked at him.

"Maybe it has to do with motive," Detective Ames said, quickly collecting himself as he flipped to another page in his folder. "It seems that Mr. Ludlow had taken out a pretty hefty insurance policy."

I shrugged.

"It names your daughter as the beneficiary," he pointed out. "That's a nice chunk of change for a single mom, don't you think? That kind of money could make a big difference in your life. Make raising your daughter a bit easier?"

I rolled my eyes. Single mom stereotypes didn't vary too much - poor, struggling, and frazzled.

"We do alright," I told the detective through my clenched teeth.

He raised his eyebrow as if to say "really?"

I leaned forward. "Look, you've got a lot of coincidences. And that's it. We happened to be in the wrong neighborhood when a police officer dies. Not my fault. We happen to break down near my ex's home around the time that he dies. Not my fault. You get a tip that points me out in a murder I'd never heard about. This is starting to sound like a conspiracy."

Detective Ames flinched.

"You're never going to find evidence of me committing murder because I didn't commit any murder," I said. "So what's next? Planting evidence?"

Detective Ames face turned several shades of red and the fury rolled off of him in waves.

I gasped at the sudden emotional shift, taken back by the force of it.

The detective stood up and leaned forward with his hands planted on the table. His glare was so angry I could see the red from his emotion in his eyes.

"I don't plant evidence," he snarled. "I may be a lot of things, but I ain't a dirty cop."

He continued to glare at me for another minute before he snatched up the folder and stormed out of the room, slamming the door shut behind him.

I stared after him, my eyes wide. I must have really hit a nerve for him to have such a strong reaction. I wondered what could have happened to him that it was such a sensitive subject.

The door opened and I shook myself out of my thoughts.

Officer Smug had returned. He took me back to my cell without a word. His grip on my arm was tense, though, and I wondered what he knew about the way my interrogation had ended.

I spent the time remaining before lunch going over the interview and trying to clear my head. I still had work to do. I dozed off at some point, waking when a new officer brought me a tray with another lunch meat sandwich.

I ate quickly before setting my tray aside and sitting on my padded bench with my legs crossed. I focused on my breathing, clearing my head. I wasn't going into the astral plane this time, but the preparation was pretty much the same.

I focused my thoughts on the embrace of Mother, feeling the love and protection. I went to the night sky, focusing on the pure blackness speckled with lights. I felt the barrage of life energies fade, allowing the objective energy of the stars to wash my mind free of distractions.

I wrapped myself in a cloak of that objectivity as I began searching my memories.

I remembered going into the astral, retracing my journey step by step. I frowned as I replayed attempts to get the answer through the Akashic Library. The frustration of those attempts brushed against my detachment.

I recalled my search through the layers of worlds. I noted the things that stood out in my mind: the flag on the castle, the grains, the cow-horse creature. I carefully pulled out as much detail as I could from each of those memories, mentally turning them over, examining them for anything I might have missed.

A tendril of doubt floated around me, pointing out that I could just be making things up. But I knew that what I was doing had a basis in science - people never actually forget anything, they just don't have the ability to access it consciously.

Also, keeping clarity and objectivity in the forefront of my mind meant that I would be less likely to have an emotional taint on the memories, which could cause them to merge and meld with other memories, changing the details. I was pretty good at accurate recall, prioritizing the facts and details over emotional desires and wishes. And, frankly, this was the best thing I could do under the circumstances.

I went back to the search, finding where it ended, acknowledging but not feeling the frustration. I recalled the crazy, world tilting sensation, carefully noting the discrepancy of that experience with my previous treks into the astral plane. I replayed the fuzzy mindedness of Lucifer's seduction, reviewing his words for clues.

Suddenly, my memories jumped away from my trip to the astral plane and I was remembering a conversation with Mercy. We'd been driving in the car and talking about the gods.

"Even the gods need gateways to enter the bifrost," she'd said. My memory then jumped ahead to my conversation with the ravens in the astral plane. Huginn had said "Gods travel the astral, but only through the bifrost."

I latched on to those memories, examining them closely, looking for meaning in the words. If I was right, then my encounter with Satan in the astral plane could not have happened. As a creature of the gods, a fallen angel, he wouldn't be able to enter the astral plane itself. There had to be more to that encounter than I'd realized.

I picked apart my recall of the seduction, searching for clues, noting scent and sound. I'd had my eyes closed for most of it except...

I remember a glint of golden amber on the tip of a finger. A finger that had just wiped a tear from my cheek. I considered that for a moment, but I couldn't make any connections with the devil and amber.

I reviewed his words again, my objectivity allowing a little awe at his manipulation of my deepest desires - to simply walk away from the responsibility. But I found nothing in his words to give a clue to the Runespells.

I just couldn't shake the feeling the he had more to do with the situation. Otherwise why would he have tried to tempt me away? I sighed mentally. The Satan thing was a puzzle, but it wasn't the priority. I set it aside the memories to examine later.

I noted the world tilting again, and went through the conversation with the ravens. The birds had been relatively straightforward, if a little metaphorical in places, explaining just enough for me to understand what was being offered.

I took a deep breath and pulled more of the objectivity around me, fighting back the fear and nervousness I felt in anticipation of my recall of the implanted memories. I put myself back into the experience of the pearl being jabbed into my throat. I allowed the sensations to wash around me, keeping my shield in place between myself and the full experience.

This time, it was more like a movie or an observation tank at the aquarium. The sharks were still there, but I wasn't in danger of being bitten. I replayed the experience, trying to pull out snippets of sound, specific scents, an isolated emotion, single images. When it ended, I replayed it again, pulling at individual sensations. And when it ended, I played it again. And again. And again.

Over and over, I struggled to find any kind of discernable clues in the overwhelming waves of sensation. Over and over, I pulled my objective cloak around me and replayed the barrage on my senses.

Over and over, I swallowed my frustrations and did it again.

"Ms. Crandall!"

I gasped, sitting up straight and popping my eyes open. I could feel the energy ripping from my grasp at the shock.

I blinked owlishly at the officer standing in the doorway to my cell. He was holding out a tray. I pushed myself off of the bench and stumbled forward to take the tray from his hands, mumbling my thanks. More lunch meat sandwiches. I sighed and sat back down to eat.

I went over the few clues that I'd recovered in my memories while I chewed my food. The ones that stood out the most were the smell of dried grass, the blue flag, the field of seven grains, the cow-horse, a roaring explosion, a stinging sensation on the skin of my face, and an odd mix of fear, hopelessness and determination.

I wondered what they meant, turning over possibilities in my mind. After I finished eating, I gave up on deciphering and lay down on the pad to catch some sleep.

CHAPT 14

Very early the next morning, I was woken by Officer Smug and kicked out of jail.

It turns out, you can't be charged with trespassing when you have a membership card in your wallet for the organization that owns the property you were supposedly trespassing on. They did seem a little confused that we hadn't pointed out the membership in the first place, but when they asked me I just shrugged.

We waited for nearly two hours for the paperwork to be completed, dozing in our uncomfortable molded plastic chairs.

Joseph tried to talk to me, but I motioned for him to wait until we were out of the station. When I asked the officers about breakfast, I was reassured that it would only be a few more minutes and we would be free to leave. In other words, no cereal for us.

Finally, we were given our things back and escorted out of the secured area of the building. I hesitated, not sure what we should do next. Joseph was heading for the doors, cigarettes in hand.

"Nicola! Joseph!" a familiar voice called to us.

We turned and smiled as Hound Dog appeared, unfolding his thin body from one of the waiting area chairs. We hugged him and asked him how he'd found us at the jail.

He snorted. "Your little adventure made the news last night," he explained. "I called to find out you were still here and figured you'd be out this morning." He shrugged. "I thought you might like a friendly face when you returned to the land of the free."

I smiled. "You have no idea how much that means to us."

Joseph nodded his agreement. "I just wish we had our rental car," he said.

I shook my head. "Ames said it was towed," I admitted. "I don't know where to."

Hound Dog grinned. "Never underestimate the Hound Dog," he said, grinning. "I got a guy who works at the impound lot. He owed me a favor, so I called him up and got him to lose the paperwork and have it towed to a shop. You'll have to pay for the tow, but you got your car back."

I stared at Hound Dog. "You are the best!" I exclaimed.

Hound Dog held up his hands. "Now don't get too excited," he warned. "It's still gonna be about a hundred to get it back."

Joseph shrugged. "I got an emergency credit card that can take care of that," he said. "And Nicola can pay me back later."

I huffed. "If we live that long."

"If we don't, I don't have to pay off the card anyways," Joseph pointed out. He turned to Hound Dog. "We can catch a cab to get the car, then grab a bite."

Hound Dog sniffed at us. "I know a truck stop with a great restaurant," he said. "And showers."

Joseph threw a fake-punch at Hound Dog's shoulder as we turned towards the door, laughing. I dodged around a man coming in, mumbling an "excuse me" and glancing up at him under my lashes. I took another full step before I realized what I'd just seen.

I spun around on my heel and rushed after the man. "Excuse me, sir!" I called.

The guy turned around. He was older with the rugged, weathered look of a man used to physical labor. His jeans had faded marks and oil stains, and his button-up flannel was worn but clean. "Yeah?" he asked.

I stared up at his baseball cap. It was just as worn and stained as the rest of his outfit, a yellowed white with a logo on it, probably from a company give-away or something.

The logo was a blue triangle with the point going to the right. A faded white circle filled the center of the triangle, and worn blue stitching spelled out "AWS".

"Can I help you, miss?" the man said, showing his impatience.

I blinked. "Yes, sorry," I said, pointing at his hat. "What is that logo on your hat?"

Catching his questioning look, I grabbed at an excuse. "It looks like a cap my dad used to have. I thought if I could find the company, I could get him a new one. It was his favorite cap, you know?"

The man's face relaxed into an understanding expression. "Sure," he said. "I get it."

He took off the hat and looked at it, checking the logo. "Ah, yeah, this is AWS. Agricultural Warehousing and Storage. They got warehouses and offices on the south side of downtown, in the industrial area off-a Kennedy."

I thanked the man and grabbed his hand to shake it before turning and practically skipping out the door. Joseph and Hound Dog were staring at me like I'd gone crazy.

I waved off their questions. "Let's get the car and some food. Then I'll explain," I promised.

• • •

We grabbed some fresh t-shirts at the truck stop and got our showers while Hound Dog ordered us food. We sat down and slurped down some coffee before the plates were brought out stacked high with Denver omelets, toast and sausage, and a side of fresh fruit. We ate for several minutes before finally slowing down.

"Alright," Joseph said around a mouthful of toast, pointing his fork at me. "The hell was that with the guy's hat?"

I swallowed some coffee to wash down my last bite of omelet. "The logo," I said. "The logo on his hat. It was one of the things I saw in the astral plane."

Joseph sat back. "You think it means something?" he asked.

I nodded. "Definitely. It was a triangular flag with the white circle and writing. It was identical to the logo."

Hound Dog leaned on his arms on the table. His plate had already been cleaned and he was on his third cup of coffee. "Couldn't that just be a coincidence?" he asked.

Joseph shook his head as I answered.

"Not likely," I said. "If it was kinda the same, maybe, but the chances that I'd get a vision of something identical to that logo while looking for the sigils?" I shook my head. "There aren't coincidences that big."

Joseph took a long drink from his coffee. "I agree," he said. "In my experience, when you see things in the astral plane or other places like that, they are metaphorical, but once you make the connection it's obvious. A flag indicates a country or company of soldiers, right?" He waited for Hound Dog to nod his understanding. "Well, that's what a logo does, too. It marks a country or company."

"So what do we do with that information?" Hound Dog asked.

I grinned over my forkful of sausage. "We head down to the warehouses and keep an eye out for more clues."

• • •

I pressed my nose to the partially rolled down window, just below the top edge of the glass, staring out at the industrial buildings we were passing. Joseph was driving just fast enough to not piss off the other drivers.

"Tell me again what we are looking for," Hound Dog said, peering out the driver's side in the backseat.

I sighed and listed the clues again. "There was an animal that looked like a cross between a Holstein, one of those black and white cows, and a horse. There was a field with seven different types of grains growing. There was a smell like dried grass. And there was a feeling of something stinging my face, like when there's a super cold rain or blizzard and the stuff is hitting your face."

"And the castle with a flag," Joseph said.

I nodded. "The triangle with a circle, which is the logo for a company called AWS."

Joseph nodded at the road in front of us. "We should be coming up on their warehouse pretty soon, if the address in the phone book is still current."

We drove another few minutes in silence, looking for anything that could match up with my clues.

"I see it!" exclaimed Joseph, pointing out the windshield.

I turned to look and gasped. The white building had four tall grain elevators at each of the four corners of the building. At the top of each of the elevators was the blue triangle logo. The side facing us had a large roll-up door and dock for loading semi-trailers. From this distance, it looked a bit like a drawbridge.

"That's it," I said. "That's what I saw."

"Holy crap, look!" called Hound Dog.

I turned to find him pointing to a restaurant parking lot. Joseph slowed down and we all stared. The restaurant was one of those steak house types of places that tried too hard and ended up being just kitschy. They had placed a fiberglass statue in their parking lot. A cowboy, now broken off at the waist, rode a tan ranch horse to chase down a black and white cow. One of the cow's horns had also broken off, as well as the horse's raised front leg and tail. The effect was a kind of partial cow, partial horse with blue legs attached.

Joseph whistled in awe. I understood the sentiment. It was still really weird when the information we brought back from the astral plane or Akashic Library was so obviously accurate. Although, we hadn't found the sigils yet, the way two of the clues had manifested so closely together gave me hope.

We pulled into the restaurant parking lot and left the car there, walking along the road to the warehouse. As we crossed the concrete in front of the docking area, I paused and took a deep breath through my nose, smelling the grainy scent reminiscent of dried grass. I shot Joseph and Hound Dog a meaningful look, and they nodded.

We crept around the building, keeping an eye out for people. It seemed to be mostly empty. We found the main doors and the office hours said the building was open weekdays from 8 until 4. We shrugged and tried the doors. They opened easily and we went in.

A middle aged woman sat behind the counter, typing furiously on her computer. She glanced up and, without smiling, said, "Welcome to Agricultural Warehousing and Storage. How can I help you?"

I stepped forward and smiled. "Hi, we were wondering if you could give us a tour of this facility."

The typing stopped. The woman looked up and examined each of us. She brought her gaze to me and I lifted my eyebrow. She slowly stood up.

"A tour?" she asked. "May I ask why?"

I cleared my throat and tried not to break into a grin. "We take our grain storage very seriously," I said. "Before we could even consider using this company, we need to see what kind of operation you have."

I heard Joseph make a noise that sounded suspiciously like he was choking back a laugh, but I didn't dare turn around. Instead, I concentrated on keeping my gaze level on the woman, projecting a business-like sincerity.

She seemed to be flustered by what I'd said. "Usually people make an appointment to take a tour," she pointed out.

I nodded. "Yes, which gives you time to clean up anything that you don't want us to see." I shook my head. "We prefer to have a spontaneous tour, so we can get a more realistic look at the process."

The woman frowned. "Very well then," she said. "Let me get the warehouse supervisor."

I stood there, trying very hard to look like someone who dealt in grain, which would have been easier if I had a single clue as to what that would entail.

The woman exchanged mumbled words with someone over the phone, then hung up and looked up at us. She still seemed suspicious, but she asked us to please sit down until the supervisor came to give us the tour.

After a few minutes, an older man with the heavy muscles and belly paunch of someone who worked hard and ate too much meat and potatoes came through the door from the back. He glanced over us, shrugged and introduced himself as Gary Smithfield, manager of operations.

He gestured us to follow him and he showed us to the large docking area, a mostly empty space that allowed the two forklifts along the wall to transport pallets to trucks. I pretended interest, asking questions about their sales and shipping procedures.

"So you usually buy the grain directly and repackage it to sell?" I asked.

Gary nodded. "By selling it under a single brand name, the customers have certain assurances of quality, knowing that AWS has quality standards for what we purchase and package."

I rubbed my chin. "And where do you perform your quality checks and repackaging?"

Gary showed us to a roll up door with a regular door to the side of it, which separated another third of the warehouse into a separate room.

"We keep our grain storage and packaging separate to prevent adulteration of the product," he explained.

He ushered us into the room revealing a tall machine that looked like a spout along one wall and large bags of grain split into groups separated by metal dividers along the other. A younger man in an AWS uniform and cap was checking bags and marking a form on a clipboard.

"We aren't expecting any deliveries or pick-ups today," Gary explained. "So we only have one employee for warehouse staff, plus a security guard."

"Why are the bags divided into groups?" Hound Dog asked.

Gary walked up to one of the bags and pointed out the tag. "Each group is a different type of grain. We keep them labeled and separate to ensure there are no mix ups in putting together orders for delivery."

I ran my eyes over the groups, counting. Five, six... seven different grains. I caught Joseph's eye. He'd seen it, too. I wracked my brain trying to think of a reason to stay in the storage room, but Gary ushered us out quickly, finishing his tour with a description of the grain elevators and their holding capacity.

Suddenly, two large black birds swooped through the warehouse, diving right in front of us before flapping over to settle on one of the forklifts.

"What the hell?" Gary yelled. "How did those things get in here? Johnny! Get them out!"

The man from the storage area ran out and Gary pointed at the ravens.

I narrowed my eyes, recognizing the birds. I opened my mouth, not sure what I was going to say. But I was interrupted before I could figure it out.

The door from the front office area burst open and a group of Valkyrie ran in. Relief and joy washed over me when I spotted Mercy leading the charge with the tallest of her sisters. Misty was holding the woman from the front desk by the arm, dragging her along. Kara was dragging a man in a slate blue shirt that said "security" on the left pocket.

"Gary!" the woman called. "They just shoved their way in. I couldn't stop them..."

Mercy stepped towards us, cutting off Gary's hesitant step forward. She looked at me. "Did you find them?"

I shook my head and pointed to the door to the storage room. "They may be in there."

Gary turned to look at me with an expression of hurt. "What do you want from us?"

"Everyone freeze!" a familiar voice interrupted.

I stared at Detective Ames standing just inside the door, holding his gun out. His eyes shot hard glares at everyone, noting each person. He was probably trying to figure out the threats.

"This is turning into a damn party," Hound Dog muttered.

"I knew something was going on," the detective said. He locked his eyes on me. "Now you are going to explain yourself."

"Thank god the police are here," the front-desk woman said.

"Quiet!" Ames shouted.

I frowned at him and turned to Mercy. "Why are you here?" I asked her.

Mercy leveled her gaze at me. "They are coming," she said.

"How long?" I asked.

"Minutes. Maybe."

A shattering, crashing noise sounded from the office area. Detective Ames jumped and turned to look. One of the Valkyrie pushed him back towards us and three of the Valkyrie pressed themselves against the door, holding it shut. Their bodies shook from the impact on the other side of the door.

"Time's up!" one of the women yelled. "Get them somewhere safe!"

"What the hell..." Detective Ames began as Misty pushed him and the front-desk woman towards the storage room.

"This is ridiculous!" Gary shouted over the detective. He glared at the Valkyrie herding him. "Let us go now!"

The pop-pop of gunfire halted the protests, and we all dropped into a defensive squat. Waves of fear washed over the warehouse employees. I could feel it brushing against me, pushing me to act. I resisted, knowing my instinctive fear reactions would probably be the wrong tactic.

The Valkyrie pushed the humans into the storage room, with the detective protesting uncertainly and the AWS employees looking shocked and terrified. Just before I entered the room, I caught a glimpse of two Valkyrie straining to lift one of the forklifts between them. Mercy grabbed the door to shut it on us, pausing for a moment.

"Find them," she told me. I nodded and she turned to Detective Ames. "Shoot anything that tries to come in."

She slammed the door and we heard a loud crashing noise as something was pushed against it.

Detective Ames stared for a moment. "Any... thing?" He turned to face me and Joseph. "She meant any one, right?"

I shook my head. "No, she didn't."

The woman from the front desk had actually passed out. I thought that only happened in the movies. Johnny from storage was hovering over her, so I ignored them.

"I need something to cut open these bags." I looked at Joseph. "And I need to concentrate."

Hound Dog found a box cutter and handed it to me. I tuned out the noise of fighting outside the room and the high pitched questions of the people inside. Joseph responded to the questions in his deep, calm voice. Relief and gratitude for him washed over me, and I let it push away the fear that had snuck into my energy.

Fear, hopelessness and determination. I was in the right place.

I closed my eyes, focusing on the memories of my friends. I remembered finding Joseph on the side of the road next to the stalled out rental car, relief and happiness on his face when he recognized me. I felt the wash of pride and confidence, knowing that he'd had my back through this entire adventure, standing up to Rowan, facing down Keith, and running around just surviving.

I brushed at a tear running down my cheek and recalled Hound Dog, greeting us at the bridge that first day, welcoming me despite the years since we'd seen each other. I smiled at the memory of Hound Dog appearing at the police station, giving us direction when we had no idea where to go. I embraced the gratitude for how he'd given us food and water for our hide out. He had no idea he had probably saved our lives with his generosity.

I wrapped my arms around myself, needing the feeling of being held for a moment.

I turned my memories to Mercy, smiling at the way she'd been so cynical of us when we'd met. She had turned out to be a good friend and invaluable help to us throughout the last week.

I thought about the ravens, too, their humor and the wonder I felt in knowing them and about them. I felt the pride and satisfaction at being trusted with their secrets and shown some small bit of their knowledge.

I wrapped myself in the feelings that my friends gave me, topping it all off with the joy and love I felt for Ella, my daughter and the reason I even considered trying to save the world. Because I wasn't trying to save the world, really. I was just going to save her.

I felt the positive emotions filling me and washing over me, pushing out fear and doubt until there was nothing of them left.

I opened my eyes and let my vision change to my second sight. I grabbed at the feelings of confidence, applying that confidence to finding the sigils. I directed the feelings of joy and pride to the triumph of winning the day. I let my gaze drift over the bags of grain until I saw several of them stand out with a kind of hazy glow, like an afterimage in my vision.

I opened the box cutter and walked over to the grain bags, quickly marking each of the ones that had popped in my vision by scratching through the label. I mentally tallied the bags as I did this - four.

But my studies of the Hávamál said that there were 18 spells.

I moved to a different position in the room, giving me a new line of sight on the bags. I repeated the process, finding my emotional center, pushing the positive emotions towards my desired goal, and looking with my second sight for any other bags.

Nothing. I shook my head. I'd have to get the four I'd found and figure out what to do about the others later.

I turned and found Hound Dog staring at the door. Detective Ames was standing in front of it, gun drawn. He seemed ready to shoot. I only hoped he really would.

The sound of fighting was really loud now, with gunshots, metal clanging, shouts and growls. Joseph was in front of the large, free-standing ventilation fan, hovering protectively over the three AWS employees who had huddled in the back corner behind the grinding and bagging machines. The woman had woken up, but still looked pale.

I grabbed Hound Dog's arm. "Help me with these," I said.

I showed him the markings and helped him lay out the first two bags on the floor. He started hauling the third over as I ripped one of the bags diagonally from corner to corner. Pale tan grains spilled over the edges as I pulled them apart. I plunged my hand into the bag, working my fingers into the shifting granules.

Nothing.

I pulled my hand out and moved closer to one end. I forced my hand into the pile of grain, rough edges and grain dust abrading my skin.

Nothing.

I moved to the other side and repeated the process. I dropped the box cutter and plunged both hands in. The dust stirred up as I moved my fingers through the grains. I sneezed three times in a row and sniffed.

Still nothing.

I pulled my hands out to try again. My pinky finger brushed against something that felt different than the grains, and I froze. I wriggled my hands around, trying to find whatever it had been, half convinced it was just a seed rubbed free of dust and bran.

My hand closed around something that was harder and larger than the grains, and I closed my eyes, hoping. I pulled it up and opened my hand.

It was bright silver, almost white, about the size of a quarter. It was in the shape of a hollow circle, with the lines of runic symbols in the center. I stared at the lines crisscrossing the circle. I could feel it pulling me in.

"Nicola!" I heard Hound Dog calling me. "Is this -"

The breath caught in my throat. I heard a chanting voice, deep and powerful, singing the words into being. I knew the language was not English. It sounded more guttural, like German but not quite that harsh. Despite that, I could understand the words perfectly.

The voice repeated a verse over and over. "Learn to carve them, learn to read them, learn to stain them, learn to validate them, learn to summon them, learn to modify them, learn to share them, learn to use them."

I felt my pulse beating in time to the rhythm of the words from the Hávamál, the words of Odin, and I started to fall into them, but they changed to another verse.

"I have learned the seventh spell: For if fire burns around me, if it threatens my friends and family, I know the song to sing in my heart and mind and blood, the song that controls the flames."

I listened to the words, my eyes going wide. Each word burned into my memory, and I began to understand how to use the Runespell. I knew what it could do, and what I was capable of with it in my hands.

My muscles were frozen with shock, which was a good thing, because otherwise I might have dropped, or even thrown, the sigil.

The words finished one last cycle then stopped, the echo of them ringing in my ears. Then, just as suddenly as my breath had caught, I was pulling in the air that had frozen in my throat.

"- all the bags you needed?"

I blinked at Hound Dog, trying to catch up to what he'd been saying before time had frozen. "Oh, um, yeah." I nodded, brushing off the extra grains and putting the sigil in my pants pocket.

I crawled over to the next bag and slit it open. I took a moment, hesitant to plunge my hands in after the last experience. I shook it off.

"Gotta do what you gotta do," I muttered, thrusting both hands into the grains.

This time, the grains were shiny and dark brown, with almost no dust on them. The ends had little sharp points, though. I winced as I was stabbed by a hundred tiny pokes.

I caught Hound Dog's concerned look. He must have seen me flinch. I smiled reassurance at him.

"I'm gonna need a manicure when I'm done with this," I said.

He tentatively stepped forward. "I could..." he started, gesturing to one of the unopened bags.

I shook my head. "The conditions of finding them are pretty limited," I explained. "You might not be able to find them, or you might even trigger them moving somewhere else."

Hound Dog looked confused, but he nodded and stepped back.

I dragged my hands through the grains over and over, wiggling my fingers to try to cover as much of the space as I could with each pass.

Finally, I felt something. I dug it out as quickly as I could. It was much the same as the other had been, with a slightly different arrangement of the runic symbol's lines. And as before, I felt the pull and then my breath stopped in my lungs.

The same voice spoke the same words, "Learn to carve them, learn to read them." It repeated until I felt myself falling into the words, then it changed again.

"I have learned the third spell: When I must fight an enemy, the blade he carries will not cut my skin and the club he swings will not bruise my body."

Again, the words repeated over and over, burning the meaning into my mind. My muscles had locked up once more, preventing me from escaping the chant.

My lungs released as time moved forward once more, and I gasped. I let the loose grains fall and put the sigil into my pocket with the other one and moved on to the next bag.

I glanced at the door, which was shuddering with random impacts. I could hear female voices screaming in rage and pain. Monstrous voices roaring with rage and hate.

I pressed my lips together and dug into the round, yellowish grains. It took even longer to find the sigil this time. I dug and dug, nearly ready to give up before I pulled out the silver pendant. I barely had time to brace myself before I was frozen and falling.

"Learn to share them, learn to use them," chanted the voice before launching into the second part. "I have learned the fourteenth spell: If I want to, I shall know, by name and function, every god and demigod and creature of the gods; I know all their stories, while others know only a few."

My eyes stared helplessly into nothing as the Runespell branded itself into my brain. I felt the tears leaking down my face as I understood. I gasped in air as my body was released from the time warp.

I collapsed on the floor this time, my whole body shaking with what I'd learned.

Hound Dog bent to help me and I instinctively recoiled from him, curling around the hand that held the sigil.

This Runespell gave me the knowledge of the truths behind all myths, throughout the world and throughout history. It would reveal each god's name, lineage and weakness. I could destroy entire pantheons with this Runespell. I choked on that thought. No mortal should have that kind of power.

I took a moment to regroup, then I shoved the sigil into my pocket, tiny round grains and all.

I shot an apologetic look at Hound Dog and shakily made my way to the fourth bag. I sat for a long moment, trying to block out the shrieks and snarls of the fighting outside. I finally got my courage back and shoved my hands into the light reddish brown grains.

I felt the pressure to finish and I began shoving grain out of the bag as I dug through. Finally, a glint of silver caught my eye and I ground my teeth as I snatched it up, taking a deep breath before everything stopped.

"Learn to share them, learn to use them," the voice said. "I have learned the eleventh spell: When my friends and I must fight, whether in war or battle, I know the song to sing in my heart and mind and blood, for strength and rage and luck and skill, for my allies to return unharmed."

As the meaning melted into my brain, I began smiling. When the time warp released me, I kept the sigil clutched in my fist as I jumped to my feet.

"Joseph! Ames!" I cried. "Everyone gather around!" I rushed around the room pulling the detective away from the door and helping Joseph herd the AWS employees forward.

I looked around at everyone with an evil smile on my face. I could tell the exact moment that Joseph caught my look and understood. He stood straighter and leaned in as I explained my plan.

CHAPT 15

I looked around the room, checking people, places and equipment.

Johnny was feeding grain into the grinder, while Gary shoveled the resulting flour into the bagger. Their foreheads were sweaty and their noses and mouths were covered with thick white dust masks, which we'd found in a small supply cabinet near the door.

Veronica, the lady from the front desk, and Dwight, the security guard, were positioning the ventilation fan to point at the doors, their eyes glittering with fear over their own masks.

Detective Ames was crouched down with his gun pointing at the doors, and Hound Dog was at the control panel, a metal bar in hand and ready to open the large roll up door. Both of them had dust masks on, as well.

I looked to my left over at Joseph, with his mask over his face, and a plastic trash can lid in one hand and a large metal bar in the other. I met his eyes and he nodded, acknowledging the part of my plan I hadn't told any of the others. They knew we were going to try to get out, but they didn't know my plan B.

I clenched my fist around my own metal bar and lifted my other hand to feel the sigils against my chest tucked into my bra. I'd already sung over the group to give them the powers of the eleventh Rune spell, which should protect them from all but the most serious wounds. The blade one, I could only use on myself and anyone I was touching, and the fire one... well, there had to be fire for that one.

I glanced at everyone again. Gary gave me a thumbs-up and Veronica nodded. I looked at Hound Dog and nodded for him to begin.

The doors squawked and creaked as they began to open, revealing one of the forklifts leaning against the smaller side door. I heard the bagging machine start up, then the fan. By the time the doors were halfway open, the air was full of grain dust, blowing around, getting in my eyes and stinging the skin on my face, the same feeling I'd had in my visions from the ravens.

I took a deep breath through my mask, lifted the metal bar over my face and yelled with all my might, running forward into the swirling dust.

I immediately lost sight of Joseph, and I hoped he was following the plan. We weren't supposed to go too far, just enough to distract any monsters away from the door behind us. I stopped running and began counting. At 100, the rest of the group was supposed to run for the exit.

I saw shadows to the right, appearing to struggle with each other. I moved in that direction, trying to make out who was what. I caught a glimpse of a long golden braid and I focused on that, singing the protection of the eleventh Rune spell over the Valkyrie.

23, 24... I shook my head, surprised at how thick the dust had gotten so quickly, as I searched for more fighters. I spotted another Valkyrie running past, and I sang the spell on her.

39, 40... A huge bulky shape crashed down in front of me and I gasped, certain it was a body. My sudden intake of breath sucked some grain dust through the edges of the mask and into my lungs, and I spent several seconds coughing it up. When I finally got a good look at the bulk, I saw that it was just a bag of flour.

That explained the extra dustiness. The demons and Valkyrie had already been lobbing "smoke bombs" at each other. When we added more flour and grain dust, plus the fan, visibility was nearly nothing.

51, 52... I spotted another shape in the dust and trotted towards it. It spun towards me and I realized its color was bluish and its size that was too big for a Valkyrie. I swallowed, fighting the sudden rush of fear and panic, and backed up, one step, another step.

I bumped into something and froze. I slowly craned my head up and around to look into the drooling jaws of another demon, this one green. We all froze there for a second, then the green demon behind me drew back its arm to strike at me. The demon in front of me launched itself into the air at me.

I felt the power of the protection spell wash over me, slowing down time. I had expected the shielding effect that I felt cover me, but the other effect was a little unsettling. The power guided my muscles into a drop with my arms crossed on my chest. My legs pushed me into roll to the side. Once clear, I finished the roll in a squatting position and swung my metal bar out, backhanded.

The jumping blue demon landed on the outstretched arm of the clawing demon, and I heard the cracking crunch of breaking bone in the green demon's arm a mere second before my swing connected with the blue demon's face.

Another cracking crunch and twin howls followed me as I turned and ran towards what I hoped was the bagging room door. I had lost count and I wanted to be sure that I was around when the others made their break.

A shape appeared in front of me. I eyed it for size and relaxed.

"Joseph," I called. "Is that you? You'll never believe what that protection spell did..."

I trailed off as the shape came closer. It was Bob, with several dark, lumbering shapes appearing behind him.

He smiled. "Actually, I would," he said. "I've had the pleasure of that particular sigil's power. A power I will get to keep when I continue God's plan."

I took a step back. "You mean, Jehovah's plan? I take it Keith wasn't the only one in contact with him then."

Bob laughed. "Keith knew God existed, but he still wasn't a true believer. I was always the one that Jehovah trusted to get the job done. Keith was just a..." he waved his hand, "distraction."

I glanced at the shadows now taking shape behind Bob. Purple and orange demons growled and snarled. Even more shadows appeared behind them and my heart sank.

"You never intended Keith to survive this, did you?" I asked, already sure of the answer.

Bob barked a laugh, throwing back his head. "I chose Keith," he said. "I chose him and Jehovah chose me. And that's as close as Keith could have ever gotten to being Saved."

I glanced at the demons and the shadows behind the demons again. My mind raced with jumbled thoughts of what to do, how to escape, and trying to understand what Bob was telling me.

Bob sneered at me. "I did him a favor," he said, pulling out a gun. "You don't get that privilege."

My eyes were drawn again to the demons and shadows, and I knew what to do. I began singing the spell song of protection, directing my focus to the shadows in the back. Shadows that were much smaller than demons. Shadows with blonde hair and swords.

I relaxed my body and let the protection spell direct me as I dropped and rolled to the left a split second before Bob shot. He tried to track me, firing, but I managed to stay just ahead of his aim. Mostly.

I felt the burn along the back of my left shoulder a split second after my right calf exploded in pain. It felt like a rug burn, only a thousand times worse. I let the spell take care of my movements while I moaned in agony. Each movement reignited the burning, as if someone kept laying fresh, hot pokers on my skin, one after another.

I pushed at the pain, trying to clear my head. I knew Bob wouldn't stop with bullets. He wouldn't stop until I was dead. I blinked my eyes, clearing the tears from them, trying to see through the dust. I grabbed hold of a moment of clarity and wrapped it around my mind as quickly as I could, my gaze finally landing on my enemy.

With an enraged cry, Bob launched himself at me. I rolled to my knees and twisted, swinging my metal bar out. It connected with Bob's knee just before he reached me, and I felt something crack. His attempt at a tackle turned into him grabbing a loose section of my hair while he fell on his side. My cry of pain as the hair was ripped out of my head melded with his scream of agony.

I stood and kicked downward with one foot onto the knee I'd just broken. The sickening crunch under my foot told me that Bob wouldn't be coming after me. I glanced at the demons who were engaged in close fighting with the Valkyrie. The women looked like they'd taken a beating, but they seemed to be holding their own now.

I shot Bob another glance before I headed for the bagging room. He was lying on his side, rocking and clutching his knee, muttering under his breath. I briefly wondered if he was praying.

I dodged a Valkyrie fighting two demons at once and stumbled through the thick grain dust to the bagging room. The fan kept the dust from settling too much, but it wasn't quite as thick as it had been earlier.

The bagging room was empty. I quickly headed along the wall towards the exit we had decided on. It only took a few seconds before the group came into view, huddled near the door. It was still shut.

"Sweet baby Baldur, what now?" I cursed under my breath, certain that something was wrong as I rushed up to them.

Detective Ames leveled his gun at me and Hound Dog hefted his metal bar. They both relaxed a second later, recognizing me.

"What's wrong?" I asked. "Why aren't you out of here?"

Gary, Johnny and Dwight were working on the door, but the handle appeared to have been twisted.

Joseph leaned close to yell in my ear. "It won't budge! We are trapped."

I glanced around, my eyes falling on the forklift.

Dwight came up. "Thought of that. The forklift won't go fast enough to break through the doors."

I noticed a pile of pallets nearby, and I turned to Joseph.

"Time for plan B," I said.

Joseph nodded slowly.

I pulled Gary and Johnny away from the door and told them to get the forklift ready to drive into the dusty warehouse floor.

While Gary showed me how to get the forklift running, Joseph directed Dwight and Hound Dog to grab some heavy plastic pallets from nearby and pull them into the corner. He pushed Veronica into the corner first and helped the other two lean pallets against the wall around her.

Joseph pulled a greasy rag out of his pocket that we had found earlier in the bagging room. We tied it around the tubing of the propane tank that fueled the forklift.

Gary grabbed me. "You can't light that," he yelled. "With all this grain dust..."

I looked him in the eye. "I know," I said. "I'm counting on that."

The color drained from his face as the realization hit him. He stumbled back a few steps, then grabbed Johnny and started pushing everyone into the little fortress of pallets.

Joseph stood next to me with his trusty Zippo in hand. I took it from him and pointed him towards the pallets. He looked under them, counting heads and looked back at me and nodded. I returned his nod and waited until he was under the pallets, too.

I climbed up on the forklift and started it running before I turned to light the rag. It took me a minute to get it to light, mostly because I kept jumping each time I thought it had caught.

Finally, the rag began burning and I jumped from the forklift, jarring my injured leg, but I managed to start running for the pallets. I was sure with each limping step that the propane would blow.

I reached the pallets and turned to look. I noticed the shadows of the fighting Valkyrie and demons. The creatures were getting closer and the Valkyrie looked like they were about done.

I turned to look at the forklift. It had stopped moving forward and I could see the flame on the rag, but nothing was happening. I started to panic. If nothing blew before the fire went out, we didn't have much chance of getting away from the demons.

"Detective Ames!" I called. "I need you out here!"

The detective huffed his way out of the pallets. He stood up and caught sight of the demons fighting, drawing his gun. I realized that this was the first clear looked he'd gotten of the monsters that had been chasing me all week.

I grabbed his arm, getting his attention. "Ames! I need you to shoot the propane tank!" I pointed at the forklift. "Can you do that?"

He squinted through the dust at the large machine for a second and nodded. He moved over to get a better line of sight and leveled his gun to aim at the tank.

I took a deep breath behind my mask and pulled it down to let my voice project. "Valkyrie! To me! To me!" I cried.

The Valkyrie immediately dropped back, running towards me as I put up my hands, ready to sing the spell song. Three loud cracks sounded from beside me, where the detective was firing. And then a huge boom followed by the loudest roar I'd ever heard, as the propane released, caught the flame and ignited the grain dust.

It was the sound from my memories, the last clue in place.

The concussive blast hit us first, knocking the Valkyrie face-first into the warehouse floor. The warriors slid and rolled several feet farther. Detective Ames staggered back until he hit the wall. He dropped his gun and put his hands up to protect his face.

I pulled the power of fire control from the sigil on my chest and pushed against the blast, feeling the slowing of time once again as I sang.

It's an instinctual thing, I think, using one's hands in spell casting. After all, the hands aren't intrinsically necessary to use the energies that make up spells. But, as with robes and candles and other ceremonial symbols, certain gestures have meaning that impress so heavily on the human mind that it is almost impossible to do a thing without making the motion.

Putting up your hands and pushing makes things go away or keeps things away. So when you try to make things go away with magic, your mind triggers that pushing away movement. It wasn't necessary, but I pushed at the fire with my hands.

I almost expected a visible line, as if there was a physical shield between us and the flames, but that wasn't what happened. The flames simply stopped coming towards us, licking at the air barrier between the fire and the people that I was protecting. The heat was intense against my face, but not enough to burn our clothes or flesh.

There's another thing that is instinctual for humans: the awe and fear that we have of fire. I felt the familiar pull of the fire's beauty, the perfect blending of red and orange, yellow and white, with tongues reaching up and around and even sideways.

I saw Detective Ames pull off his mask out of the corner of my eye, staring up at the flames surrounding us, flames held back by nothing but the sigil's magic and a few feet of space. I glimpsed Joseph as he stepped up on my other side, face turned up. He had taken off his mask, too. He raised a hand as if to reach out to the curling tongues of fire.

Grain dust burns quickly, and it was only a few more seconds before the flames evaporated from the ground up. I dropped my hands and time resumed, taking our breath away.

The fire had used up all of the oxygen and we all fell to the floor, gasping and choking on the ash and remaining grain dust in the air.

We sat there for several minutes, on hands and knees, struggling to hold on to consciousness, before the oxygen levels normalized enough for us to clear our heads. I sat back on my ankles, wincing when the move put pressure on my injured calf. I looked around, seeing the damage but unable to get myself to move.

The air was hazy with dust, ash and smoke, but I could see the blackened bodies on the warehouse floor. I mentally counted twelve and tried not to guess if any of them were smaller than demon-sized.

The Valkyrie were coughing and dragging themselves upright. Mercy had dark smudges on her face and clothes, and a deep gash across one cheek. Her shirt was torn in a few places and I guessed there would be slashing wounds behind each rip.

The other Valkyrie appeared to be in more or less the same condition as they staggered to their feet, one by one, and limped around helping each other.

I noticed a stinging feeling on my face and I glanced over at Joseph. His pale complexion had darkened to a bright red. He was likely going to come away with a nasty sunburn from the heat of the fire. Other than that, he appeared to be in pretty good shape. A bruise was darkening under his right eye, but his clothes weren't showing any blood.

I turned to check on Detective Ames. He had suffered a lot more than Joseph. He was wheezing heavily and he had a bright red spot slowly spreading on his left side. I crawled over to check on him.

"What happened?" I asked, looking closely at the bloodstain. It appeared to be a deep gash along his ribs.

"Goddamn propane tank," he gasped. "Shrapnel hit me when the blast knocked us back." He barked a dry laugh. "Didn't even feel it until just a minute ago."

"I'll call an ambulance," I said.

"Don't bother." He stopped me with a hand on my arm. "Fire department will be here soon." He waved his hand around at the ash settling on the floor. "Kinda hard to miss this."

I nodded. "You gonna die?" I asked.

Detective Ames leveled his gaze at me. "Not on your life," he assured me. "You owe me an explanation, though."

Joseph and Hound Dog stumbled over to us. "The others are

okay," Joseph said. "But we need to figure out what to tell the police..."
He trailed off, meeting Detective Ames' gaze.

"Leave that to me," the detective said. "You all were too confused
and shocked to remember anything but gunshots and the fire."

I slowly nodded. Looked like Ames wasn't going to be following
me around accusing me of murder any more.

I looked over at the AWS people. Veronica was weeping with
hiccoughing sobs in Gary's arms. The security guard just stared at the
mess, and Johnny sat with his head in his hands.

I felt sorry for them. This had been a huge ordeal for everyone, but
at least Joseph and I had had some experiences that prepared us for it.
I wondered if there was anything that could be done for them. No
doubt they would be recovering from the psychological shock for
months. Maybe even years.

I looked up as Mercy came over. "How are you and your sisters?" I
asked.

"We'll be fine." She shrugged. "Two were lost."

I felt tears building up in my eyes. "I'm sorry."

Mercy looked me in the eye. "Don't be," she said. "This is what we
do. Besides, they were reabsorbed into the essence of Valfodr and will
be renewed."

Valfodr. Father of the Slain. Odin. He had soaked them up and
they would exist again.

I took a shaky breath. The whole dying without dying thing was a
little hard to grasp, even with all the other stuff that had happened.
Another Valkyrie walked up and spoke to Mercy so softly that I
couldn't hear what she said. Mercy nodded after a moment and
responded just as quietly. She turned back to me.

"Wasn't that horrible man with the desert god's creatures?"

I nodded. "Yeah, Bob was here." I looked over at the Valkyrie, who
seemed to be checking out the barbecued bodies. "Why?"

Mercy sighed. "No human body has been found," she admitted.

"Odin's left eye," I cursed. I stared at the Valkyrie. "What are they
doing?"

"Glamours," Mercy said. "Making the bodies appear human. It's the best we can do in the short time we have."

I nodded. I could hear the sirens in the background now. Help was on its way. I wondered what Detective Ames was going to say happened.

"We can't stay, but I will see you again soon," Mercy said, stepping back to rejoin her sisters. They vanished a few seconds before firemen in full gear rushed through the doors.

CHAPT 16

During the first day of my stay at the hospital, Joseph and Hound Dog came to see me.

I was still wearing an oxygen mask, and I was groggy from the doctors poking and prodding me. I was convinced they'd given me more tissue damage in their efforts to fix me up than I'd had when the ambulance brought me in.

I smiled weakly and struggled to sit up until Joseph grabbed the bed controller and raised the head of the bed to help me sit upright.

"Hey, guys," I croaked out. My voice had finally given up after all the abuse I'd given it.

"Hey, rich girl," Hound Dog said, hoarsely.

"How are you doing?" Joseph asked.

I shrugged. "I'll live."

They pulled a couple of chairs up to my bed and we spent several minutes catching up. Neither they nor the AWS employees had suffered any major lasting damage, although everyone had a mild case of smoke inhalation. Joseph ended up with a bright red, first degree burn on his face and hands from the heat of the flames.

We fell silent, each of us thinking about the past week and the last few days. Finally, I tried to speak, but my throat had gone dry. I grabbed my water and sipped the lukewarm liquid.

"I want to thank you both," I said. "This turned out to be so much bigger than I ever expected, but you guys... I couldn't have done it without you."

Joseph grabbed hold of my hand, his eyes shining with tears.

Hound Dog nodded at my words. I noticed he had more lines on his face than I remembered him having before. The set of his mouth and the look in his eyes gave him a slightly haunted but wise quality.

My heart broke for my two friends. Their goodbyes when they finally left had a hint of pleading, as if they had accepted the certainty of death and wanted assurances that we would live to meet again.

• • •

During the second day of my stay at the hospital, my mother brought Ella to visit me.

I was sitting in bed, trying to decide if I should watch the soap opera on TV or take a nap. My hip and shoulder hurt from the stitches used to seal the wounds from Bob's bullets and my head ached from the constant, middle of the night interruptions from the nursing staff.

"Mama!"

I turned towards the little voice and held out my arms to the bundle of energy running towards me. She climbed up the bed and wrapped her little hands around my shoulders. For the first time in days, I cried.

I spent an hour talking to my mother before Ella fell asleep on my chest. They had gotten the package that I'd sent them, and my mother had already contacted a lawyer to review the paperwork, but it looked like everything was in order.

My mother very carefully avoided asking me what had happened, and I wasn't about to offer up the information, but I could feel the question in her gaze every time she looked at me. I just shrugged it off. There was no way I was involving these two in this mess in any way, not even after the fact.

After Ella fell asleep, I faked dozing off, until my mother left the room. Knowing her, she'd be hunting down the nearest coffee shop. That woman loved her coffee, black and sugary.

I lay on the bed, the head raised to an upright position, and smoothed Ella's hair with my hand. My nosed was buried in the crown of her head and I stared at a corner of the room, just thinking about how our lives had changed so drastically.

It probably says something that I didn't even flinch when the ravens appeared. They turned towards each other from a not-there, back to back position until they faced me, fully present and standing side by side. Their heads were both tilted at a slight angle to the left.

I raised my eyebrows at them, but I refused to speak and break the peace that I'd just found. After a moment, the twins each took a big step to the side, opening up the space between them.

Mercy was suddenly there, looking much better than the last time I'd seen her, with an older, familiar looking man.

I frowned, trying to place where I'd seen him before. He smiled at me, glancing down at Ella's sleeping form. One of his eyes didn't move.

"Mr. Corvus, was it?" I said, softly, keeping my voice down so I wouldn't wake Ella.

He chuckled. "I go by so many names," his deep voice rumbled. I recognized that voice, from my dream and from the visions that came from each of the sigils. "You may pick any that please you."

I smirked. "How about 'that guy who leaves me the hell alone'?" I asked.

The Wanderer laughed louder. "I do like you, Nicola," he said.

I shook my head. "You want your sigils back?" I asked.

Odin looked at me for a long moment. "We do not control the Runespells," he said. "It is your choice what to do with them. I would recommend, however, that you keep them for future use."

I narrowed my eyes. I didn't like the sound of that. "Future use?"

Mercy cleared her throat. "Nicola," she said, stepping forward. "We..."

She glanced at the god beside her. "I came to tell you, we couldn't find Bob's body. There's no sign of him anywhere."

I nodded. I had already figured that not so good ol' Bob hadn't finished messing with my life.

"And you only recovered four of the sigils."

I nodded again.

"There's nothing that indicates that Keith had more than the four. So, the others might not have been part of the spell you and Joseph did."

I shrugged.

"And there's something else," Mercy continued. She stared at a spot on the bed sheet as she spoke.

I had a sinking feeling that she didn't want to meet my eyes when she told me this other news.

She took a deep breath and spoke in a rush. "You have accepted the role of hero to the challenge of the quest. As such, you will finish the crusade unto completion or until you are dead."

One of my monitors beeped, suddenly loud in the silence following her words. I stared at her, trying to understand what she had said, afraid I had understood her just fine.

I breathed in deeply through my nose. I spoke quietly. I knew there was a deadly tone in my voice, but I didn't care. "What are the exact conditions to be met to complete the quest?"

Mercy closed her eyes. "The discovery and retrieval of all of the Runespells. Or die trying."

My eyes narrowed. "And how many are there?"

"Eighteen."

"And we only have four."

She nodded.

I shifted my eyes to the Wanderer, fixing his one good eye with my glare. I allowed the silence to stretch out, demanding that they break the standoff first.

Odin simply stood there, no doubt having had some kind of precognition as to how this would end.

Mercy, however, was soon nervously shifting her weight from side to side. Finally, she opened her mouth to speak.

"I don't have a choice," I said, cutting her off. "I have to finish this, right? But I can choose my timeframe."

I paused, letting that sink in. "I could wait until it's too late and whoever is behind this gets Ragnarok started, or I could wait until I die of old age, fulfilling the alternative result."

Mercy's face drained of color, and I saw alarm flash across One-Eye's face. He hadn't expected that.

I lay there a moment, chin raised, and my daughter in my arms, facing down a god of gods, a ruler of a pantheon of all-powerful beings. And, after a long moment, he blinked.

"But I won't," I relented. I smiled, tight lipped. "I just want you to know, one hundred fucking percent, that I am choosing to finish this quest."

I sat up just enough for effect, but not enough to jar Ella from her sleep. I glared at One-Eye, a snarl on my face. "You will remember this, and remember it well. You don't fucking control me, and you don't fucking try to manipulate me like that. Ever again."

I sat back, relaxing against my pillows. "But I ain't going anywhere until the dust settles from this last week, 'cause I'm wiped out."

The Wanderer nodded once, the patronizing look gone from his one eye. He slowly turned away from me, fading into not being.

Mercy hesitated a moment.

"Nicola, if you need me to help..." She trailed off.

I rubbed my chin against Ella's head. "I would be honored to have you at my side at any stage of this little adventure," I assured her.

She smiled and turned to follow Odin, stepping back between the silent twins and vanishing. The ravens winked at me and grinned before turning away from each other and disappearing, too.

•   •   •

During the third day of my stay at the hospital, I let a nurse push me in a wheelchair down the hallway after I'd talked them into letting me visit Detective Ames. He was recovering from surgery after having had a piece of shrapnel, a section of the propane tank, to be exact, taken from his side.

If the yelling coming from his room was any indication, he was going to be just fine. We paused in the doorway just in time to see a single-serve cup of orange gelatin hit the TV screen.

"Goddamn Pacers better pull your heads from your asses!"

I bit back a laugh and waved away the nurse, taking control of my borrowed set of wheels. I rolled into the room and pulled up beside the bed.

"Game not going well?" I asked.

Detective Ames shrugged. "Eh, we're up by 5." He took a swig from his water jug and looked me up and down. "You're lookin' better."

I smiled. "It's the hospital food."

I looked down and picked at my nails, suddenly shy about saying what I'd come to say.

"Spit it out, girl," Ames said without taking his eyes off the TV.

I leaned forward, speaking quietly. "I just wanted to thank you for all you did. At the grain warehouse. You didn't have to stick your neck out so much, but I appreciate it."

The detective snorted, shifting his heavy frame in the narrow bed. "I'm not ready to retire," he said. "Certainly not a retirement forced on me because some crazy shit went down and I was stupid enough to tell everyone."

He turned to me and I could see a haunted look in his eyes. "I always thought myself a God-fearing man," he continued. "But that was something else. I don't know what it was and I don't want to know."

I nodded my understanding.

"At least I'm pretty sure that you didn't murder those people, am I right?"

"I told you the truth, mostly," I assured him. "The cop and Keith were killed by those creatures and Bob. I don't know anything about the other guy. A former friend turned enemy probably called in that tip to try to convince me to leave town." I raised my right hand. "On my honor."

Detective Ames nodded sharply once and turned back to his game. "Then I don't want to hear any more about it."

I nodded slowly and awkwardly turned the wheelchair around to leave.

"Keep in touch." Ames' voice called out just as I reached the door. I waved over my head and kept going.

When I got back to my room, there was a small box on my side table. It looked like a box from a jewelry store. I opened it up and pulled out a sturdy silver chain with a toggle clasp and a folded piece of paper. I eyed the chain warily while I unfolded the paper. I wasn't a fan of jewelry.

"Accept this gift – a piece of the chain of the Wolf. It cannot be broken nor removed but by the wearer." The signature line was a pair of ravens facing each other.

I turned the chain over in my hands, tugging at it to test its strength. I pulled one of the sigils from my bag and tried to figure out how I would attach it. I held the sigil to the chain, trying to see how it would look, and the next second, the sigil was a charm on the chain.

I shrugged and muttered under my breath about magic, but I

pulled out the other three sigils and repeated the process. I latched the chain around my neck and felt a sense of relief that the chain was the perfect length and weight so that I barely noticed it was there.

At least I could stop stashing the sigils in my bra during battles.

I yawned, still exhausted from my adventures, so I hefted myself back into the bed and quickly fell asleep.

•   •   •

During the fourth day of my stay at the hospital, I was released. I immediately went home to my daughter. And I didn't hear from any gods for several months after that.

View other Black Rose Writing titles at <u>www.blackrosewriting.com/books</u>
and use promo code PRINT to receive a 20% discount when purchasing.

BLACK ROSE
writing™